There was a small thud again̲s̲t̲ ̲t̲h̲e̲ ̲d̲o̲o̲r̲. ̲T̲h̲e̲n̲ ̲s̲o̲m̲e̲ ̲v̲o̲i̲c̲e̲s̲. The four froze, not moving a muscle. A soft glow appeared on the door, then a puff of smoke followed by a stream of sparks. An acrid cloud of smoke seeped into the vault and eddied around the ceiling.

"Get down!" Gunny ordered needlessly. All four crouched behind the table, protected from the steady stream of sparks shooting into the vault. There were four simultaneous clicks as four safeties were clicked to "fire." Sweaty hands nervously gripped the weapons.

A cut was being made at the very top of the door, cutting through the heavy steel bar there. After a moment, the bar was cut, and the torch shifted to the locking bar on the floor.

There was a shout of triumph, then gloved hands came in to grip the door at the new opening. Gunny motioned to the other three, and they came up, weapons aimed. As the door was pushed open a crack, Gunny opened fire, followed by the other three a split second later.

At least one set of hands was hit as the other two sets jerked back. There was some furious shouting down the passage and footsteps running from further down toward the other offices. They could hear an excited exchange right outside the door. A hand appeared around the edge of the partially opened door and threw in a round object.

"Down!" shouted Gunny as the four crouched behind the table. A horrible four or five seconds followed, which stretched for an eternity. There was a deafening blast as the grenade detonated. Gunny and Van Slyke immediately sat up, weapons over the edge of the table. Three men tried to rush in, but their concerted burst dropped all three in their tracks.

"Good shot, you two. Thanks." Loralee coldly looked down on the gunman.

The voices outside stopped. Gunny knew they were regrouping, ready to try and end it all right there in the bottom deck of the embassy. All four turned to the opening and raised their weapons.

Loralee Howard, diplomat's wife and sister to a Marine, Private First Class Peter Van Slyke and Gunnery Sergeant Jacob McCardle, United States Marine Corps, and Michael Eduardo, President of the United States of America, lifted their weapons and faced their incoming fate.

The Few

A Tale of the Marines in the Near Future

Colonel Jonathan P. Brazee

USMCR (Ret)

iUniverse, Inc.
New York   Bloomington

The Few
A Tale of the Marines in the Near Future

iUniverse books may be ordered through booksellers or by contacting:

iUniverse
1663 Liberty Drive
Bloomington, IN 47403
www.iuniverse.com
1-800-Authors (1-800-288-4677)

ISBN: 978-1-4401-8120-7 (pbk)
ISBN: 978-1-4401-8121-4 (ebk)

Printed in the United States of America

iUniverse rev. date: 10/19/2009

Prologue

The Military Reform Act of 2018, which merged most of the Marine Corps into the Army, consolidated the various service intelligence agencies, and brought logistics and procurement under one joint agency, was primarily passed as a means to lower the federal budget.

Without the Islamic Renaissance, however, it is unlikely that there would have been support to pass the act. When the leaders of All major branches of Islam, inspired by the efforts of such men as Prince Ghazi bin Muhammad of Jordan and Sheik Ali Gomma of Egypt, announced an end to terrorism as a means to promote religious causes, the US military seemed at once too expensive of a luxury to maintain.

The prime directive of the fatwa was that no violence could be conducted against innocents. That meant no more indiscriminate bombings, no more indiscriminate attacks, no more kidnappings, torture, and executions. Suicide was announced as a sure step into hell, as expressed in the *Qur'an*. Any Muslim who ignored this fatwah would be hunted down and killed as being false followers of the Prophet.

There were other parts of the Renaissance as well, such as the re-establishment of the university at Timbuktu (once the greatest university in the world), equal (if separate) rights for women, and a movement to the non-aligned sector of world politics. The rest of the world wondered if this was merely fodder for public consumption or if it was for real. Some Islamic religious leaders decried the fatwa and issued their own, but the public had grown tired of the years of violence and continued poverty when the rest of the world improved its standard of living. Western forces in Iraq, Afghanistan, and the Sudan drew back to their bases. Navy ships off the coast of Iran and Malaysia withdrew. The world watched as small flurries of violence erupted and as stubborn imams and their small forces were overwhelmed by local military forces joined by farmers, businessmen, students and shopkeepers. A few weeks of spasms, and calm entered the scene. It seemed the Renaissance was for real.

Within a year, all US forces in the Muslim world were deployed back to the US and the final cost of the War on Terror was being tallied.

That cost was high: years of deploying forces abroad, years of expenditures in equipment; years of military men and women coming home in body bags; years of increased security on the homefront. Years of politicians trying to justify the sacrifices.

With the removal of Islamic Extremism as an enemy, there wasn't a strong, obvious reason to keep a large military to a public weary of years of fighting. Who was the enemy? Why keep such a large military? A resurgent Russia was not considered a military threat to the US, and China's "threat" was economical.

Now, some politicians saw their opportunity to make their mark on the nation. A triumvirate of three legislators, Congressman Thomas Eddy (D-NY), Senator Katherine Brooke (D-MO), and Senator Michael Eduardo (R-CA) felt this was their opportunity. Although coming from different directions, all three had the same goal—a drastic reduction in the military. Congressman Eddy had always felt that violence was not the answer to anything, and that the show of military force always damaged the interests of the nation showing the force. Although he toned down his rhetoric somewhat to get elected, he was still an opponent of militarism. Senators Brooks and Eduardo thought that the vast expenditures made on the military could be used either in other programs or to reduce the budget.

Together, these three fairly junior politicians, with behind-the-scenes support from politicians in greater positions of power, were able to ramrod through the act. Large numbers of servicemen would be de-mobilized. Units were to be disbanded. Weapons programs shut down. Bases closed. And the Marine Corps? The Marines would cease to be.

The Marines might not have been on the skyline to get disbanded had it not been for Senator Eduardo. The Senator published report after report on how much savings would be realized without a separate Marine Corps. He pointed out that in the War on Terror, Marines and Army units had been used interchangeably. One Army Division, one Marine Division. Same mission. With only a handful of former Marines still in public office, it seemed as if Eduardo would succeed where Harry Truman had failed.

Although not a former Marine himself, Secretary of State Zachary Dischner's father had been a Marine, and Zach remembered his father's pride at being part of the "Frozen Chosen." Truth be told, he also liked having his own military, in a sense, with the Marine Security Guards at his embassies. He approached then President Holt and suggested that they shouldn't let Eduardo gain too much traction with this. By keeping alive the Corps as the Presidential and Embassy Guards, they would seem in touch with the needs to reform the military, they would somewhat appease those who served in the Corps, and would be able to have their own praetorian guards, so-to-speak. President Holt liked the idea of special presidential guard, but he liked more the idea of throwing a fly in the ointment of Eduardo's rise.

When the Act was finally signed, the Corps was alive—barley. Reduced to a single regiment, one battalion was to serve as embassy guards around the world, one at the White House and Camp David. The Marines would keep Quantico and the museum at the Washington Navy Yard. The Marine reserves would be reduced to the staff at the museum and a very small IMA detachment. Of the 180,000 active duty and 120,000 Reservists, most would be either released or transferred to one of the other three services. A select few would be retained as Marines to man the regiment.

Chapter 1

Early Tuesday Morning, Marine House, New Delhi

Gunnery Sergeant Jacob McCardle, USMC, sat in his skivvies on his easy chair in his quarters and sipped his Thums Up Cola, savoring the sort of cough medicine aftertaste that so many other Americans detested, but he sort-of liked. The cool air from the wheezing air conditioner rendered his room bearable, but only just. He glanced at his watch, and with a sigh, he realized it was time to get dressed.

He checked his dress blues blouse one last time as it hung on the hanger. On his blouse were the dual "toilet bowls" of a Marine basic marksman, the Marines' lowest level of basic shooting competency. Twice, Gunny Mac had qualified sharpshooter, but both times, he had fallen back to marksman the next year on the range. Of the 16 Marines in the detachment, only the Gunny and PFC Ramon were "dual stool." Above his shooting badges were the ribbons denoting his good conduct medals (seven awards), his National Defense Service Medal, Global War on Terrorism Service Medal, Iraq Service Medal, and the ubiquitous Embassy Duty Service Ribbon. Not really that much for 22 years in service, he thought, but at least he kept the Marine uniform when so many others had not.

Satisfied with his blouse, he carefully took his trousers off the hanger, trying not to wrinkle them, and cautiously stepped into the legs and raised them up to his waist. He zipped them and fastened the belt, then slid into his shoes. Lifting his blouse off the hanger, he slowly put it on and fastened the buttons. The tightness of the fit around his belly was more evidence that he might be putting on a little weight. He wondered if he was going to have to finally give in and get the blouse re-fitted. Well within Marine weight standards, Gunny was none-the-less unhappy with the overall "softening" of his physique over the last couple of years.

Gunny Mac stepped to the mirror for one last check on his appearance. Getting ready for an inspection was always harder on the inspector. Each Marine getting inspected had one set of eyes checking him or her out-- his. But he had each and every Marine checking him out as well. And for this inspection, the stakes were even higher. Although he had seen the former president many times while on White House duty, he had never seen this president, and he had never seen a president in another setting. Personally, Gunny Mac would never forgive the president for his part in the dismantling of the Corps while a senator, but the man was his commander-in-chief, and the office carried a solemn weight in its own right. And the fact that the company XO would be there as well only added to the pressure. Gunny Mac was up for one of the two E-8 slots open this year, and there were a lot of other gunnies seeking those same slots. If this didn't go off well, he could kiss E-8 goodbye forever.

He took one last swig of The Thums Up then walked out the hatch and into the passageway. He looked at his watch—two more minutes to go. Down the passageway and out the main entry of the Marine House, he could see the ceremonial honor guard easing into position. The detachment had gone on a port and starboard watch to get ready for the visit, and the ceremonial guard was merely the planned off duty watch plus LCpl Saad. Four Marines in the color guard itself, and four in the cordon. The rest of the detachment would be on post when the president arrived. Gunny had already inspected them and sent them off to relieve the honor guard so they could get ready. Normally, for a POTUS visit, the other detachments in neighboring countries would send augmentation, but there had been problems with the Indian government and entry visas, so the New Delhi detachment had to make do with the personnel on hand.

The honor guard had been practicing for a week. Every one of the actual guard had already served at the White House and had performed honor guard duties time and time again for visiting dignitaries and ceremonies. So this should have been no problem. However, no matter how much the Corps had changed, some things never did. So they were instructed to practice and practice for their thirty seconds when they might be in view of the president.

The hatch to the duty office swung open and Captain Leon-Guerro walked out. The Company C XO had been hovering around for three days, trying mightily to let the Gunny do his job but worried that some detail would slip through the cracks.

Gunny knew that Captain Leon-Guerro was a Guamanian, a third-generation Marine. His grandfather had been a general, and it was accepted among the other Marines that that had been a major factor in his getting into the Corps. Slots for junior officers after the dismemberment were very hard to get, and Captain Leon-Guerro hardly looked like a stereotypical 8th and I Marine. At 5'4", the captain was one of the shortest male Marines in the company. But he wasn't a small man. His chest and arms were huge, and his legs were like logs. No one who saw him doubted his raw animal strength. It was common knowledge that he had played for the American Eagles Rugby team as a loosehead prop while in school, and it wasn't hard for Gunny Mac to imagine him charging down the rugby pitch in search of a victim.

The company headquarters was located in Nicosia, so the captain (or any officer, for that matter) was not normally at the detachment. Due to the presidential visit, however, he had come to watch over things. Gunny thought the Captain was OK, if somewhat prone to worrying. And he appreciated that the captain stayed mostly out-of-the-way and let the Gunny do his job. Major Morrisroe, the company commander, might have come instead, but he had chosen to go to Amman to oversee that stop in the president's itinerary. Gunny rather preferred having the captain come, if I had to be anyone. Major Morrisroe was rather demanding and hard to please, and he just didn't want to have to deal with that particular stress-bomb along with the rest of the rigmarole.

Captain Leon-Guerro seemed to have a permanent warrior's scowl on his face, but he was actually quite soft-spoken. He had the habit of chewing his fingernails when under stress. As he spied the gunny and walked over to him, he was chewing away.

"Gunny Mac! I need to talk to you."

Gunny came to almost-attention and faced the captain.

"I just got a call from Major Ingersoll in Amman, You are not going to believe this. The advance team told him that the president did not want the Corps Colors in the color guard. Only the US Colors. They had to ditch the Corps Colors at the last second."

Gunny Mac's mouth dropped open. "You've got to be shitting me, sir?"

"No, It's true. LtCol Duhs told him to call us and give us the word. No Marine Colors today."

Gunny Mac felt as if he had been pole axed. "That doesn't make sense, sir. We had the Marine Colors at the White House and Camp David. We've used them here. What's going on?"

"I don't know. But we have the word from CO. We've got to lose the Colors."

"So we go with three Marines? The US Colors and two honor guards?

"That's what they want."

"Aye-aye, sir." Gunny Mac came to full attention, performed a left face, then marched down the passageway to the awaiting team, scowling as he went.

Opening up the front hatch, Gunny walked out onto the parking lot where the Marines were in a semblance of a formation. Staff Sergeant Child brought them to attention.

"Guard, atten—HUT!"

Gunny Mac decided to inspect them first, then give them the news. He marched over to Staff Sergeant Child who saluted.

"Honor Guard formed and ready for inspection!"

"Very Well."

Gunny Mac looked at Staff Sergeant Child. Joseph Child. A modern day Marine hero, of sorts. The only living Marine of the modern era to receive a silver star when he was the lone survivor in his detachment of the attack on the embassy in La Paz. At 6'3" and 220 pounds of muscle, it wasn't hard to imagine him dragging the ambassador into the crypto room and holding off the attackers with a chair until the Bolivian police arrived to restore order. Walnut-colored skin, square jaw, and now with a slight scar from the attack crossing his chin, he was the poster-book Marine. Literally. He was the Marine currently on the posters still used by recruiting. Enlisting weeks before the dismemberment, he was technically "Old Corps" even if he didn't hit the fleet until after the dismemberment. He was the only Marine in his San Diego boot camp class to keep the Marine uniform. Brighter and more intelligent than just about everyone else, his future looked promising. Many thought him to be on the track for Sergeant Major. Gunny Mac tended to agree with that thought.

As usual, Staff Sergeant Child was immaculate. Gunny Mac nodded at him and said "Precede me."

Stepping in front of Sergeant Tony Niimoto, Gunny felt a small misgiving. Sergeant Niimoto was to bear the Corps Colors today. Gunny Mac felt a little outclassed intellectually by Korea Joe (a nickname he had picked up in bootcamp by a drill instructor who obviously did not know the origins of his family name.) It wasn't that he showed off his intelligence. In fact, he seemed like any other Marine, if rather talkative and prone to break out in a loud, donkey-like laugh at the slightest provocation. But he was a graduate of Stanford, and that daunted the gunny a bit. He was also the best marksman in the detachment, if not the company. While at Camp David, he had been on the depleted Marine team which won the National Rifle Championship trophy at Camp Perry against all the other service and civilian teams. Now, on his chest, he had the gold-colored distinguished shooter medal.

Gunny Mac nodded at Sergeant Niimoto and moved on the next Marine, Corporal Samantha Ashley. Corporal Ashley was taller than Gunny Mac, slender and hard. In uniform, she seemed to have a runner's body, but in the weight room, she revealed corded muscles that could push a surprising amount of iron. Quietly competent, she did what was asked of her in a determined and thorough fashion. She rarely joined the rest for a beer or cards, but spent most of her time reading or working out. She went out in town to worship at a local Christian church, and she had been taking Hindi lessons. Gunny Mac could never get a feel for her. Not overly attractive, she had pale blonde hair and piercing blue eyes. The rest of the detachment often speculated about her—her background, her goals, even her sexual orientation--but since she pulled more than her own weight, they let matters lie.

Next in line was the other rifle bearer, Corporal Seth Crocker. Corporal Crocker loved two things in life—the Red Sox and Sam Adams beer. He somehow convinced someone at the embassy to have his Sam Adams piggybacked in with the embassy's booze shipment, and he kept that as his private stash. Technically against regulations, the previous detachment commander had chosen to ignore it, and when the battalion commander joined Crocker for a brew on one of his visits, Gunny decided to let that dog lie. Corporal Crocker also had Lance Corporal Steptoe take his PDA and hack past the subscription firewalls for the Sox games. A good Marine, he still needed to be watched. He should have received office hours for listening to a game while on post, but he had gotten off with a warning. Gunny Mac still kept track of when the Sox were playing and checked up on Crocker if he was on post at the same time.

On a sudden impulse, Gunny Mac turned quickly, without warning, to see if he could catch Staff Sergeant Child unawares. Child smoothly executed his own right face as if physically connected to Mac. The gunny almost smiled, struggling to keep on his game face. He wasn't going to catch Child that easily.

Stepping in front of the first member of the cordon, Gunny wiped the hint of the smile from his face. Lance Corporal Saad had his usual nervous look on his face. This was his perpetual countenance. LCpl Mahmoud Saad was actually part of the other watch, but he was in the cordon to make the numbers right. A logistics specialist, he was a natural linguist. Speaking English, Spanish, Farsi, Arabic, Chinese, Hindi, and who knows what else, he was the duty dictionary. Now he was studying Bantu. He was also the detachment pool shark. Many modern era Marines were athletic and fit enough to max out the PFT, but Saad could crank out 120 situps in two minutes and do 50 dead-hang pull-ups. He had trouble maxing out the run, though. He would offer smirking encouragement to Gunny when he was struggling to get his 20 pull-ups, so Gunny took a perverse satisfaction on running him into the ground during detachment runs. He knew it wasn't professional, but driving Saad in the humid New Delhi heat until the guy literally puked gave Gunny a small degree of satisfaction. But he could find no fault with Lance Corporal Saad's uniform, so he moved on.

No one would take Lance Corporal Harrington Steptoe for the twisted genius that he was. Tall and big, he had a look of softness about him and a dull expression which might make some think he was the village idiot. The Marine Corps got it right when they gave him the

2802 MOS. Steptoe was a genius with anything electronics. In another era, he would have been a master hacker. Now, he merely invented ways to make his life and that of his peers easier.

An African American, he had a small splash of freckles across the bridge of his nose. This caused him no end of grief from other African American Marines who pulled his chain constantly about how that proved he wasn't really black. When he finally gave up defending himself and began his own jabs back, the teasing on that aspect faded away. However, one aspect did not fade away. Lance Corporal Steptoe had a serious case of hero worship. He looked in awe towards Staff Sergeant Child. His feelings were so obvious that the other Marines started calling him "Stepchild." He took it as a badge of honor.

Then there were the two newbies, Privates First Class Ramon and Van Slyke. Both on their first duty station. Both going to see the president for the first time.

Gunny Mac stepped in front of PFC Ivy Ramon, known as "Princess" by the detachment. Princess was short, about 5'2" with a cute, very young-looking face. But there was nothing child-like about her figure. Her Alphas seemed to strain to contain her rather large breasts. Gunny Mac did not know where to look when inspecting her. He looked down at her while she stared straight ahead into his chest. As he looked down, his eyes were drawn to the swell of her chest. He looked away quickly, but then felt his eyes being drawn back.

Truth be told, Gunny was rather attracted to PFC Ramon. From the second she marched into the duty office to report in, he felt something stirring inside him. He really hadn't had a serious girlfriend in years, and seeing this pert, smiling woman with an amazingly curvaceous frame brought to the surface longings he thought he had suppressed. But Gunny Mac was a professional, first and foremost. She was a PFC in his command, and he would not step over the boundaries set by years of tradition in the Corps. So no matter what he wished, he tried to treat her like any other Marine.

But Princess was not like any other Marine. How she made it through boot camp was a topic of much discussion. Princess always seemed to just get by. On her first PFT, she barely passed. She barely passed her marksmanship training. She barely passed her drill. She had been counseled about laughing when on post. She picked up her nickname because of her obsession with her appearance and living quarters. She lightheartedly complained about any training that messed up her nails or hair, then would rush back at the first opportunity to give herself a manicure. She shared a room with LCpl Wynn, but there was little doubt as to whose rack was whose. Princess had a stuffed pink dog, a frilly pillow, and a pink comforter on her rack and a poster of some young movie star-of-the-moment (Gunny didn't even begin to recognize who it might be) posted above her desk. She was like a high school girl suddenly transported into wearing the Marine uniform.

Gunny Mac looked down at Ramon. He was surprised to see that her marksmanship badge was off kilter. The surprise was that Staff Sergeant Child had not corrected it. He started to reach for it, but then stopped. He wasn't sure how he should fix it lying as it was on the platform of her left breast. He decided to ignore it for now and make sure it was fixed before the president's arrival.

Private First Class Peter Van Slyke stood awaiting inspection. A Maine Military Academy graduate, he was a legacy Marine. Five generations of Van Slykes had preceded him. His Great-Grandfather had been awarded the Medal of Honor in Vietnam, and his father was killed in Iraq. Van Slyke wanted to be an officer, but family tradition required that he serve as an enlisted Marine first. Of average height and with flaming red hair, Van Slyke had an earnestness about him which made the other Marines back off of riding him about his desire of being an officer. He had been pretty impressive so far in his short time on station.

Gunny Mac stepped away from PFC Van Slyke and moved slowly to the front of the formation, giving Staff Sergeant Child enough time to get in position. He stepped up to Child.

"They look good. As always. I need to talk to them, though. Have them form up in a school circle."

"Aye-aye, sir! Detail. Fall out and form up round the Gunny."

The Marines each took a step backward, executed an about-face, then moved forward to gather round. Gunny Mac looked at each one before beginning.

"OK Marines, you look good. For most of you, this is not big deal. But for you newbies, this is your first time with POTUS. Remember what they taught you at Quantico, though. He is not here to see you.

You don't exist. You don't look at him. You are a statue. Once it is over, you can e-mail home and say you were two feet from the President of the United States. But until then, just do exactly as we've rehearsed over the last week. Nothing more, nothing less." He paused a second. "And there is a change. We are not going to have the full Color Guard. Only the US Colors will be presented." He looked at Sergeant Niimoto.

"That's bullshit, Gunny!" cried out Corporal Crocker. "We always have a full guard. Always!'

The grumbling started up in echo of Crocker's outburst.

"First he fucks the Corps, then he fucks us. Spits on us." That was Saad. He understood just where the decision had been made.

"I say fuck this piece of shit. He can march in with his Secret Service. He doesn't need us."

Gunny knew he should have stopped it right away. But he wanted to vent, too, and he let them vent for him. After a few moments of this, he considered it to be time to stop the complaints.

"OK, zip it. I don't want to hear about it. The Battalion CO is over in Amman now, and he gave us the word, and that came right from the president himself. He doesn't want the Corps Colors. Period. We go with the National Colors and the two honor guards." Gunny glared at the Marines around him.

Sergeant Niimoto looked up. "What am I supposed to do, Gunny?"

"Well, you aren't going to be in the guard. Just make yourself scarce. I'm going to watch from the Cultural Affairs office. Why don't you join me there? Or go to Post 2 and hang out there." Gunny Mac looked around. "Any more questions?"

The Marines stirred, but no one spoke.

"Staff Sergeant Child. Take charge. I want everyone in place by 1400." With that, Gunny Mac wheeled around and walked back into the Marine House. He could hear Child speaking behind him as he entered the building. Captain Leon-Guerro stood in the passage waiting for him.

"How'd they take it?"

"Like shit, sir. How'd you think they'd take it?"

"Yea, I know. I'm taking it the same way."

Gunny Mac didn't reply but walked past him and into his room.

Chapter 2

Tuesday Morning, Marine House, New Delhi

When Gunnery Sergeant Jacob McCardle   enlisted into the Marines, he entered a Corps which was a full member of the US military. Three active duty divisions, three air wings, and three FSSGs formed the offensive power that had served the nation so well over the years. Another reserve division, wing, and FSSG augmented the active forces, and had been in combat in Iraq, Afghanistan, and the Sudan since the turn of the century. The Commandant was a full member of the Joint Chiefs of Staff. One Marine, General Pace, had even served as Chairman of the Joint Chiefs.

Jacob had been a cross-country star in high school in Billings, Montana, earning All-State honors. Looking ahead past graduation, he didn't see much of a future for guys who could merely run fast. When his cousin, a soldier in the 101st Airborne Division was killed in Afghanistan, Jacob decided that he needed to step up. So he marched down to the Army recruiting office.

The Army recruiter had stepped out of the office to use the latrine. With Jacob standing waiting, looking at posters of "An Army of One," he felt a tap on his shoulder. He looked to see a Marine Staff Sergeant standing there.   Staff Sergeant Woleski smiled and escorted Jacob into the Marine recruiters' office. Thirty minutes later, Jacob was signed up as a Marine.

At the Marine Corps Recruit Depot, San Diego, recruit McCardle fared well. Being a natural runner gave him a certain degree of "cred." He performed well enough to be assigned as recruit squad leader, a position he held until marksmanship training at Camp Pendleton's Edson Range. Recruit McCardle just couldn't shoot well, and when he had to endure marksmanship extra instruction, he lost his billet.

What was strange about his shooting abilities, or lack thereof, was that he excelled in other weapons. During the mortar orientation, he found he could hit any target at will. One spotting round, and he could call for fire for effect.

Recruit McCardle qualified with the rifle with his platoon—barely. During the Gauntlet, his recruit squad leader was injured, and Recruit McCardle was promoted back up. Standing on top of Mount Motherfucker, looking down at the mountain he had just humped, he felt a lump in his throat. Exhausted as he was, he had just become a Marine. He had joined a brotherhood.

With the War on Terror, most new Marines moved into combat MOS. Recruit Jacob hoped to become an artilleryman, or if going infantry, a mortarman. But he had also shown an ability to write. So the powers than be decided Recruit Jacobs would become a Public Affairs Marine.

All newly graduated recruits attended a four-week course at the School of Infantry. One precept of the Marines was that every Marine was a rifleman. That is the prime purpose of any Marine, be they aircraft mechanics, cooks, or computer jocks. All of that is secondary—being a rifleman is primary. So Private McCardle become a rifleman. He also became known just as "Mac."

Private "Mac" actually preferred to be called "Jake." He thought the name had power, an élan. "Mac" was so common. It seemed like every Marine with a "Mac" or Mc" before their name became known as "Mac." He told several fellow Marines to call him "Jake," but names either stick or they don't. "Mac" stuck. "Jake" did not.

Four weeks later, Private Mac was off to Fort McNair, Maryland for the Public Affairs Specialist School. This was an intense 20-week school, and Private Mac was the junior person in the class. Normally, most services, including the Marines, sent to the school students who had already served a tour of duty in another specialty first. Private Mac and Airman Cynthia Conners were the only two students right out of basic training. Other students ranged up to E-7. Understandably, both Mac and Conners got pretty much every shit detail.

But Mac liked the school. He learned structure to his writing. He learned how to look at things in the way others might view it. And the proximity of the school to Washington, DC made liberty enjoyable. A Marine sergeant, John Willis was also a student. Newly back from Iraq, Sergeant Willis had a car. On their first liberty, Sergeant Willis ordered Private Mac to get in the car. Private Mac had never been east of Montana before, so he had no idea where they were going. When the car finally stopped near a small, heavily windowed apartment building surrounded by trees, Private Mac still didn't know where they were. Until he steeped out of the car and turned around. There, down a slight rise and across an open expanse of manicured lawn, stood a statue of five Marines and a Navy Corpsman raising the US flag: the Iwo Jima Memorial. Mac felt a lump in his throat. This was the Marine Corps. This was his history now. Sergeant Willis didn't say anything. He let the moment speak for itself.

An hour later, at Boomerangs in Georgetown, Private Mac bought a beer for Sergeant Willis. He figured it was a small price to pay for that gift. Boot camp, Mount Motherfucker, graduation—all hinted at what it was to become a Marine. The Iwo Jima Memorial cemented what it was. And Private Mac knew then he wanted to be a Marine for life.

After graduation from Public Affairs Specialist School, now Private First Class McCardle was given order to the Second Marine Expeditionary Force (Forward) at Camp Fallujah in Iraq. Assigned to the MEF newspaper, *The Globe*, PFC McCardle began penning articles. Some of his articles made it as far at *Leatherneck* and *The Stars and Stripes*. He began to make a small name for himself. As the junior Marine in the office, he was also sent to driver's school and got his license. His extra duty was to drive Colonel Parks, the MEF PAO, or sometimes visiting dignitaries. Colonel Parks was an infantry officer who was now assigned to Public Affairs. A platoon sergeant in the first gulf war, and a company commander in Iraq for the invasion, he was now back—but not as a regimental commander. PFC Mac knew the colonel would rather be holding the point of the spear, but he did his best shepherding VIPSs around. Although technically in charge of the newspaper as well as the television station, Colonel Parks spent most of his time babysitting visiting politicians and public figures. He knew he didn't know the first thing about running a television station, but he also knew that he could shoulder the burden of every VIP Division threw at PA and let the PA experts do their jobs with the paper and television programs. PFC Mac rather admired the colonel for that.

It was after his tour in Iraq that the world according to the Marine Corps changed. The Muslim World rocked the planet, and the US military lost radical Islamic terrorists as a foe. Then the Military Reform Act of 2018 regulated what became known among the Corps as the "Dismemberment."

Much to his surprise, Corporal Mac was selected to remain a Marine. He didn't think he stood much of a chance, so he was already planning his transition to the 1st Civ Div. When his notice came in, his joy was tempered by an almost sense of guilt. No one else in the PA office was selected. In fact, upon his arrival at Quantico for school, he found out he was the only Marine with a Public Affairs MOS to remain.

Over the following years, Gunny Mac served at the embassies in Tokyo, Phnom Penh, Buenos Aries, Quito, Vienna, and Helsinki. He served tours at Camp David and the White House. Now, he was assigned as the detachment commander in New Delhi. And his detachment was on the skyline with the planned arrival of the 48th President of the United States, the former Senator Michael Eduardo: the man who had gutted the Corps.

Chapter 3

Late Tuesday Morning, US Embassy, New Delhi

Gunny Mac left the briefing room where Diplomatic Security Agent Thomas had given a last-minute briefing to the embassy Regional Security Officer and the Agent-in-Charge of the U.S. Secret Service detail. Now they wanted the cordon backed up to the main entrance to the embassy. The Secret Service had wanted to eliminate it altogether, but Major Defilice, the Army assistant attaché, had stepped in and mentioned that after all their preparation, it would hardly seem fair to deprive the young Marines of their chance to see the president. Agent Thomas relented and agreed, but only if the Marines were back off the courtyard (read—where they would not show up on photos of the president's arrival.)

Gunny Mac was pissed on principle. However, he did not envy Agent Thomas his job. Part of the State Department advance team, he was to get the president from the airport through the streets to the embassy in a nation where the US had been becoming increasingly unpopular. The Secret Service had wanted the president to helo onto the embassy's roof, but this was President Eduardo's second trip abroad, and he wanted to be seen. So this resulted in super headaches for the DSS, the Secret Service, and the RSO.

Gunny passed Post One on his way to the courtyard. Sergeant Patricia McAllister ("Little Mac" to the detachment upon the arrival of

Gunny Mac) nodded. Private First Class Jesus Rodriguez was standing beside her, nervously adjusting his blues. Other than the Standard Operating Procedures doubling of the posts for a VIP visit of this magnitude, PFC Rodriguez's main mission was to open the hatch for the president and his entourage after Sergeant McAllister buzzed it open. From the look of him, this was akin to lining up on the 40 yard line to kick the winning field goal with 4 seconds left on the clock. He looked terrified.

Little Mac winked at the Gunny. For a second, he had the perverse fear that Sergeant McAllister would take the advice of the other Marines who'd told her yesterday that she should ask the president for his ID, and if he didn't have it, refuse him entry. That would be something to see, but Gunny rather doubted that neither he nor Little Mac would be around much longer after that. Little Mac had a streak of the ornery. An Arizona honest-to-goodness cowgirl, she had no fear. So if anyone would do it, she would.

Gunny started to turn back to her. She winked again. With a sigh, he turned back around and walked out. He knew in his heart she was digging at him.

Walking out into the bright afternoon sunshine, Gunny had to admit that the new embassy really looked good. The front courtyard was paved in granite brought in from New Hampshire. Entering by vehicle or by foot through the front gate, the huge circular courtyard drew the eyes to the vast embassy itself. In reality, the embassy was nothing more than a squat, square building. However, the architect, in what Gunny felt to be a spasm of creativity, added awnings, mirrors and abutments so that the whole building looked like it was almost ethereal. There was a helicopter pad on the top of the building, but that fact would not be evident to a casual observer. Windows in the outer offices were also mirrored, and it was hard to tell where the windows actually were, where the windows began and the embassy walls ended.

Gunny glanced to the left. The consular building, on the other hand, looked like it belonged in another era. Over the fishpond at the edge of the courtyard, and over a lawn, it rose with columns like a Southern plantation house. Gunny wondered which government agency gave the OKs for the two buildings. It had to have been two different agencies, because no single source could possibly have approved both.

They just clashed too much. Separate from the consulate, adjacent the embassy walls and near the street, was a communications tower, disguised poorly to look like a bell tower, or a *campanile*, as the embassy guide termed it. Oh, there was a bell in the belfry, but it wasn't fooling anyone. Under the bell, there was a platform which gave technicians access to the equipment in the tower's cupola, and there were several rooms below the cupola with more equipment in them. The Marines of the detachment liked to go up there and sit. This was probably not allowed, but since the view and breeze were nice, it fell under the don't ask for permission rule. And until someone said anything different, the Marines would continue to use it.

Post 2 was in the consular building. Staff Sergeant Harwood and Sergeant Chen were at the post right now. Harwood was the SOG and should actually be at the embassy checking Post 1, but Gunny Mac knew he was probably trying to stay away from the procession. In days gone by, he would be leading a react force, but the DSS and USSS now took over that function. Gunny would have to speak to him later about hiding out at Post 2. He didn't have time now.

One of the Secret Service agents went up to Crocker and Ashley, asking to see their weapons. Crocker rolled his eyes, but handed his M18 over. The agent checked to see that there were no magazines in the weapons, then checked the chamber. As the agent stepped away, Crocker held up four fingers and mouthed that to Gunny Mac that this was the fourth time he had been checked. Gunny smiled back. He also had been checked three times so far, and although he had no round in the chamber, his three magazines were full. Regulations, he told both the Secret Service and the DSS. They chose not to make an issue of it.

Gunny Mac went up to the cordon and had them move back almost to the embassy's front entrance, under the awning. Two on one side of the walkway, two on the other. He checked out Princess. Her marksmanship badge was straight now. Someone had fixed it. Standing further back was cooler, at least. The overhead covering which provided protection from the elements kept the sun off of them. Staff Sergeant Child and the two honor guards were stuck standing out in the full brunt of the late morning sun's heat.

He walked down the red carpet that had been laid an hour ago, and approached Child. "Everything OK?"

"Sure Gunny. We're ready." Staff Sergeant Child didn't even look like he was sweating, unlike Crocker who had a dark patch forming between his shoulder blades.

Gunny looked out at the street through the Embassy's main gates. There were a couple hundred protesters mulling about out there, listless without someone upon whom to focus their attention. Lance Corporal Shareetha Wynn was manning the front gate with a DSS agent. Although in reality the purview of the Indian security employees, Captain Leon-Guerro had suggested a Marine be at the gate when the president arrived, and since the detachment was on a temporary port/ starboard watch, there was the manpower to do it. Lance Corporal Wynn had just reported for duty two weeks earlier, so she got the job with the easiest requirements—come to attention when the president drove through, salute, and go back to parade rest. Of course, coming from Camp David, this was old news to her, thought Gunny Mac.

Looking back at the protesters, Gunny remarked, "Well, I guess he isn't getting a popular reception."

"No, I guess he wouldn't," responded Child. "His campaigning on bringing jobs back to the US and his stance on the Kashmir issue sure wouldn't have won him any friends here."

Gunny looked up at Child. He really didn't know much about that issue. Oh sure, he was briefed about the decades-long problem in the Kashmir, but jobs? What was that all about? Child continually surprised him.

The shoulder mic of the Secret Service agent standing at the head of the red carpet came to life. "Grizzly turning onto Sadar Patel Marg. ETA 5 minutes."

Chapter 4

Late Tuesday Morning, US Embassy, New Delhi

"Grizzly turning onto Sadar Patel Marg. ETA 5 minutes."

Staff Sergeant Child looked at Gunny Mac. The Gunny obviously had not understood his comment about the president's popularity in India, or lack thereof. Gunny was a good Marine, a good guy. But for someone who had been a reporter, he really did not seem to follow the news or world events much.

Staff Sergeant Child straightened up. "Well, here we go."

"I guess I had better get out of the way. You've got it." Gunny turned and walked back up the red carpet and into the embassy.

"Crocker, Ashley, let's form up." It felt a little strange standing there without the Marine Colors to his left.

Staff Sergeant Child had been in more than a few Color Guards in his career. And, God willing, he would serve in many more. So standing there with only the National Colors and flanked by two riflemen felt disjointed. But he could adjust. He always did.

Joseph Child came from Detroit, from an area where, if pressed, he would admit was "perhaps not the best." That was an understatement. He lived with his mother and father in a small tenement, where electricity was seemingly out off more often than it was on. He walked to school past the corners, amongst pushers and hoodlums, past gangbangers and hookers. Yet even then, there was something about him that made him special. People knew he was going somewhere, he was going to be somebody, and they left him alone.

His teachers knew it, too, and they felt validation for long hard hours in trying conditions when they saw Joseph (never "Joe," always "Joseph") soak in the knowledge. By high school, he knew more about certain subjects than his teachers. They knew he was destined for college where he would shine.

So it took them all by surprise when he enlisted into the Corps. How could he waste such an opportunity to become a mere soldier? That was OK for other kids who needed to escape the ghetto, kids with no other choices. But not for Joseph.

But Joseph was more than a child of the classroom. He was more complex than that.

Joseph's father, Will Child, had served in the Navy as a young man. He hadn't seen combat, but he had participated in a humanitarian relief effort in Bangladesh. When his tour was up, he got out and returned to Detroit where he was never able to land a good steady job. He regretted leaving the Navy, and he let young Joseph know that. He also instilled in Joseph a love of the country. Even though Will never seemed to get the break he wanted, he never blamed anyone else for that. He insisted that the US was the land of opportunity, and it deserved the love and support of all of its citizens.

Joseph was a bright kid with a quest for answers, but he also loved to compete. A natural athlete, he ruled the b-ball courts for his age group, and he was able to play with the older guys. He found an old skate board, and he loved to play tricks on it. The school had long dropped its wrestling program, but Joseph found a dojo where he learned taekwondo. It seemed whatever he wanted to try, he succeeded.

Truth be told, Joseph liked to fight. There was something so basic, so primeval about being able to vanquish your opponents. When he was 9 years old, walking home from school one day, a stoned fiend was mugging strange Old Lady Williams who refused to let her purse go. This was in broad daylight, but no one moved to stop it. Something came over Joseph, and he dropped his books and charged. The suddenness of his attack, his fury, (and the fact that the mugger was stoned, most likely) overcame his youth and undeveloped body, and he beat the mugger into unconsciousness. He then dragged the body up the steps of the crack house nearby and dropped him on the stoop, a warning to others.

The neighborhood gangbangers thought it was funny and called him Little Big Man. He became sort of a mascot, so the dope fiends left him alone for attacking one of their own. Later, as his body matured and he picked up taekwondo, he didn't need anyone else. He could take care of himself.

In the back of his mind, Joseph also had the beginnings of an interest to serve in government. He knew he would have to go to school for that. But serving in the Marines certainly would not hurt should he want to go into politics. And it would give him a chance to see more of the world. But most of all, it was a challenge he could not pass up. So he enlisted.

During boot camp at Parris Island, Recruit Child shone. It seemed he could do no wrong. Well, almost no wrong. Initially, he worried about himself, and his performance became a competition against the other recruits. During week 3, after a junk-on-the-bunk one evening where he excelled and his bunkmate failed miserably, Sergeant Parton, one of his junior DIs, took him aside for some "extra instruction." Five hours later, after some "patient explanations" and arms which could barely move any longer, Recruit Child realized that the Corps was a team. Individuals can shine, but they shine more when the team shines. A renewed Recruit Child became the driving force in the series. It was a forgone conclusion that he would be the series honor grad.

Then the dismemberment became a reality. The series was in flux. What was going to happen? Graduation was both joyous and somber⊠joyous for making it through, somber because only one recruit would stay with the Marines, Private First Class Child. And for the graduation parade, Will Child, leaving Detroit for the first time in years, wiped away the tears as PFC Child led the entire company in the pass-in-review.

Going to Quantico, PFC Child was given odd jobs until the incoming Marines arrived for re-training at the Security Guard School. And despite being in class with Marines up to E-7, he was once again the honor grad. Marines looked at Child and knew he was going places.

PFC Child's first duty station was the White House where he served an uneventful tour. It was at his next duty station at the Embassy in Lima where Child became part of Marine Corps history.

One aspect of the dismemberment was that Marines on Embassy Duty would not carry firearms. Carrying firearms was deemed too "militaristic," and an insult to the security forces of the host country. Colonel Byrd, the new Marine Commandant, resigned over this in protest. But the Marines were disarmed. "Every Marine is a rifleman" became hard to defend anymore.

Then on April 26, 2022, in a coordinated attack, mobs overran the embassies at Lima and Caracas. The local "security forces" either disappeared or joined the mob. Without weapons, the Marines were overwhelmed. In Caracas all the Marines were killed along with the ambassador and all but 3 of the American staff. A large amount of classified material also disappeared into the hands of the mob.

At Lima, the mob hesitated for a few moments as the ambassador, Hank Stellars (a political appointee who had contributed heavily to the then president's election) confronted them and asked for their grievances. This gave the Marines time to destroy the classified materials. Coming back out, the Marines arrived just as the mob surged. The Marines, aided by some members of the staff, charged the mob and dragged back the ambassador who had been knocked to the ground and injured. In a running retreat, Lance Corporal Child and others brought the ambassador back to the crypto room. Down to Child, another Marine, the RSO, and a Navy ensign on temporary duty to the Naval Attaché, the three stood over the ambassador and beat members of the mob who tried to enter the door with pieces of broken furniture. By the time the Peruvian Army arrived to drive the mob back, only Child and the ambassador were alive.

Lance Corporal Child was meritoriously promoted to Corporal and was awarded the Silver Star for his actions. And the regulations were changed. Marines would be armed again. The doors to all the Army's armories were opened, and the new Marine Commandant could take what he wanted to arm his detachments.

Corporal Child could have left the Corps then. He was a minor celebrity with his 15 minutes of fame, and he could have gotten into any university, or possibly even skipped school to enter right into politics, if he really wanted. But he liked the Corps. He liked being around others like him. He had found a home.

He was observant, too. He was aware that others thought he could make Sergeant Major. Sergeant Major of the Marine Corps. It still had a nice ring to it.

Several years later, Staff Sergeant Child stood in the courtyard of the embassy in New Delhi waiting for the president to arrive. He was well-trained, and he was thoroughly capable. Nobody could throw anything at him that he couldn't handle.

Special Agent Freely, whose shoulder mic had just announced the president's imminent arrival, turned to Child and needlessly announced, "The president will be here shortly." Freely had been part of the advance team, and Child had formed a rapport with him. It was Freely who had told him that while the president's code name was "Grizzly," some members of the secret service had pushed for "Enchilada," as in "The Grand Enchilada." Given that the president was the first Hispanic to hold the office, cooler heads prevailed. Still, some agents privately referred to him as "TGE." Child thought it was rather funny in a lame sort of way.

Staff Sergeant Child gave Crocker and Ashley one more look. Crocker was sweating heavily now, but there was nothing to do about that. He took his place at the edge of the red carpet, flanked by the other two. He could see the new Marine, LCpl Wynn come to a more formal position of parade rest. Evidently the DSS service agent standing next to her had given her the heads up.

Over his left shoulder, he could see some of the higher ranking embassy officials and their spouses milling in loose order against the front of the building to the right of the main entrance. Most of the staff and guests from the diplomatic community were already over at the consulate for the reception, but these select few would be there to bask in the twenty seconds it took the president to walk from the vehicle down the red carpet to and into the embassy.

There began to be some motion outside the gate. The Indian police were moving the crowd further back off the road. Sensing something was about to happen, the crowd started chanting "Down with Eduardo, down with USA." They pronounced the president's name as "e-dar-do," instead of "ed-war-do." They seemed to lack the fervor he experienced before the attack in Lima, so Child was not too concerned. Demonstrations against Americans were common happenings.

The front gate began to open. The chanting grew louder, but the local police seemed to have things in hand. Staff Sergeant Child could glimpse the flashing lights of the motorcycle cops coming down the road. "Detail, atten—HUT!" Child brought the three of them to attention.

The motorcycle cops stopped at the sides of the gate, and the first black Suburban entered the courtyard. It drove past the red carpet, and several secret service agents hopped out. The next Suburban entered the courtyard, then pulled to the right. More agents got out along with some staff members holding briefcases or talking on phones.

The third Suburban came right up to the red carpet. An agent rushed over to open the door, and President Michael Eduardo stepped out. He turned and waved to the chanting crowd as the Ambassador and the Embassy Staff Secretary got out of the other side and hurried over to lead the president down the red carpet.

"Detail, present HARMS!" Child heard Crocker and Ashley bring their rifles up.

The final Suburban entered the courtyard. Child could hear the gate begin to close. In the corner of his eye, he could see Ambassador Tankersly place his hand in the small of the president's back and point down the red carpet. The president took a step down the carpet, not acknowledging the Color Guard. Staff Sergeant Child felt anger rise up within him. He knew the president did not like Marines. But this was the US flag he was holding.

On the other side of the red carpet, Special Agent Freely was pacing the president, eyes not looking at the president but rather glancing back-and-forth at just about everything else. He suddenly stopped and looked up.

Chapter 5

Late Tuesday Morning, US Embassy, New Delhi

"Grizzly turning onto Sadar Patel Marg. ETA 5 minutes." The Special Agent in the front passenger seat spoke into his shoulder mic.

Michael Antonio David Eduadro, 48th President of the United States, settled back into the soft leather of the Suburban. He ran his hands over the seat, taking in the texture. There were Suburbans, and then there were Suburbans. When he was a child, his father had had a Suburban, taking him to the ranches and tracks where he made his living as a farrier. A work truck, his father's Suburban rode like it, even with the heavy-duty suspension installed to handle the extra weight of the equipment. Now this, this was different. This was like riding a tank—a luxury tank, to-be-sure. Even sitting in the back, he could feel the vehicle's power. During one of his first briefings by the Secret Service in the time after the election leading up to his inauguration, he had seen a video of one of the Suburbans on a test range somewhere withstand a direct hit from a rocket-propelled grenade. He really didn't know much about military weapons, but that impressed him.

But this Suburban was hardly just a fortress on wheels. It was plush, from the roses in the sconces to the chilled Dr. Pepper (bottles, not cans, and flown in from Texas using the original recipe with cane sugar, not corn syrup), to the incredibly comfortable seats, this was riding in style. As a senator, he had ridden in many limos, but for a boy from California's Central Valley, this was it. This was the one thing which really brought home the fact that he was the most powerful man in the world. Not living at the White House, not addressing Congress, not attending G-10 Conferences. Just riding in one of the many Suburbans stashed around the world. Somehow, this was something to which he could relate. Deep in his heart, he felt that he had somehow lucked into the presidency, that he wasn't really up to the job, that someday the nation would wake up to that fact. But in the Suburban, with his Secret Service in tow, he felt like a president. He felt "presidential."

As they rode through the streets toward the embassy, he tuned out most of what Ambassador Tankersly was saying, nodding at times to make it seem as if he were listening. Tankersly was a political appointee, but not one of his. He hadn't been president long enough to put in his own supporters in positions like these. And Tankersly obviously was angling to keep his job. Approaching 60, Tankersly was into pulp timber in North Carolina. From the briefing the president had received on Air Force One, he reveled in the diplomatic social scene in New Delhi, but he also seemed to be holding his own navigating the tricky path between the US and India, where job loss, trade imbalances, and most of all, the Kashmir and the US's tacit support of Pakistan has caused some serious rifts between the two nations. Looking at Tankersly's round, florid face, the president would not guess him to be that capable, but then looks could be deceiving. The president had many favors to fill, and an ambassadorship was one of the accepted rewards for political and, more importantly, financial support. And it might be that a career diplomat would be a better choice for India given the current situation. But perhaps Tankersly had earned the chance to keep his position. The president hadn't really thought about it enough to make up his mind.

It still amazed him that this was even something on which he had to make up his mind. He had come a long, long way since his childhood in Modesto and Bakersfield. Driving down the sun-dappled streets in New Delhi, his thoughts went back to his childhood, to his dream of playing ball for the Giants. Well, he never made it that far, but baseball scholarship to UC Davis had gotten him his veterinarian degree and introduced him to Jennifer. He smiled at the thought.

He tried to listen to Ambassador Tankersly, but he really could not focus. He held up a hand to stop the Ambassador.

"Sorry, Ambassador, but can we hold that thought for a second?"

"Of course, Mr. President, of course."

"Thanks. Ron, can I have the phone? I want to speak with Jennifer," he asked his Staff Secretary.

Ron Neal took one of many phones out of a briefcase, hit a speed dial, and handed it to the president.

"Hello?" said a sleepy voice on the other end.

"Hi baby. Just thinking of you."

There was a contented sigh. "That's nice, darling."

"I miss you. I want you to know that. I was riding here, and I was remembering how this all started, getting into the school board, with you putting up campaign signs with the kids in tow. Anyway, I just wanted to let you know you and the kids are in my thoughts."

"I saw you on CNN giving that speech in Amman. Nice job."

"Thanks baby. Nick wrote it, of course, but I can take the credit," he said with a laugh. "Hey, next State trip, let's think about you coming with me. I know you've got your education initiatives, but I think it would be good. OK?"

"Sure, if you think it is a good idea. I would like that." She still sounded sleepy over the phoe.

"OK baby, I'll let you get back to sleep. Give the kids my love, and I will see you the day after tomorrow. Kiss, kiss."

He heard a "kiss, kiss" in return as he handed back the phone.

Looking back at the Ambassador, he shrugged. "Family takes precedence, even to running the country. Got to keep the homefront happy."

"I understand, Mr. President, and I fully agree. I don't know if you have been briefed on this, but we have implemented a number of family-related initiatives for lower income Indian families. I would be happy to put together a short briefing on them." The ambassador looked anxious to please.

"That would be great," he said, trying to put some degree of sincerity into his voice. The ambassador droned on as the president thought about his last few days. This was only his second trip abroad as president. The first one was a G-10 conference in Halifax, hardly an exotic location.

This trip started with a day in Amman, then he had planned to overnight in New Delhi before heading to Beijing and Tokyo. The president was somewhat surprised to learn that he would be the first serving president to visit New Delhi since Bill Clinton back in 2000. He realized that the US and India had a love-hate relationship (a little more hate over the last several years) but as the second largest country in the world population-wise, and as the world's largest democracy, he would have expected some more attention from the executive branch.

Ambassador Tankersly's voice caught his attention. "This is Chanakyapuri, Mr. President. Most of the embassies are located here." The president looked out of the heavily tinted windows as the ambassador played tour guide. They turned right down a wide, tree-lined road. The president was impressed by the amount of greenery. This looked nothing like what he expected the capital of a major nation to look like. With traffic moved off the route for the motorcade, it rather reminded him of a typical Ohio small town. "Our embassy is right ahead of us."

Up ahead, as they neared the embassy, he could see people lining the road. "I see we have a reception committee ahead?"

"Uh, yes sir. As I told you at the airport, there have been sporadic protests against your visit. Pakistan and jobs, sir."

The president had never really seen foreign protests aimed at him before. At Halifax, all protestors had been kept far way for the resort acting as the summit's headquarters, and most of them were protesting against the Chinese delegation anyway. And in Amman, there has only been a handful of environmental protestors, barely enough to be noticed. Here, there had to be hundreds, if not thousands lining the street around the embassy. He looked on with interest. As the Suburbans drove by, the people seemed energized, holding signs and shouting out. The Indian police kept them off the road proper, but they lined it on the broad sidewalks for several hundred yards from the traffic circle up to the embassy gates.

As they drove into the gates and up to a red carpet, the ambassador needlessly said, "The building in front of you is the embassy itself." As if it could be anything else. "Over to the right is the consulate. That is where the reception will be."

The Suburban stopped and a secret service agent rushed over to get the door. The president stepped out. One of the Marine guards alongside the carpet shouted out "Detail, present "HARMS!" as they did their saluting thing with their guns. He ignored them as he wondered, as he had done since being sworn in, why they couldn't speak normal English. "HARMS?" What the heck was that? He turned to look at the protestors, then raised his arm to wave at them as if they were welcoming him.

The ambassador and his Staff Secretary hurried out of the other side of the Suburban. The ambassador pointed down the carpet. As the president started walking down, the secret service agent, (Special Agent Freeman? Freely?) began to pace him. Suddenly, the agent stopped and looked up.

Chapter 6

Late Tuesday Morning, US Embassy, New Delhi

Gunny walked down the red carpet back into the embassy. He motioned for PFC Rodriguez to leave Post 1 and take his position by the front entrance. Rodriguez licked his lips and came out, running his thumbs along the front of his dress blues, removing imaginary wrinkles. He patted Rodriguez on the shoulder and walked into the passageway to the left. As the detachment commander, he really didn't have a mission. His Marines were at their positions, but he wasn't important enough in the embassy hierarchy to stand outside or even to join the crowd at the consular building.

He walked down the passage to the Ambassador's office where LCpl Jeb Kramer waited at parade rest. "Head's up. The president is about two minutes away."

"OK Gunny."

He checked over Kramer. A former jock, Kramer was voted "Man for All Seasons" at his high school in Des Moines. Despite having heard this from Kramer about half a million times, Gunny still didn't know quite what it meant. Something akin to homecoming king, but having to be a multi-sport star. Regardless, Kramer was still athletic, and he always looked good in uniform.

Inside the ambassador's office, Gunny could see one of the local Indian staff, an older man named Dravid, laying out the antique Russian tea set. He guessed the president would get tea in the ambassador's office when he arrived, tea a few minutes later at the reception, and probably tea when he went to the head (which he would need after drinking so much tea in the first place). Gunny liked coffee better, but Ambassador Tankersly loved tea, and he thought drinking tea showed deference to India.

Gunny nodded to Kramer and walked back down the passage to the Cultural Affairs Section. This was a large office with windows overlooking the courtyard, so he felt this would give him a good view of the president's arrival. As he walked in, he was only somewhat surprised to see Major Defilice and the DSS Agent-in-Charge agent already standing at the window. Most of the embassy staff was at the consular building for the reception.

The major turned around. "Ah, Gunny! Coming to slum with the peons?"

"I thought you'd be at the reception, sir. There's food there, you know?"

"Ah, but half the diplomatic community is there, too. A mere major could never hope to fight off the Romanian Assistant to the Deputy Science Advisor when there is a buffet line in front of him."

Gunny laughed and turned toward the window. The DSS agent eyed the 9 mm at his hip but said nothing. Directly in front of the windows and below were various embassy staff and spouses waiting for the president to arrive. Although he could not hear them through the reinforced windows, he could see the crowd outside the gates starting to intensify its actions. Both the color guard and LCpl Wynn came to attention.

"Well, I guess its showtime!" murmured the major. The gate swung open and a line of black Suburbans drove in. There was a flurry of people jumping out of the first two Suburbans while the third drove right up to the red carpet. A secret service agent moved to open the door, and the President of the United States stepped out. Gunny had never seen this president in person, but he thought he rather looked just like he did on television. Overall, a handsome man, he looked trustworthy. Hard to believe this was the man who'd destroyed the Corps.

SSgt Child brought the color guard to present arms, but the president did not acknowledge them. "*Bastard!*" thought Gunny. He did acknowledge the crowd, though, waving like he was on the campaign trail. Ambassador Tankersly came around form the other side of the Suburban and started to direct the president down the red carpet. One of the accompanying secret service agents suddenly stopped and looked up.

Gunny thought that rather odd, still odder when the agent suddenly flung himself at the president, knocking him to the ground. "Did you see that? He tackled the president!" He felt a jolt as the agent standing beside him swore an oath under his breath and pushed past him, bolting for the door. Out in the courtyard, SSgt Child faltered, slightly dipping the colors as he took a hesitant step toward the prone president lying at his feet with an agent on top of him.

The next few moments seemed to slow down to a standstill. They just couldn't register on his mind.

There was a blinding flash in the courtyard. Gunny stared dumfoundedly as the color guard, the ambassador, and the staff secretary seemed to be pushed to the ground. In quick succession there were four more blasts, rocking the window. Small ticks sounded as shrapnel peppered it, but the window held. The group of people standing outside in front of the window, though, collapsed almost en masse where they stood.

Major Defilice grabbed Gunny Mac by the arm. "Let's go, come on, let's go!" They ran out the door and down the hall toward Post 1. Inside Post 1, Little Mac was standing up staring open-mouthed out the front and down to the courtyard.

Seeing him, she started shouting "Gunny, Gunny!"

LCpl Saad was lying alongside the steps leading up to the entrance. He was holding his right shoulder, and Gunny could see the blue fabric of his blouse turning red. His mouth was open, and he was panting. Princess and Stepchild were huddled behind a stone column flanking the left side of the entrance. LCpl Van Slyke started to follow the agent, who was now rushing toward the president with a small, lethal-looking automatic weapon in his hand.

Rodriguez had taken a step or two following Van Slyke and the secret service. The agent charged toward the president when there was a rattle of fire and a burst of rounds cut him down. He pitched forward with the boneless flop of someone dead before he even hit the ground.

Van Slyke went down as well halfway between the entrance and the president.

Gunny grabbed Rodriguez and pulled him to ground, sliding in back of the other stone column flanking the entrance. There was a blast of answering fire from a secret service agent, and a shadowy figure on the other side of the front gate collapsed. A single shot rang out, and that agent fell.

Gunny glanced around the column. There were a number of prone bodies lying on the ground in the courtyard. A couple agents, whether DSS or USSS, he couldn't tell, were upright and returning fire. One agent rushed toward the president when he stumbled and fell to the ground. He tried to get back to his feet when another round struck him, and he fell back motionless.

Off to the left, Gunny saw movement coming from the consular building. It was Captain Leon-Guerro, running through the fish pond and into the courtyard. Several shots rang out from unseen sources, but they merely kicked up chips of brick and stone at the captain's feet. Gunny watched in awe as the captain ran, powerful legs pushing him along toward the red carpet. A round hit the captain's leg, instantly shredding his blue trousers, but he didn't let that stop him. Then, two rounds hit his chest. This wasn't Hollywood. Captain Leon-Guerro did not go flying backwards in the air. He just collapsed. His momentum kept his body sliding across the ground after he fell, past the president, shoving up the red carpet, and up against SSgt Child and Cpl Ashley. He looked up and lifted his arm toward the US flag and tugged on it, as if he wanted to take it away from the scene. Then his body stilled.

Within a few short moments, the remaining agents in the courtyard were down as well. The gunfire slowed and ceased.

Gunny had pulled his 9 mm and with fumbling hands, inserted a magazine and chambered a round. But he couldn't see a target. The crowd, which had rushed backward after the first blast and gunfire, was now crowding forward, looking inside the fence. Gunny could see Indian police joining them, taking in the carnage.

Then he saw three men push themselves through the crowd up to the gate and spray the courtyard with automatic fire, even though there was no obviously moving target. They started climbing the gate. Gunny tried to get in position for a shot, but that was a long shot for a handgun, especially when made by a piss-poor marksman.

Over at the gatehouse, LCpl Wynn picked herself up off the ground. Even from this distance, Gunny could see the blood streaming down her face and neck. She calmly walked up to the gate as if she were back at Quantico getting ready to qualify on the range. The three men saw her and started scrambling to get their rifles in position to fire, but Wynn coolly shot all three, one after the other, one shot apiece. The men fell back over the gate into the pressing crowd.. She turned around, holstered her 9 mm, took a few steps back towards the embassy, then fell face first to the ground.

Gunny had five Marines down. And the president, and the ambassador, and a shitload of secret service agents. In the momentary lull after Wynn's shots, he jumped up yelling for the Marines near him to follow. Rodriguez, Steptoe, and Ramon jumped up and ran with him. Major Defilice rushed down the red carpet as well.

Gunny reached down to Van Slyke, but the Marine was pushing himself up. His face was covered in blood and his upper lip seemed to be hanging off. "I'm OK Gunny, I'm OK," he managed to get out of his mangled face, blood spraying. Gunny kept going to the end of the carpet.

The closest person to him was Crocker. The right half of Crocker's face was gone, sheared off. His left eye was open, and looked completely normal, as if nothing had happened. But it would never see again. Crocker was gone.

Staff Sergeant Child was moving slightly, but he was obviously hurt pretty bad. Blood was soaking his blouse and trousers, and a pool of blood was forming on the courtyard stones. "Rodriguez! Help me here!" Rodriguez started to kneel next to Gunny Mac when LCpl Steptoe pushed him aside.

"I've got this, Gunny." He reached down and slung Child over his back, exactly as outlined in the Marine Handbook. He could have been demonstrating to a class. He stood up and started back down the red carpet to the embassy entrance.

Cpl Ashley was lying on her back. She didn't look obviously hurt. "Take her back, Rodriguez." Rodriguez grabbed her by the collar and started dragging her. As he dragged her past him, Gunny Mac could see a broad swath of red form under her, as if someone was using a paintbrush to paint the courtyard.

Major Defilice had gone right up to the president. Lying underneath the secret service agent, his left arm was outspread, and there was some blood on it. Defilice and the Princess rolled the agent off the president, who moaned and tried to sit up.

"Take it easy sir. We've got you." Defilice got his arms under the president's shoulders while Ramon picked up his legs. Together they carried the president back.

Gunny looked around. The agent who had covered the president was quite obviously dead. Ambassador Tankersly lay in a pool of blood, his right arm blown off and lying a few feet from his body. The man who he would later learn was the staff secretary lay on his back wheezing, blood pulsing out between his fingers which were pressed up against his neck. As Gunny moved toward him, the wheezing stopped, and his hand fell away. The pulsing blood slowed to a flow. One hand still clutched the handle of a badly mangled briefcase, broken electronic components falling out of it to lie scattered across the ground.

Van Slyke came staggering across the courtyard, Wynn over his shoulders. A shot rang out, and Gunny could see another man pushing himself through the crowd to fire into the embassy grounds. Gunny stepped behind the president's Suburban, then cranked off a few rounds at the man. He didn't know if he hit him or not, or if he hit someone else in the crowd for that matter, but the firing stopped long enough for Van Slyke to make it to the red carpet. Gunny's natural instinct was to help him with Wynn, but he stayed at the Suburban and scanned the crowd outside the gate for another shooter.

Looking back at the embassy, he could see Saad step up to help Van Slyke into the building. Feeling quite vulnerable out there alone, he decided it was time to get back himself. He turned to run and almost fell over the US flag, lying in the blood on the courtyard ground. Looking at Crocker's body, he mouthed a small apology for abandoning his body, picked up the flag, then sprinted for the entrance. Little Mac waited until he got through before hitting the release to lower the emergency door.

Chapter 7

Late Tuesday Morning, US Embassy, New Delhi

Gunny Mac placed the flag up against the emergency doors and took in the scene. The President of the United States of America was sitting down, back against Post 1, with Major Defilice and PFC Ramon kneeling beside him. A few feet away, Corporal Samantha Ashley lay on her back. PFC Rodriguez was holding her hand in his. Gunny raised a questioning eyebrow. Rodriguez shook his head and looked back down.

Staff Sergeant Child was also on his back. His breathing was steady, but small bright bubbles were forming at the corners of his mouth. LCpl Steptoe stood by him, as Child's skin took on a sickly, gray cast. Saad was sitting on the other side of the passage, hand pressed to his shoulder, an angry look on his face.

PFC Van Slyke had lain Wynn down next to Child. Mac could see blood in Wynn's hair, and what looked to be bits of brain matter. But the shallow rise and fall of her chest assured him she was still alive. Blood streamed down Van Slyke's face. Gunny wondered how he could have taken a shot to the face and be standing alertly, looking toward him for orders. They all were looking toward him now, even the major.

A sense of weariness crept over him, of hopelessness. This wasn't how it was supposed to happen. How could this happen with the president of the freaking United States? Where was the secret service? Who was going to take charge?

He looked to Major Defilice. "Sir?"

The major seemed to understand. "I'm an assistant attaché, a logistician by trade, not a line officer. I'm in no one's chain of command. You're in charge here. You know what to do. Tell me what you want, and I'll help. But you've got the training for this."

Gunny Mac knew the major was right. He had the training. And he had to do two things first. Find out who was where, and destroy the classified. When he had run back down the red carpet, the crowd was still outside the walls. But someone had planned this, and it was only a matter of time before they and/or the crowd took over the embassy grounds.

Falling into the steps drilled into him over and over was better. Let the routine take over. This was just like a drill. He wheeled to the glass of Post 1. "Sergeant McAllister. Hit the Mayday. Then pulse Battalion and let them know what happened. Tell them we need help right now."

"Rodriguez, go inside Post 1. Get a hold of Post 2 and get a sitrep from them. Let's find out where everybody is."

"Major, maybe we should get the president out of the passageway here." He looked around. "How about the Admin Section's office? It's an inside office, no windows." When the major nodded, he added, "Ok let's get everybody in the office."

Major Defilice and PFC Ramon helped up the groggy president. At least he seemed to be able to walk under his own power⊠sort of. Steptoe and Saad carried Child, and Gunny helped Van Slyke with Wynn. He glanced at Ashley's body, but decided to leave it there for the moment. Entering the office, he told Steptoe, Kramer, and Van Slyke to push the desks together and clear them off so they could lay Child and Wynn on them.

PFC Rodriguez came running in. "Gunny! Sergeant McAllister told me to get you. None of her circuits work." Gunny ran back out, and up to Post 1 where Little Mac buzzed him in.

"What's going on?"

"Gunny, I can't contact anyone. And the pulse doesn't look like it went out."

Gunny Mac looked at the control screens in the booth. The video monitors seemed to work. He picked up the telephone. The line was dead. He pulled his cell out of his pocket and checked the screen. The "No Network Available" message flashed at the top of the screen.

"What about the land line?" This was a protected communications line connecting the embassy posts. This line did not use transmissions and was buried several feet below the embassy grounds as it ran to between the posts.

Sergeant McAllister picked it up and pressed the talk button. "I've got them Gunny!"

Gunny grabbed the handset. "Post 2, this is Post 1. Give me a sitrep."

He could hear Sergeant Chen's excited voice coming over the line. "We're OK Gunny. What the hell happened over there?"

"Chen, give me a sitrep. Who is there with you? Are you under attack?"

"No, we are not under attack. We saw the explosions, but nothing over here. Some secret service agent tried to run over to the embassy, but I think he got shot. He is over in the fishpond right now."

"Who is with you right now? Give me a head count."

"Uh, me and Staff Sergeant Harwood are here in the post. Niimoto and Fallgatter are in the garden with the civilians."

"OK. Get Niimoto and Fallgatter. Tell them to come here using the service tunnel. Do not let them cross the courtyard. Understand?"

"Sure Gunny. I'll get them over."

Gunny turned to Little Mac. "Keep trying to get out a pulse. And let me know if you see movement out there. Oh, and give me the first aid kit." She reached under the counter and handed it to him. He left the post and went back into the Admin Section's office.

Major Defilice walked over to the president, who was sitting at the Protocol Officer's desk. He took off his jacket, tore a large piece from his t-shirt, and began to wrap the president's arm. . The major had obviously torn the bandage from the bottom edge of his t-shirt. Above the torn strip, there was a silk screen saying "Money Can't Buy You Happiness But it Can Buy You Beer, Drugs, and Women!" Despite the circumstances, that struck him as pretty funny. All the more so as the most professional Major Defilice was wearing such a shirt under his uniform when the President of the United States was coming. He almost broke out into a laugh despite the present circumstances.

As he walked up, the president looked at him and said, "Sergeant, the major here tells me you are trying to find out what happened. What the hell is happening?"

"We don't know yet, Mr. President. We have been hit by some sort of attack. We've got you back in the embassy, and no one seems to be storming the grounds yet. We need to secure the embassy until the Indian authorities arrive. We have tried to call them as well as pulse Quantico to let them know what's happening, but we have no com. Ambassador Tankersly is dead, but the foreign civilians and other Americans are in the consular garden and are OK for now."

"No communications? Where is Neal? He has my direct communications with the White house." Gunny looked blank for a second. "Ron Neal, my Staff Secretary?"

"Sir, if that the man with you and the ambassador, well, he is dead. And the briefcase he was carrying looked like it took a direct hit."

"Ron is dead?" he looked stunned, then swallowed hard. "Well, use your backups then. I want the White House, and I want it now."

"Gunny, Sergeant McAllister needs to open the emergency doors," Rodriguez's voice came in from the passageway.

"Excuse me sir, but I need to take care of this." Gunny handed Major Defilice the first aid kit, turned from the president and went back into the passageway where Rodriguez was holding open the hatch into Post 1. Gunny went inside and up to Little Mac who was looking at the monitor which covered the front of the emergency doors. When Gunny Mac looked for himself, he could see an older woman, covered with blood, who had managed to crawl up the side of the steps and was knocking on the emergency doors. Gunny realized she had been one of the favored few who were allowed to wait in the courtyard for the president's arrival.

Gunny looked at the other monitors. He could see the bodies in the courtyard and the mass of people still outside the gates, but no one else seemed to be around the embassy entrance.

The emergency doors were two tons of reinforced derma steel, impervious to most anything. They were intended to slam shut at the onset of any emergency. Once closed, though, they could not be opened without a code. Gunny Mac was one of five people at the embassy who had the code. He walked up to the console to punch in the code, shielding the touchpad with his body so no one could the numbers. Then he almost laughed. What was the use of keeping it secret now?

The door started inching up. "Rodriguez, help her in."

Rodriguez lay down on the deck and reached under the door as it continued its slow process up. "I've got you ma'am, Lie down and I'll get you in."

He kept reaching, sliding his head under the door, then started pulling back, half assisting, half dragging the woman under the door and into the embassy. There was a loud crack, and tile chipped on the floor. Gunny, who had taken a step forward, jumped back. "Fuck, they're shooting at us. Slam the door, slam the door!"

Sergeant McAllister hit the release, and the door slammed shut once again, barely missing the outstretched leg of the woman. She lay on the floor in Rodriguez's arms. She was about sixty-five years old and heavy set. Gunny had seen her before, but really didn't know who she was. Her obviously tailored suit was now bedraggled, with a large tear in the shoulder and blood seeping from her face and shoulder gave its cream color a pinkish, tie-dyed look. There were what looked to be globs of blood and flesh sprayed across her skirt. She was pale and breathing heavily, the signs of shock evident on her face. She looked up at Gunny, took a breath, and with a seemingly forced bravado, asked. "Are you going to help me up, or what?"

Gunny snapped out of his daze. "Yes ma'am!" He reached down to take her hand, which was cool and clammy, and the woman stood up. She had on a black lacy bra, which was visible through the tear in the shoulder of her suit. Blood was running down her shoulder and over the curve of her breast, which was also exposed, then soaking into that bra. Her face showed every wrinkle of her years, but her chest seemed somehow younger. Maybe it was the bright blood. Gunny wondered why the hell he even noticed that, given the circumstances.

"Gunny Mac, is there someplace a little more appropriate where I can go?"

She knew his name? Not impossible, he thought, but most at the embassy never addressed him by name, and those who did usually used his full last name, either as "Sergeant McCardle" or "Gunnery Sergeant

McCardle." Gunny Mac thought he sort-of recognized the woman, having seen her at functions, but he could not place the name.

"Yes, ma'am. Let's go back to the Admin office. The president is there."

"Is he OK?"

"I think so, ma'am. Rodriguez, McAllister, stay here on post. No one comes in. No one." He assisted the woman down the passage to the office.

"In case you are wondering, I am OK." She looked like she was forcing a stern appearance, but in back of it, her eyes were in somewhat of a daze.

Gunny looked back. "Uh, right. I'm sorry ma'am. Anyone else with you make it?"

She softened the look in her eye somewhat, and she almost seemed to break before she gathered herself. "I don't think so. I think I have a lot of the charge-de-affairs' blood on my skirt here."

They walked into the office. The president was still sitting on the desk, but he looked up, still obviously dazed, but somehow defiant at the same time.

"Where is my secret service?"

"I don't know Mr. President. Some were killed out there, but the others should be here soon, I hope."

The woman brushed past Gunny to hold out her hand. "Mr. President, I am Loralee Howard. I'm married to Stan Howard, the charge-de-affairs here."

Gunny looked at her sharply. Loralee Howard? Stan Howard? Yes, he was the charge-de-affairs, but didn't she just tell him that she had his blood on her skirt?

Despite the circumstances, ingrained political behavior kicked in. President Eduardo reached out and took the hand. "Pleased to meet you."

"Well Mr. President, we are up shit river right now. I hope you have some sort of Secret Squirrel hotline which is going to get us out of this."

The president, still holding and shaking her hand, looked slack-jawed at her.

Chapter 8

Late Monday Night, Executive Office Building, Washington, DC

Vice-President Jennifer Wright was in her office with her chief-of-staff, discussing an upcoming trip to Dallas when she saw the attack live on CNN on the television hanging on her wall. She stopped dead, her mouth falling open. David Spears, her chief, had his back to the wall and kept talking, not noticing her expression.

"David, look!" He turned around and saw the images of bodies on the ground on the screen.

"What....?"

Right then, Special Agent Mel Greene rushed in. "Ma'am, we have a situation here. Will you please follow me?" He grasped her arm and lifted her to her feet, belying to his phrasing that he was asking her permission rather than giving her an order. Several secret service agents preceded them as they walked down the hall, others watching the intersections. He escorted her down the stairs and through the tunnel to the White house and into the Situation Room, the Marine Guard waving them inside.

The room was empty except for the duty officer, who stood wringing his hands and looking at the vice-president. "The key staff are being informed and instructed to come here. Most of them are home at this late hour."

She didn't know the duty officer's name, so she just asked "What do we know? Do we have communications with them?"

"No, Madame Vice-President. We have no communications with the president. But it looks like the president is alive. We saw him on CNN being helped into the embassy building. He might be hurt, though."

She sat down in the President's chair. Well, it was up to her now. He certainly was not going to be sitting in the chair during this crisis. This was on her to fix.

Jennifer Wright had been in politics for a long, long time. If someone had told her while she was a Congressional page while in high school or when she was working as a young volunteer for Ronald Reagan's campaign that she would someday be vice-president, she would have been overjoyed. But now that she was vice-president, she wanted more. She wanted the Oval Office. Oh, she jumped at the offer of being Eduardo's running mate. She knew her credentials as chairman of the House Armed Forces Committee and then her subsequent executive experience as governor of Virginia shored up some perceived weaknesses in what Eduardo brought to the table in the election. But after getting to know the man, she was sure that she would make a better president. She didn't really have anything against him as a person, but she thought his idealism and adherence to budgetary issues made him less than the right man for the job. And while she realized that the vice-presidency could be the final boost she needed to make a run of her own for the presidency, finally putting a woman in the oval office, she was getting older. The voters were far more forgiving of older men running for office than older women. It was possible that after eight years of an Eduardo presidency, she might be considered too old for the job.

She didn't feel the slightest bit of guilt at the surge of excitement that flowed through her upon hearing the news. Could her chance at the Oval Office be coming sooner rather than later?

Chapter 9

Late Tuesday Morning, US Embassy, New Delhi

Sgt Niimoto and LCpl Fallgatter rushed into the room. They took in the scene in split second then rushed up to Gunny Mac.

Gunny realized that everyone was looking at him. He took a deep breath and then let it out slowly, calming him down a hair. "Sgt Niimoto, everything OK in the tunnel? Any problems?"

"It was fine, Gunny. No problem." He was breathing hard, whether from excitement or from running, Gunny couldn't tell.

"OK, Niimoto, Fallgatter, Steptoe, Kramer, start a security sweep. Check for any classified, but do it quick. Meet me at the vault. Saad, you OK?"

"Sure Gunny." His dress blues blouse was off and someone had bandaged his shoulder.

"OK, join them. Meet me at the vault." Saad nodded, then rushed out of the room to join the others. Gunny Mac looked at Van Slyke. It still looked like half of his face was a mess of blood and tissue. "How about you?"

"I'm OK," he sputtered, drops of blood spraying as he spoke.

"Stay here with the president. You too, Ramon. Major, can I ask you to stay here as well?" Major Defilice simply nodded.

"Sergeant, where are you going? Shouldn't you be staying here protecting us? Or calling for help?"

Gunny looked up at the president, who was glowering at him. "With all due respect sir, we have to destroy the classified. This area is fairly secure right now, and the major, PFC Ramon, and Lcpl Van Slyke will watch you and Ms. Howard. We'll work on getting us out of this once the classified is destroyed."

"You are leaving me here with a soldier who has had his face blown away, and two other soldiers who aren't even armed?"

"Private First Class Van Slyke and Private First Class Ramon are Marines, sir, not soldiers." He looked to Major Defilice. "Nothing derogatory intended, sir," he said. "And as far as arms, we'll take care of that shortly. " He came to attention, did an about face, then marched out, ignoring the protests arising from the president.

Actually, he felt embarrassed that the president had brought up the fact that only he was truly armed with both a weapon and ammunition, even if it was only an ancient 9 mm pistol. He should have thought of that himself. He ran to Post 1, barely glancing at the body of Sgt Ashley, which still lay up against the bulkhead.

"Rodriguez! Run down to the auxiliary weapons locker and get weapons and ammo for everyone. Everything you can carry." He pulled out the electronic key for the weapons locker and gave it to Rodriguez.

"Do we have any battle gear left?" he asked, already knowing the answer but asking anyway.

"No Gunny, me and Van Slyke helped SSgt Harwood and Cpl Ashley box all that up last week and got it ready for pick-up."

The Army was under contract to the Department of the Navy to provide body armor and weapons to the Marines. The new body armor was to be delivered the prior week and the old shipped back to the States. The problem was that the new armor was held up in Indian customs, something to do with it being shipped via DHL as normal supplies when the Indian customs agents thought they were "instruments of war." Gunny Mac had tried to keep possession of the old body armor until the new actually arrived, but the shipping arrangements had already been made, and the company First Sergeant in Nicosia had told him they didn't have the authority to stop an Army shipment. So the old body armor had been boxed and shipped.

He really wished he had that battle gear now. But there was no use stressing over it—it was what it was. He grabbed PFC Rodriguez by the shoulder and gave him a light push. "Well, get what you can and meet us down at the vault."

Gunny rushed back down the hallway, swiped his card at the hatch to the stairwell, then ran bounding down the steps three at a time. He turned the corner and sprinted to the end of the passage and swiped his card again. Down one more set of steps, then back up the corridor to the vault. Putting in his key, he waited, but nothing happened. Taking it back out, he carefully inserted it again. The five lights went one by one from red to green, then a voice prompted him to put his chin in the cradle. He did, and a puff of air blew on his right eye. The voice let him know he was who he should be, and the hatch to the vault opened. In front of him, the barred doors remained closed, but perversely, these doors would open to anyone with an embassy card. He swiped the card, and the bars slid back.

In front of him was a room about 20 feet deep and 10 feet wide. The shelves to the right held an assortment of ciphers and hard drives. The shelves to the right held files of paper. All were labeled, and all had individual RFID transmitters. Each time a piece of classified material left the vault, the radio transmission from the RFID let the tracking software know the classified material had left the vault. All existing materials were tracked this way, and newly created materials were logged in when they were first taken to the vault. With the president's visit, almost all material should have been returned, but a quick look at the monitor showed Gunny that there was a hard drive from the Commercial Attaché's desk missing. Gunny hoped Niimoto would find that as well as anything else not yet logged in as classified.

Each shelf was covered with a piece of metallic-looking plastic. And on each shelf, there were folded-up bags. These bags looked like normal paper bags, but upon closer inspection, they had a series of wires embedded in them. Gunny had never used the new Classified Neutralization System before except in training, but it sure beat the old system. Just put the classified material in the bag, be it paper, crypto gear, or hard drives, seal the bag, place it on the shelf, then flip the switch on the right hand side of each shelf. Without heat, the classified material is destroyed. Utterly. Gunny didn't really know how it worked, only that it did.

Staring on the lower right shelf, he started stuffing the paper in the bags and then sealing them. He was about half-way through when the rest of the Marines arrived. Saad had the missing hard drive, and Niimoto had some papers. Together, they were able to prep the rest of the materials in another two minutes or so.

Despite the fact that the destruction released no heat nor gases, the Marines stepped back. "Everyone ready?" There were nods all around. "OK, here goes." Gunny flipped the master switch. There was an audible puff as each bag seemed to shudder.

Even having done this in training, this still seemed anti-climatic. Sgt Niimoto opened one of the bags containing paper. Inside was what looked like grey ash. He opened one of the bags which had held hard drives. The drives inside had obviously fused. "Well, I guess that's that!"

Gunny set the vault controls to open access so he wouldn't have to go through the entire procedure again to open the hatch. This was normally only used for allowing large amounts of items to be brought in and out, but Gunny wanted instant access for any member of his detail. He would have to remember to reset the access though, as open access was limited to two hours before reverting to normal.

They backed out of the vault, and Gunny was surprised to see the Indian staff member he had seen earlier dutifully waiting for him. Sgt Niimoto said, "This is Mr. Dravid. We found him in the Ambassador's office ready to serve tea."

"Sir, can you please tell me what is happening? Is Ambassador Tankersly well?" The man seemed genuinely worried. Gunny had a moment of strong suspicion, which he suppressed.

"The ambassador is dead." Dravid stopped wringing his hands and his mouth dropped open. Gunny wondered what to do with the man. Well, he could decide that later. "Follow us for now."

They moved as a group back up the stairs to the upper deck. On the second deck up, they met PFC Rodriguez already there burdened, with weapons. Rushing forward, they (except for Dravid) relieved him of the rifles, grenades, and magazines of ammunition.

"I left some of them in with Van Slyke and that Army major already." Gunny nodded, realizing he should have told Rodriguez to do that in the first place.

Feeling a little better for being armed, the six Marines retraced their steps and returned to the office with the president. Things did not look good, but having a weapon in hand with the ability to cause somebody, anybody, grievous bodily harm, did wonders for the Marine psyche.

Chapter 10

Late Tuesday Morning, US Embassy, New Delhi

Gunny led his Marines back into the office. Major Defilice, PFC Ramon, and LCpl Van Slyke jumped up, weapons at the ready. The president was still sitting on the desk, not looking like he had moved since he first sat down.

"Hey, you might want to take a look at this." Loralee Howard was in the back of the office near a coffee mess. Gunny went over to find her watching a television. He looked at it for a second before realizing that it was a live shot of the embassy.

"CNN at work." Major Defilice had moved up in back of Gunny Mac and was looking over his shoulder at the TV. The scene was evidently shot from one of CNN's ubiquitous satellites, and it clearly showed the mobs outside the embassy and bodies still lying on the ground in the courtyard. The mob seemed to be all facing the same direction, listening to a man up on the roof of a parked car. An announcer kept saying that the fate of the president was unknown at this time, and that the vice-president was meeting with the cabinet in Washington to deal with the crisis.

"I bet she is." The president had moved off the desk and joined the group at the TV. He seemed a little unsteady, but otherwise in control. "Well, what now? Have you been able to contact anyone?"

"No sir." We seem to have been cut off." Gunny stared at the screen for a few seconds longer.

"Sgt Niimoto, do you think you can take the sniper rifle and climb the bell tower? Think it would do any good? It seems to me that a few well-placed shots could stop the mob from coming in."

Niimoto's face lit up. "Sure Gunny, I imagine I can do that."

"Take Rodriguez with you."

"Gunny, you're going to need everyone you can here. I'll go it alone."

Gunny Mac hesitated a second, then nodded. "OK, but hook up to the landline jack as soon as you get there. Call Post 1 and let me know when you're set up."

"Aye-aye, Gunny." Sgt Niimoto turned around and walked out to go to the weapons locker to pick up the sniper rifle, then to wend his way through the service tunnels to the bell tower.

"Where are the Indian police?" Gunny turned around to Loralee Howard, who was watching the television. "Shouldn't they be coming to disperse the mob? Doesn't look like they intend to do much." She pointed to the screen where men in uniform seemed to be simply watching the crowd.

"You are right ma'am," put in the major.

"Honey, I am no one's 'Ma'am.' Call me Loralee. Seems to me getting out of this mess is a little more important than protocol." She gave a measured glance at the president, who seemed not to notice.

"OK, ma'---, uh, I mean Loralee. But you're right. They should be blasting away the mob. But they aren't doing anything."

The president seemed to pull himself together. "Sergeant, I need to contact Washington, now. I'm going to see an end to this."

"Sir, we don't have communications. Even our Mayday didn't get out. They've got to be jamming us somehow."

"How can they be jamming us? Doesn't this place have our best, most secure equipment?"

"Well, yes sir, but we aren't getting anything out."

"This is bullshit! I am the President of the United States of America, still the most powerful nation in the world. How the hell am I stuck in an office in the US Embassy with eight soldiers and a diplomat's wife? Just how the hell does this happen?"

"One soldier, sir. One soldier and nine Marines." Gunny Mac hooked his thumb to point at Childs and Wynn, lying on the desks.

The president looked perplexed for a moment. "I don't care if you want to call yourselves Campfire girls, you are just soldiers. I have dealt with you Marines before, and you always thought you were special, but you are just soldiers, just public servants. Now get me some communications!"

Gunny Mac looked at the president, not knowing how to respond. He finally did a mental shrug, then simply said "Aye-aye sir." He walked out of the office and back to Post 1. Sgt McAllister looked up as he came. And yes, she winked. Gunny snorted in disbelief. McAllister was some sort of crazy!

"Do you have any com with anyone?"

"Just with Post 2. They keep asking what they should be doing."

"Nothing with anyone outside the embassy?"

"Nope. Nobody wants to talk with us."

"Well, fuck. We've got to get somebody. Niimoto should be on the landline as well once he gets into the tower."

"Yea, he told me. Korea Joe's got balls."

"So do you, McAllister, so do you." He turned to walk back to the office, McAllister letting off a hearty laugh as he left.

"Big enough for the both of us, Gunny!"

LCpl Steptoe was waiting for him at the hatch into the office. "I know how they are jamming us, Gunny. It's the software."

Gunny stared at him without comprehension. "What?"

"It is the software. Who does all our programming? The Indians. We send all of it to India."

"But this is not Windows. These are highly critical, highly secure programs."

"Doesn't really matter. They are great programmers, and they do probably all of our programs in our non-secure systems. It doesn't take a genius to hack into our system and jam us. They might have a hard time breaking into our com, knowing what we are saying. But they don't have to do that. All they have to do is block our systems. Turn off a few switches. Walla! We can't talk."

Gunny stared hard at Steptoe. "Are you sure? Shouldn't it be harder than that?"

"I never said it'd be easy. But with an entry into the system, a talented programmer could shut us down."

"Can you fix it?"

"Give me a couple weeks, maybe. But I think I have another way. You know Crocker likes the Sox? Dang, of course you know that. But do you know how he gets the games?" When Gunny shook his head, Steptoe went on. "I took his PDA, and I programmed it to work as a repeater for very low frequency transmitter and receiver I built at the Marine House. Really low. Lower than anything we have here. It travels pretty long distance, even with the low power. I've got a buddy of mine in Katmandu. He works there for Oracle. He just hooks up a netcast of the game, then retransmits it to our receiver at the Marine House, then it goes to Crocker on his PDA. If I can get his PDA, I can probably reach my buddy. I don't think the Indians would be blocking anything that low from here."

He looked expectantly at Gunny Mac as he digested what he had been told. Gunny's eyes lit up. "So we can get com out!" Good job!" Then as a thought crossed his mind, his countenance fell. "But where is Crocker's PDA? Back at the Marine House?"

"Gunny, Crocker never went anywhere without his PDA. He probably had it on him when he was hit."

"He had his PDA in an honor guard? What was he thinking?" Then realizing that Crocker would not be thinking anything else, ever, Gunny fell into silence. He also realized that Crocker now lay in the courtyard, in plain view of the mob.

"Well, I guess we'll just have to have to go get it. Meet me at Post 1. As soon as Niimoto is ready with some cover, we'll do it." He returned to the office and walked up to the president, who looked up expectantly.

"Sir, I think we might have a way to re-establish communications. Sgt Crocker, one of the Marines who was killed out there, has a PDA which should work. We just need to get out there and get it."

"Well, what are you waiting for? Go get it."

Gunny felt a wave of revulsion sweep over him. That was a US Marine, out there, a person who was now dead. The president's cavalier attitude struck him as just plain wrong. "Sir, there are still gunmen out there. Going out now would be suicide. Sgt Niimoto should be in position soon up on the bell tower, and he can give us cover. It should only be a few more minutes."

The president looked at him for a few seconds, then saying nothing, turned back to watch the television.

"Gunny, who is going to get Sgt Crocker?" PFC Ramon had come up and stood in front of him.

Gunny Mac hadn't really thought of it. But now that he was thinking, he didn't want to send anyone else out where he or she could get killed. He certainly did not want to risk getting shot himself, but that was better than sending someone else to get shot.

"I am," he said with a surprisingly strong voice.

"Not disrespect intended, but that is not such a good idea. You're in command here, and we need you safe and sound. I'll do it." She looked at him assuredly.

Gunny's mind reeled. He looked up to see Major Defilice nodding in agreement. The rest of the Marines were also looking at him, waiting to hear his response. Even the president turned back around to look at him. But a leader led from the front, right? He would not order anyone to do something he wouldn't do himself, right?

Then he remembered a conversation he had with Col Parks back at Fallujah, one of many he had while driving him around base. Col Parks told him one of the hardest things he had had to do was to send Marines into the line of fire. But he realized that a leader leads. Not necessarily from the front, leading a charge just to show his bravery. A leader leads where and how he can best accomplish the mission. Where he can have the most impact on the mission, keeping the most number of his Marines alive, where he can secure the objective.

He now understood Col Parks. He needed to be in the embassy. He was going to have to send someone else, and that hurt.

He looked at the still waiting Princess. If the PDA was right where it could be grabbed, then Princess could probably do the mission. But Crocker knew he wasn't supposed to have a PDA while in an honor guard, so it was probably hidden. Crocker was going to have to be brought back inside the embassy. And Princess just did not have the mass to pick Crocker up and carry him back inside. He looked at the rest of the Marines. Steptoe was needed to use the PDA. Van Slyke was missing half his face. Rodriguez was also on the slight side. Saad would be a good choice, but even if he said he is fine, he had still taken a hit. Fallgatter, possibly. He caught the eyes of Kramer, who nodded slightly. Kramer, the former jock.

"LCpl Kramer, you're up." PFC Ramon frowned, started to say something, then evidently thought better of it and said nothing.

"Kramer, Rodriguez, Fallgatter, Ramon, come with me. You two stay here with the president," he told Van Slyke and Saad. He nodded to the president, then left the office to go back to Post 1.

"OK, once Niimoto is ready, we are going to have him provide cover from the bell tower. Kramer, you need to haul ass, grab Sgt Crocker, and get back here. The rest of us will provide cover as well. Sgt McAllister, any word from Sgt Niimoto yet?"

Little Mac shook her head.

"OK, now we wait." He put his back against the bulkhead and slowly slid down until he was sitting. He looked up to see Sgt Ashley's slack face staring at nothing. She still did not seem to be dead, somehow. Hell, Van Slyke looked much worse. But the total lack of tension in her skin and muscles told the tale better than anything else.

"Rodriguez, Fallgatter, take Sgt Ashley into the ambassador's office. Put her on his couch. Then come on back." He did not want just lying there, like a discarded piece of rubbish.

They shouldered their weapons. Rodriguez put his arms under her shoulders, and Fallgatter grabbed her legs. As they lifted, there was a slightly ripping sound where her blood had congealed on the floor. Gunny felt his stomach lurch. They carried their burden down the passage, then turned into the ambassador's office. A few moments later, they re-emerged and made their way back to Post 1.

As they sat on the deck waiting for Sgt Niimoto, each in their own thoughts, the magnitude of what was going on hit Gunny Mac hard. This was tantamount to a declaration of war, wasn't it? The Indians had attacked sovereign US soil, they had attacked the President of the United States of America. Where would this end? What would they do next?

The hatch to Post 1 opened. "Gunny, it's Korea Joe," reported Sgt McAllister.

He jumped up and grabbed the landline. "You OK? You in the bell tower?"

"Yea, Gunny. I've got good fields of fire, but man, there are a lot of targets out there. This place is packed!"

"Ok, listen up, this is what I want you to do…" Gunny briefed him on what was going to happen.

The hatch opened again. "Gunny, it is the Canadian Ambassador. He is at Post 2, and he wants to talk to someone in charge."

Gunny rolled his eyes. "Not now, McAllister. I'm kind of busy right now!" He motioned for his team to gather round, waiting until Fallgatter and Rodriguez returned.

"Ramon and Fallgatter to the right of me and Rodriguez to the left. We aren't going to be able to see much from here, but if they fire on Kramer, we fire back. Watch what you're shooting at, though. Kramer will be coming right back. Sgt Niimoto is in the bell tower giving covering fire, too. You ready Kramer?

LCpl Kramer licked his lips and nodded. A thought struck Gunny Mac. "Hey, you better stretch first. You pull up in a cramp, and I'm going to have to send Ramon here out to haul in your ass."

There was a nervous chuckle from the group, but LCpl Kramer dutifully went into a sprinter's stretch. It seemed sort of surreal, the four of them (five counting Sgt McAllister) watching Hank Kramer stretch as if he was back in high school getting ready for the Friday night game. He finally got up and merely nodded his readiness.

"Nothing fancy. Just grab Crocker and get back inside. Let's get into position. Prone Fallgatter! We are not John Wayning this. Get on your face!" He started over to enter the code, hesitated, then walked back to the Post.

"Give me a piece of paper, McAllister." She put a pen and paper into the slot and sent it out. Gunny grabbed them, then wrote the code for the door on the paper, then put them back in the slot. He went back to the code-box, entered the code, then lay down beside Rodriguez.

As the door slowly started to rise, the bright sunshine almost blinded him. He could make out the tops of the Suburbans, but from his angle, he could not see any of the bodies. He could hear the chanting of the mob, though, very loud and very clear. "OK Kramer, as soon as you can, go."

The door continued its slow climb up. As it reached about 18 inches, LCpl Kramer slid underneath it and was outside. Gathering his feet under him, he started off on a dash.

"Hold your fire. Let's see if anyone will notice him first."

LCpl Kramer sprinted down the front steps and looked to be almost to the Suburbans when the tone of the crowd changed. "Ah shit," someone whispered from the left, Ramon or Fallgatter.

There was a very faint soft chuff, which could have been the sniper rifle, then several cracks of rifle fire.

"Fire, fire!" The four Marines opened up, but without specific targets. Gunny Mac could see Kramer's head and shoulders, then he disappeared. Had he been hit? He started to get to his knees when Kramer stood up with Sgt Crocker on his shoulders. He started running back, bounding up the steps in one giant stride, then running down the entranceway. As he approached the door, now open by about three feet, he threw himself forward, shoving Sgt Crocker's body through the opening and sliding in after it.

"Close it, close it," shouted Gunny Mac, but Sgt McAllister had already hit the emergency release. As it slammed shut, PFC Fallgatter still fired, sending a number of rounds zinging around the inside of the entrance.

PFC Ramon smacked Fallgatter on the shoulder. "Cease fire you moron!"

LCpl Kramer lay huffing on the deck. Sprawled in front of him was Sgt Crocker. He had been out in the hot sun for over an hour, and his body was already showing signs of deterioration. His skin looked pale but puffy, and his uniform unnaturally tight. Gunny walked over to him. Where would the PDA be? Where should he look?

PFC Fallgatter evidently knew already. He soberly reached over, pulled up Sgt Crocker's right trouser leg, and unstrapped the PDA attached to his ankle. Wordlessly, he handed it over to the gunny.

Gunny looked at it for a moment, then back at Sgt Crocker. "Take Sgt Crocker and put him in with Sgt Ashley." He turned around and walked off to the Admin Office, not waiting to see them lift the body. "Good job Marines," he shouted over his shoulder. He should have faced them and told them so, but he really did not want to see more of Sgt Crocker's bloated body.

He walked into the office, handed LCpl Steptoe the PDA, and said, "OK, get to work." Then he walked over to the coffee mess and threw up in the sink.

Chapter 11

Late Tuesday Morning, US Embassy, New Delhi

Sergeant Anthony Niimoto climbed the last few steps into the rotunda of the bell tower with a sigh of relief. After grabbing a sniper rifle from the weapons locker and a box of ammunition, he had checked in with Little Mac before going down the access to the service tunnels. He had been in the service tunnels many times, the last time just 30 minutes ago when he'd made his way to the embassy from the consulate. But he really did not like them, and now, with what had happened, he felt more stifled in them, more aware of how good this would be for an ambush. He was relieved when he finally reached the access into the base of the bell tower, then made his way up the ladder into the campanile's belfry.

Tony Niimoto had joined the Marines for no particular reason. He'd gone to Stanford, much to the joy of his parents, and majored in philosophy, much to their dismay. Tony liked to experience life, but he did not have much of a blueprint for his future.

After graduation, he went back south to his parents' home in Pacific Beach, or "PB" as it was known in the San Diego area, living in his old bedroom, surfing most days away. One dismal January day, cold and rainy, he was out surfing, hoping to catch some nice rides. Sitting on his board out in the water he was drawn into a conversation with an old man. This old guy was rather scrawny, but he was interesting could hold his own in the water, so when the old guy offered to buy Tony a burger at Hodad's, he accepted. Sitting in the ancient burger joint, under all the license plates from around the world hanging on the walls, the old guy regaled Tony with stories, claiming to have been a Navy SEAL. His stories of death and mayhem were rather intriguing to someone recently out of the brick walls of Stanford, and his stories of whoring around in the Philippines, Kosovo, and Korea were even more fascinating. San Diego was a conservative community with not much in the way of adult nightlife, and the tales of Fire Empire and Jolos in the Philippines piqued his sense of adventure. Tony spent the afternoon alternating between open-mouthed astonishment and braying his donkey laugh at some of the old guy's stories.

It was almost 4:00 when he left Hodad's. Something made him go across the bay and into downtown San Diego. Subconsciously, he was soon standing outside the Federal Building. With a sudden sense of determination, he walked inside and turned to the left where the military recruiters had their offices. It was about quarter-to-five, but when he went up to the Navy recruiter's office, it was already closed, even though the sign on the door said it was open from 8:00 AM until 5:00 PM. He felt a sense of deflation, as if something, something he really could not put his finger on, had evaporated away.

"Can I help you son?"

Tony looked up, and standing in the next doorway was a Marine. Tony did not know it, but since the dismemberment, the Marines really did not have to recruit much. In fact, they had recruitment offices in a few select locations, and these were primarily process centers for getting the recruits to Quantico for boot. There was something about Tony, though, that caught the attention of Staff Sergeant Mike Santiago, something that his instincts made him speak out.

Tony walked over to the Staff Sergeant, walked into the office, and 45 minutes later, had signed on the dotted line. Tony was going to be a Marine.

And Tony found out he liked being a Marine. The Corps gave him a purpose in life which Stanford never gave him. He liked doing "manly" things. He found out he could shoot. He found out he liked the camaraderie. He liked the uniforms. He liked being part of a team. And despite his initial objections to being called "Korea Joe," somehow, even that formed bonds with his fellow Marines. Although he may have joined because of an old man's tales of whoring, to be honest, he had found a home.

And Tony was now thinking of applying to be an officer. He had not mentioned that to anyone, else, of course. But the thought of putting on gold bars was rather appealing.

Sgt Niimoto looked around the belfry. While it looked like a bell tower from the outside, from inside the cupola it was obvious that the stacks of locked cabinets with large cables leaving from the bottom and disappearing into the floor were the real reason the tower was built. Yes, there was a bell hanging there, but it couldn't even ring. There wasn't a clapper.

The Marines often wondered as to the exact nature of the cabinets, or why they were not in a secure location. Sgt Chen seemed to think that since they weren't guarded, they were not important. But Sgt Niimoto felt they would not have built the tower unless there was a good reason. Regardless, the off-duty Marines often liked to come up and hang out, and no one ever told them they couldn't.

Sgt Niimoto eased over to the rail and looked down over the courtyard. He could see the Suburbans and the bodies lying there, which caused a small lump in his throat. And arrayed outside the wall, there were what seemed to be thousands of Indians packing the street. There was some chanting, but most seemed to be listening to several men speaking on microphones. Niimoto didn't speak any Hindi, so he could not understand what was being said.

Sgt Niimoto looked down at his M48A1 sniper rifle. He checked the baffles of the rifle, the most obvious change from the appearance of the M40A1 rifle on which he had initially been trained. The M48A1 still used the Remington 700 receiver group, but the baffles around the muzzle of the barrel, when used in conjunction to the special M124 ammunition, made the report of a shot quite subdued. He had to make sure the baffles were clear, though. They easily picked up dirt and bits of detritus. He then checked over his ammunition the boat-tailed, 178 grain round, making sure there were no dents in any of them, that they were in good shape. Although an intelligent man, Sgt Niimoto was not quite sure how the baffles and new ammunition worked, but the rifle was essentially silent out past 100 or 150 meters, depending on the conditions. Closer to that, the rifle made a softer chuffing sound rather than the sharp crack of a normal rifle.

Taking a headset from his pocket, Sgt Niimoto hooked it up to the landline jack. He dialed Post 1.

"Post 1."

"Pat, this is Tony. Let the Gunny know I am in position."

" 'bout time. They're all here waiting for you. Hold on a second."

Sgt Niimoto could hear McAllister call out for the gunny, then a few moments later, the gunny came on line. "You OK? You in the bell tower?"

"Yea, Gunny. I've got good fields of fire, but man, there are a lot of targets out there. This place is packed!" He looked back out over the crowd.

"OK, listen up, this is what I want you to do. We've got to get Crocker's PDA, Without it, we can't talk to anyone. I've got four of us here at the front hatch, but we really won't be able to see much. I am sending Kramer out to grab Crocker and bring him back in. You've got to provide cover. If you see anyone shoot, if you see anyone about to shoot, take him out. Don't hesitate, just take him out. You've got that?"

"Roger gunny."

"OK, we're going in just a minute or so. You be ready. Out."

Sgt Niimoto felt a wave of emotion well up. He could look down on the courtyard and see Seth's body. That could have been him down there. It would have been if the president hadn't canc'ed the Marine Colors. He subconsciously stroked the seam of his dress blue trousers. And he could see Capt Leon-Guerro sprawled across the ground as well. Sgt Niimoto didn't really know the Captain that well, but he was still a Marine, and that was what mattered.

He knew he could shoot, but shooting at a range was different from shooting real people. Flesh and blood. He felt a little queasy. Then, looking at the two Marines, the ambassador, and the others lying dead in the courtyard, he felt a degree of hardening. They started this.

Looking through his scope, he picked out several men who were armed and watching the embassy, not paying attention to the speakers. These were his targets. He put his crosshairs on the chest of a gunman standing on a concrete block up against the embassy wall, right at the base of his throat. Taking a couple deep breathes, he slowly exhaled.

He sensed more than saw the doors open. A moment later, his target looked startled, shouted something over his shoulder, then raised his weapon. Sgt Anthony Niimoto smoothly squeezed the trigger. They rifle kicked, the vents chuffed, and there was an explosion of blood on the man's chest as he fell back into the crowd.

Another man had an ancient AK leveled and was firing into the courtyard. Sgt Niimoto swung his weapon around as a burst of fire came out of the embassy. Squeezing the trigger again, Sgt Niimoto watched the round hit the man lower in the chest, but he, too, fell back. Through the scope, he could see one more man jumping onto the same concrete block the first man had been standing on. Taking a breath, he squeezed the trigger once more. Kick. Chuff. The man's face burst into a pink mist before he fell back into the now panicking crowd.

Taking a quick glance back, he could see Kramer disappearing under the awning, carrying Seth on his shoulders.. A couple more steps and he would be safe. Tony scanned the crowd again, but no one stood out as a target. People rushed the wall and gate, pointing and gesturing, but none were an immediate threat.

Sgt Niimoto leaned back and took a deep breath. He had just killed three men. Yes, he was a Marine. Yes, every Marine is a rifleman. But he never thought he'd have to kill anyone. And right now, he felt elated. Maybe he would feel something later, feel some regret. But now, he felt like he had just caught the perfect curl, had just sunk a 40-foot buzzer beater. He felt great.

Admittedly, the distance involved was not that great. But he was shooting at a severe down angle and increasing shadows, and he had shot quickly. He had done well. And it looked as if no one had realized they were taking fire from the bell tower.

Sgt Tony Niimoto edged back down some and went back to scanning the milling crowd.

Chapter 12

Gunnery Sergeant McCardle rinsed his mouth with water, swishing it back and forth before spitting it out into the sink. He turned around and surveyed the office.

Ms. Howard, er, Loralee, had sat Van Slyke down and was dabbing at his face with some paper towels, first aid kit open and ready, a look of concern in her eyes as she surveyed the damage. Van Slyke's undamaged side of his face was away from the gunny, so he could not see how he was taking this, but his body was still. Gunny shook his head in amazement.

Toward the left, SSgt Child and LCpl Wynn were still laid out on two desks. Saad was watching over Child, holding his hand. That hand, once so powerful and full of purpose, lay limply, with a pale, sickly grayish cast. But Child's chest rose with seemingly normal fashion, breathing life into the body. His blouse had been taken off, and bandages covered his chest and neck. Gunny wondered who had put them there, taking care of Child. He had been so busy, he hadn't even had time to see to the wounded. Lying next to Child, the rise and fall of Wynn's chest did not seem as strong. Blood seeped from under her, snaked its way to the edge of the desk, and dripped to the deck, pooling in a small puddle of red.

The president and Major Defilice were by the television, watching

CNN and making quiet comments to each other. MAJ Defilice was still in his t-shirt, uniform trousers and issue shoes, the president in a very nice pair of navy trousers, a white shirt, and shoes that probably cost more than the gunny made in a month, yet they huddled together, circumstances putting them on an equal footing. The president's upper arm was bandaged over his shirt, and he didn't seem to be in too much distress. Behind them, Mr. Dravid stood, trying to remain unobtrusive but watching the television as well.

LCpl Steptoe was hunched over the receptionist's desk, working on the PDA. His concentration was evident, making him oblivious to the entire scene. The hatch to the office opened, and the remaining Marines trooped in. Ramon and Rodriguez looked somewhat subdued, but both Kramer and Fallgatter looked elated. Fallgatter had his M18 at the ready, his eyes darting around the room.

"Rodriguez, go back down to Post 1. Stand by and be a runner for Sgt McAllister. Let me know if anything comes up." Rodriguez nodded and left the office.

He walked over to Steptoe. "How's it going?"

LCpl Steptoe did not even look up. "Good, Gunny. Sgt Crocker has a password protect, but I think I can figure it out."

"OK. Good. Let me know as soon as you have something." He made his way back to the president and Major Defilice. "Sir, we've got the PDA, and we should be able to talk to someone soon."

The president looked around over his shoulder at the gunny. "Good job, sergeant. Tell me, was anyone hurt getting it?" He stared at the gunny with a look of concern on his face.

"No sir. Everyone got back fine."

"Good, good." He paused. "Let me know when I can talk to Washington."

PFC Rodriquez came back into the office. "Gunny, Sgt Mac says the Canadian ambassador is back on the landline wanting to know what is going on. What should she tell him?"

"Ah, crap! OK, OK. I'll be there in a second."

Loralee stopped bandaging Van Slyke's face. "Don't tell him too much, Gunny."

"What do you mean, ma'am?"

"Do you really know who is over there? Most of the diplomatic community and half of the Indian government were waiting for the reception. Who over there had a hand in this?"

Gunny Mac gulped. That was a good point. No sense making it easy for anyone who wanted to do them ill. "I'll be careful, ma'am." He left the office and made his way to Post 1.

"Buzz me in, Sgt McAllister." He entered the post and picked up the landline.

"This is Gunnery Sergeant Jacob McCardle. Who am I speaking with?"

"I am Ambassador Tilden from Canada. What is happening out there? How is the president? How is Ambassador Tankersly? We have a lot of scared people over here, and we want to know what is going on."

"Sir, the president is secure, and we have initiated our emergency procedures. Please remain calm, and help will arrive. You've got the food and drink for the reception, so please make sure everyone is hydrated and ready for further instructions."

"I want to speak with the president."

"I am sorry sir, but that isn't possible now. The president is in a secure location. I am sure you can appreciate the situation."

There was a slight pause. "Yes, I guess I do. But we are going to need some help here, and soon."

"Sir, you have SSgt Harwood there. He can assist you or get word back to us here as need be. I have to go now, but we'll be in touch." He handed the phone back to Sgt McAllister who took it with a wry smile.

Gunny Mac walked back into the office. The president looked up expectantly. Gunny started to walk over to him.

"Gunny! I am through!" shouted LCpl Steptoe. Gunny hurried over. "He used the 'redsox2007' as his password."

"Redsox2007?"

"Yes, the last time the Sox won the series. I knew he had something like that. I'm dialing my friend now." All eyes turned toward him as he waited. "Dang, it's his answering service….Hey Trollbane, this is Elanadril. This is urgent. Call me back on Crocker's PDA. We've got big trouble, and we need your help."

"Elanadril?" asked Ramon, with a raised eyebrow.

Steptoe looked flustered. "Don't ask. Hey, the good news is that the low freqs are not getting jammed. The bad news is that he isn't answering."

The president left the TV and walked over. "Can you call anyone else on that? Can you call the White House?"

"Uh, no sir. Not on Sgt Crocker's. I have it set up only for this call. If I had my PDA, I could do it."

"And where is your PDA?"

"Back at the Marine House. We aren't supposed to have extraneous gear for an honor guard or something big like this."

"But you have this PDA."

"Yes sir. Sgt Crocker, well, uh, he didn't always follow the rules."

The president paused and actually smiled. "Well, thank God for small favors." He swung around and went back to the television.

The PDA in Steptoe's hands buzzed. He grabbed it as everyone in the office crowded around. "Hello, hello! Is this Trollbane?"

The bored-sounding voice came over the small speaker in the device. "Yea, Elanadril. What's so important that you have to call me when I'm taking a dump? The dragon's burning your fields again?"

"Have you seen the news? The Indians have stormed the embassy here, and we've got the president here, and we're stuck in the embassy!"

"What? What the hell are you talking about?"

The president leaned over to speak directly into the PDA. "Son, this is President Eduardo. I want you to listen up, because we need your help."

"Is this some sort of joke?"

"Trollbane, look at your news ticker. This is for real," Steptoe said.

There was a pause, then a "Holy shit! And this is you? That is really the president?"

"Yea, it is."

"What do you want me to do, uh, sir?"

Gunny Mac picked up the PDA. "Mr. Trollbane, this is Gunnery Sergeant McCardle with the security detachment. We need you to make a call for us. You need to call the White House." He suddenly realized he didn't have the number for the White House.

"Mr. President, what is the number?"

The president looked confused. "I don't know. I've never called the number. Someone else around me always has a phone."

"Mr. Trollbane ..."

"Mike."

"What?"

"It's Mike. Mike Dupris. 'Trollbane' is for gaming."

"OK, Mike, I want you to search the net for the number for the White House. Don't hang up this connection, but use another phone to call it. Tell them we have the president here, and he needs to talk to them."

"OK, wait a minute while I go to another computer." All nine conscious people in the room looked intently at the PDA while sounds of movement and low whispers too indistinct to make out came over the speaker. Finally, "I've got it!" broke out. "Let me see, uh, here...OK I've dialed." They hunched closer to the PDA, then the unmistakably brash tones of a busy signal could be heard. "It's busy."

"Keep trying son!" ordered the president. And Mike, aka Trollbane, did keep trying. For 30 more minutes. The line remained busy.

"There has to be another number we can use. Sir, isn't there another high priority number?" asked Major Defilice.

"Of course there are numbers like that. But I don't know them. My military aide has some. My staff sec has some. My secret service agents have some. But none of them are here."

"Gunny, what about Col Lineau?" asked PFC Ramon. Col Jeff Lineau was the Commandant of the Corps, the top Marine. "He should be able to reach the White House."

"Yes, but our dedicated com lines back to Quantico are down, and I really don't know his number."

"I can get through." She moved up to the PDA. "Mike, try dialing this number. 703 555 4543." She looked up at the rest. "In case I was going to be late from liberty," she shrugged. There was a pause, then the wonderful sound of a connection.

"Private Smith, Headquarters Company duty. This is an unsecured line. How may I help you ma'am/sir?"

Gunny moved back up. "Private Smith, this is Gunnery Sergeant McCardle in New Delhi. I've got the President of the United States with me. Listen carefully. I want you to go to the Commandant's office and get Col Lineau. Do not, I repeat do nothing up the phone. Just place the handset on the duty table there.   Then, I want you to go to the Commandant's office and get Col Lineau. Bring him back to your post and put him on your phone. Do it now. Do you understand?"

There was dead silence on the other end. Gunny could almost imagine Private Smith wondering if the small chance that this was true outweighed the consequences of this was some sort of prank.

"Aye-aye, Gunny!"

Gunny could hear the phone being placed on the table, then the sounds of footsteps running off into the distance.

Chapter 13

Colonel Jeff Lineau, the 42nd Commandant of the Marine Corps, sat in his office with Sergeant Major Mike Huff and Lieutenant Colonel Tye Saunders, his XO. None of the men were saying much at the moment, but had their eyes glued to the television and the scenes from India.

As the satellite shot panned over the scene from above, the body of what had to be Capt Leon-Guerro could be seen lying on the deck along with the rest of the prone figures. The Marine Corps was small, and most Marines knew each other by sight. Truth be told, Col Lineau had never had high hopes for Frank Leon-Guerro, but that really didn't matter now. He had proved the temper of his steel.

And now the question was the status of the rest of the detachment. Nothing much could be seen on the television screen, and attempts to reach the detachment via pulse and phone lines came up empty. There had been another Marine down, probably Sgt Crocker, but a short time ago, someone had dashed out and grabbed him. The angle and resolution weren't good enough to see just who had come out. And several Marines had earlier helped the president get inside as well. So at least a few Marines were alive and well. Hopefully more were as well.

Col Lineau looked around his office. Once the office of the Security Guard Battalion Commanding Officer, it was now the office of the

Commandant. Of course, his duties were little more than the CO of old, but he was granted the somewhat honorary title of Commandant (or the "'Dant," as the Marines now tended to refer to him.) And now, he felt helpless as he watched what was unfolding on the screen.

Col Lineau had joined the Corps before the dismemberment. A Naval Academy graduate, he had intended on being a Navy pilot, but weak eyes and an admiration of the Marines sent to be company officers and instructors at the Academy impressed him, and he chose green instead of blue upon graduation. He had his goals though. Truth-be-told, he had harbored dreams of becoming Commandant while a second lieutenant back at The Basic School in Quantico, but he had never thought it would unfold this way. A tour as an infantry platoon commander with 3/5 at Pendleton, then as the recruiting station ops officer in Des Moines followed TBS and IOC. He then went to Amphibious Warfare School, finding time to meet and marry the former Alicia Hera, a student at William and Mary. He reported to 2/4 at Camp Lejeune, taking command of Golf Company, where he led the company into Iraq, earning himself a bronze star and making a small name for himself.

Additional staff jobs followed, along with a promotion to major. He received a Legion of Merit while serving in a joint billet with Joint Task Force Horn of Africa , something rare for his rank. When he made lieutenant colonel, he was given command of 1/8 "America's Battalion," which he led into the Sudan. It was here, while at the tip of the spear, that the Marine Corps was shattered. He brought his battalion back to LeJeune, decommissioned it, and waited along with everyone else to discover their individual fates. And Jeff was one of the lucky ones. He was offered one of the few O-5 positions left in the Corps, and became the S-3. Over the ensuing years, as retirement and one heart attack took those senior to him, he moved up and was promoted to Commandant four years ago. He was looking to retire in 53-days-and-a-wake-up, to go back to North Dakota with his wife, going south during the winter to spoil the grandkids.

He looked over at the other two Marines in the room. LtCol Saunders still wore the gold wings of a naval aviator on his chest, the only Marine left who rated them. An Osprey pilot before dismemberment, he'd asked to be retained in the Corps despite there being no aviation billets.

Being a Marine meant more to him than flying. He was retained, and his tour as the commanding office of Bravo Company in Europe proved to him that his decision was the right one.

Tall with deep chocolate skin, he made an imposing figure. But he was usually soft-spoken, a man whose faith was the prime mover in his life. If he were not a Marine, he could have been very happy as a missionary. Tye Saunders hid nothing from view. What you saw was what you got. And what you got was good.

Now he was hanging up the phone after yet one more try to contact the detachment. He looked at the colonel and quietly shook his head.

Sergeant Major Mike Huff was along slightly different lines. A radio operator in an infantry company whetted his appetite for adventure, and he followed with tours in both battalion and force recon. He had combat experience with Force, and a silver star attested to his valor. Mike had confided in him on a few occasions when they had shared a cold one after work that he never should have made it so far. He had had a number of liberty-type incidents, about which he would only hint, which should have gotten him non-judicial punishment at the least, but he always had friends in high places who saw the potential in him, and his "punishments" for his transgressions were never official.

SgtMaj Huff still had the wild side to him, but he cared deeply for his Marines, and his ability to inspire their loyalty proved that those early benefactors had it right.

Admin had been undergoing an inspection, so the entire staff had stayed late. Otherwise, Colonel Lineau would already have been home asleep. When the news of the attack first broke, he had called his boss, Rear Admiral Chance Cates in N3. Chance had actually worked under him while at HOA, and, to be honest, there was not much love lost between them. He was told to stand by, and that was what they were now doing.

No one had said much for the last several minutes, each lost in thought on events taking place halfway around the world. Col Lineau sipped his coffee, wishing there was some sort of direct action, something he could be doing right now. But he was ordered to wait.

There was a pounding of feet coming down the passage, then a pounding knock on the door. Before Col Lineau could respond, the hatch burst open and Private Smith, one of the newest Marines, burst in, white duty belt around his waist, his face flushed. The three men, nerves taut, jumped to their feet.

"Sir, request permission to speak!" And before a response, "I have the Marines in India and the president on my duty phone. And they want to speak with you!"

Lineau's mouth dropped open as his mind reeled. "How did you get that call?" He struggled for understanding.

"I don't know sir. My phone just rang, and then there was a gunny, then the president. They want you now!"

Unbelievable or not, a possible prank or not, Col Lineau snapped to and started running out the hatch, Huff, Saunders, and Smith right behind as they all sprinted down the passage, out the building, and over to the company office building. Staff Sergeant Felicia Boyles saw them through the window as they ran up, and tried to call the admin office to attention, her apprehension obvious on her face. The foursome never slowed, but ran down the passage to the duty office. They rushed in, and Col Lineau paused a second, catching his breath, before lifting the phone receiver from the desk.

"This is Col Lineau."

"Colonel! This is Gunny McCardle! We have been under attack, and we're trapped in the embassy. I've got President Eduardo with me. We've got no coms, and…"

"Let me have that, Sergeant," ordered the president, taking the PDA out of the gunny's hand. "Colonel, this is President Eduardo. I'm going to give you a direct order as your Commander in Chief. I want you to get the White House on the line, and I want you to do it now. I want to speak with my Chief of Staff, and I want to speak with the vice-president. I want action taken to retake this embassy. Do you understand me?"

"Yes sir!" He frantically mouthed to LtCol Saunders to get RADM Cates on the other line. "Uh, Mr. President, can I please speak with Gunnery Sergeant McCardle? I need to make sure we keep this connection."

There was a pause, then "Gunny McCardle, sir."

"Gunny Mac! The news reported that all communications were cut, and we sure haven't been able to get through to you. How are you calling me? And why is the president calling us here?"

"Well sir, we sort of hacked to one of LCpl Steptoe's buds in Katmandu, and he is patching us through. And the duty was the only number any of us knew offhand."

"OK. Good thinking. I'm going to give this to SgtMaj Huff. Do not hang up!" He handed the phone to the Sergeant Major, then turned to LtCol Saunders. "You got him, Tye?"

Saunders shook his head and handed over the phone. Col Lineau put the handset to his ear and heard the cheery hold music. "Mike, ask Mac for the name and the number of that contact in Katmandu."

"This is RADM Cates."

"Admiral, this is Col Lineau. I am in contact with our detachment in New Delhi. They have the president with them, and he wants his chief of staff and the vice-president on the line. If we can get a number, I can have them call, but frankly, I'm afraid to lose the connection. I'd like to patch them directly through this number here."

To his credit, Chance Cates didn't hesitate or question his subordinate. And less than two minutes later, there was a click as the White House communications technicians electronically hooked into the Headquarters Company duty phone. SgtMaj Huff caught the Commandant's eye, then hit the speaker button and the voices came over to fill the office.

"Mr. President, this is Arnie. Are you OK? Are you safe?"

"Just a second sir. This is Gunnery Sergeant McCardle. Let me hand you over to him."

Arnold Hatch was the president's chief of staff. He had never met the president before the Republican Party had essentially foisted him on nominee Eduardo, and at first glance, the older, overweight Arnie seemed the antithesis of the personable, charismatic nominee, but quickly the two had forged a true friendship based on respect and admiration. Arnie was the president's man.

"Arnie, is that you?"

"Sir, I can't tell you how good it is to hear your voice. We haven't had a clear picture of what is going on. Are you OK? Are you safe?"

"I am a little dinged up, but I am safe for the moment, I guess. I don't have any special agents with me, just a few Marines and an Army major, so I don't know how secure this is. What is going on back there? What are you doing?"

"The vice-president has the principles in the situation room, but no one knows just what is going on. She called in the Indian ambassador and has tried to call the prime minister."

"Has the military been given orders?"

"Well, sir, there has been some debate as to that. No one knows just what orders to give just yet."

"Arnie, get her on the phone. I want the military to move. We cannot be seen as weak."

"They're patching her in now, too. I told them to patch me in first. She should be here in a second."

"This situation is outrageous. Why hasn't the prime... wait a second." There was a muffled sound of someone talking, then the president came back on. "Arnie, one of the soldiers here tells me that this line is not secure. He doesn't think anyone is monitoring it, but that it could be monitored. I think it's a good idea if we speak with that in mind."

"Yes, Mr. President."

"I heard that too, Mr. President. Are you safe?"

"Vice-President Wright. For the moment, I am. Ambassador Tankersly is dead, and I don't know how many other people. We've got half the diplomatic community over at the consulate, and about a million Indians outside the gates. I'd say the situation is serious. What are you doing about it?"

"Mr. President, the Indian ambassador should be here within minutes. The prime minister has not accepted my call I keep getting told that he is not available at the moment."

"What does the director say about this?" The director of the CIA, Kaiyen Lin, was a trusted advisor to the president, and had been since his days in congress.

"They're in touch with their sources right now, but she thinks that there are indications that the government is at least passively supporting the mob. At least they helped organize the demonstration."

"She thinks that? I can't believe that. They're going to attack sovereign US soil over jobs? Just get the prime minister on the hook and patch me through to him. I want to talk to him face-to-face. We are going to resolve this, and now. What about the military? What are they doing?"

"They've been placed on alert, of course, but no specific orders have been given yet. This doesn't fall under any of our contingency plans, as you know."

"I don't care what plans there are or are not," he said almost in a shout. "I'm here on the ground, and this is an attack on US soil. I hope the Indian government gets things straightened out soon, but until then, I want our military moving, and I want them moving now. That is what we pay them for, to protect US citizens."

"Of course, Mr. President. General Litz reports that we have the Ronald Reagan Battle Group in Thailand right now, and we have our units in Guam and Japan, but nothing is really close."

"What about Diego Garcia? What's there?"

There was a pause and some mumbles voices as the vice-president asked someone a question. "There isn't much there, only some support forces, ours and the Brits."

"Well then, I guess you have some work to do, Vice-President Wright. I want you to keep this line open. Have someone report back to me in 15 minutes as to what's going on."

"Of course, Mr. President. We are working it."

As the speaker on the desk became quiet, the three Marines looked at each other. Col Lineau turned off the speaker. "Mike, someone is going to think of this sooner or later, but send Gunny Cassel from the embassy in Katmandu to secure LCpl Steptoe's friend and his phone. You can be sure that State and the Secret Service and every other cat and dog will get there soon, and their priorities aren't going to be our Marines. I want one of ours there to let us know what is being passed on that line. And put someone else in here. I want a SNCO along with Private Smith to watch this phone. Tye, I want every swinging dick here in full battle rattle and ready to move in two hours."

"What is going on, sir? Where are we going?"

"Nowhere yet. I've got to make some calls first. I just want every possible body we've got here ready to go. Call Norm at Camp David and tell him the same. Every sickbay commando, every clerk, every possible Marine." He turned the speaker back on, then turned and left the office. He had work to do.

Chapter 14

Early Tuesday Morning, The Whitehouse, Washington, DC

Vice-President Wright strode back into the situation room from the communications room, where she had taken the call, Arnold following in her wake. She looked at the technicians who were feverishly connecting another phone. It was astounding, really, that in the heart of the White House, where decisions were made, they had not been able to simply transfer the call. Some problem with interoperability between the secure and non-secure lines, the communications chief had said.

"Well, I've spoken to him. He is safe for the moment, but rather agitated." She looked at the gathered movers and shakers sitting around the edge of the table. There was a face she didn't recognize. "Who are you?"

"Stacy Barnet, ma'am. Homeland Security. The secretary was on the Eastern Shore for the night and is on his way now. I'm here to take notes until he gets here."

The vice-president merely grunted. She looked around again. "Where is the Indian ambassador?" she asked to no one in particular.

"He is pulling into the grounds now," replied a staffer, a communications bud in his ear.

"OK. When he arrives, get him to my office. I want to see him right away. General Litz, the president wants our military to move on this, in case things go south on us. With everyone else in the room here, please repeat what you told me about our options."

"Yes ma'am. Well, our options are limited, actually. We have the Reagan Battle Group on liberty in Thailand, and a few scattered ships in the Indian Ocean. We have our civil affairs units in the Horn of Africa, and our air and army assets in Guam and Japan. We could bomb the bejesus out of India if we wanted, but in a situation like this, I'm not sure we have the assets to take any effective action." The Chairman of the Joint Chiefs, a former Air Force bomber pilot, looked uncomfortable and he glanced back down at his notes. "NORAD has just been placed on our highest alert posture, and the Quick Reaction Brigade in Korea has been placed on alert as well. They can be ready to move in 90 minutes, and we can get them to Thailand, Diego Garcia, or possibly even Sri Lanka, but we don't have any assets to get them all the way to New Delhi. Logistically, we could do an air drop with an airborne battalion, but even if the Indians just stood by for that, it'd be almost impossible to get them all to a landing at the embassy grounds."

"Surely you don't mean for us to physically invade India? That is ludicrous!" Simon Pitt, the Secretary of State, blurted out.

"No, Mr. Secretary, I do not. I'm just laying out our options."

"Well, that's one far-fetched option, doing a parachute invasion of India."

"Granted, Mr. Secretary. I don't think it can even be done if I thought it was a good idea, and I don't think that." The general looked annoyed as he spoke.

Vice-President Wright interrupted, "Look, no one is advocating any sort of attack here. The Indian government will have to restore order, and we'll have to craft our response to this. Let's all keep cool heads, now."

The staffer with the com earbuds moved forward and whispered into her ear. "Madame Vice-President, the Indian ambassador has arrived."

She nodded. "People, the ambassador is here. Mr. Lefever, if you will accompany me. General Litz, keep all our forces on alert as you deem fit. But get that carrier group out at sea and moving toward India."

"That could be seen as a provocative movement, Madam Vice-President."

"Storming our embassy, killing our ambassador, and keeping our president hostage are also provocative, Mr. Pitt." She motioned to the Secretary of Defense to join her. They stepped out of the door and waited for the Secretary of State to move out of earshot.

Jennifer Wright and Paul Lefever had worked together for years, he in various positions in the Department of Defense, and she as a congresswoman. He owed his current position to her, and they were as strong allies as anyone could be within the beltway. Both disapproved of the way then Senator Eduardo had cut the military budget, and neither really had a high opinion of the man.

"Paul, we need to move on this," she said quietly. "But Pitt is right, as hard as it is to admit this. We really don't want a war with India. So let's move the *Reagan*. Let the world see that. But a few ships off the coast can't really do much. And if we don't have the forces to do anything, well, then that is the fault of those who did not want to pay for a strong military. And matters are just going to have to progress as they will." She didn't say anything else. She didn't have to, and some things are better left unsaid.

Paul Lefever looked deeply into the vice-president's eyes, then nodded. She knew he understood her

The vice-president, secret service agents leading the way, walked back to her office. Her staff secretary was standing, waiting for her. "Ma'am, the ambassador is waiting in your office." Several men, obviously from the Indian embassy, were sitting on the couch in the reception area, and they came to their feet at her arrival.

"Thank you Ann. Please make sure no one disturbs us. She caught sight of David hovering off to the side, his eyes asking if he could join her. She shook her head no and walked in. The ambassador was standing facing her desk, back to the door, arms clasped behind his back. He turned around at her entrance and stepped forward, offering his hand. She ignored it and moved around him to her desk and sat down. He held his hand out for a few moments then slowly lowered it.

She looked at him, seeing a man not quite sure of himself. From the contact notes given to her by her staff, she knew he was political appointee and had been ambassador in the US for over a year. With a masters from Brown University, his success in building a chemical empire and his financial support to his political party (well, perhaps that more than anything else) had gotten him the appointment. She had seen him at a few functions, but she had never really had any contact with him.

"Well, Mr. Ghosh, what is the Indian government doing about this unfortunate situation?"

"Madam Vice-President, first, accept my apologies for this incident. The people of India abhor violence, and the government is working feverishly to find a peaceful solution to the situation at your embassy."

"A peaceful solution? I don't see anything being done there. Does that look like anything is being done?" She pointed to the television at the front of the office where CNN was broadcasting the scene.

He turned around, looked at the screen, then faced her again. "Madam Vice-President. I just got off the phone with our office of external affairs. I've been assured that progress is being made with the people outside the embassy."

"Progress? I don't want to hear 'progress!' You have police, you have your army. The life of the president is in your hands along with half the diplomatic community of New Delhi, and you talk about progress?"

"Madam Vice-President. It is not that easy. Most of these people are peaceful protesters. They have a right to be there. And if we move in rashly to secure the area, they could erupt into violence."

"Could erupt into violence? Mr. Ambassador, you don't think there has already been violence? Ambassador Tankersly has been killed, and the president is being held prisoner in his own embassy. And you tell me the 'people' have the right to 'protest.' What kind of unmitigated gall is that?"

On the defensive, the ambassador now seemed to grow a little bit of a spine. "Madam Vice-President, we are the largest democracy in the world. Larger than the US, I might add. Despite the efforts of the US to keep India in thrall, we are an independent, democratic people. Our government is not going to go in shooting, massacring perhaps thousands of Indian citizens and endangering the people in the embassy as well. We are going to do this right, with no further loss of life."

She saw the change in his demeanor and knew it was time to pull back. And while she almost would not admit it yet to herself, she really did not want a quick and safe solution. She had to couch what she said next in careful terms. History did not look kindly on leaders who let personal goals get in the way of what should be done, even if she fervently believed the nation would be better off with her at the helm rather than the current occupant of the White house.

"Mr. Ambassador, I realize that India is a great democracy. And no matter what happens, the US isn't about to do anything rash. India and the US are too close, and we are not going to let anything jeopardize our overall relations." She hoped the message that the US would not take military action was coming through, and that there would be no serious retaliatory measures taken should the worst come to pass. "This is happening in India, and we expect India to handle the situation. And we have full confidence in your government's abilities to take care of the situation" She didn't mention that she knew there were Indian government agents in the mob, and that they probably had a hand in what was going on. Let the government have an out should things go downhill.

The ambassador seemed somewhat surprised at her response, but he recovered quickly. "Thank you for your confidence, Madam Vice-President. We'll take care of this, peacefully, and without further bloodshed. The criminals who instigated this will be caught and prosecuted. And it is our fervent desire that our two great nations remain the close allies we are."

Vice-President Wright leaned over and punched her intercom button. "David, can you come in here, please." She looked up at the ambassador. "Mr. Ambassador, I hate to cut this short, but you can imagine that I have a lot to do. And I imagine you do, too. Please give my regards to the prime minister and let him know the US trusts his abilities to manage this unfortunate incident."

David came in the door. "David, please escort the ambassador back to his car. Make sure we get him all the assistance he needs. And make sure State has someone over at the Indian embassy to facilitate communications."

She held out her hand, and the ambassador took it. He looked closely into her eyes for a second as if trying to read her mind. "Thank

you, Madam Vice-President. I trust we'll have good news for you soon."
He turned around and walked out of her office.

She watched him leave. Hopefully, the Indian Office of External
Affairs would read into her comments and understand that the US was
not willing to risk direct action. Much hinged on whether Kaiyen Lin
was right. If the Indian government was actively involved with this, or
even passively supported it, then President Eduardo might pay the price.
And if the Indian government was not involved, and if they successfully
rescued the president, well, nothing much would change and it would
be back to the status quo.

The president was not an evil man. Naive, maybe, misguided
certainly, but not evil. Under normal circumstances, Vice-President
Wright would never wish him harm. But she knew the nation would be
safer and more secure if she was president, and if another nation helped
that come to pass, then who was she to deny destiny?

Chapter 15

Tuesday Evening, Phuket, Thailand

Lieutenant David Littlehawk watched the sun finally disappear into the sea. There was no "green flash," just the last bit of orange winking out. An audible sigh arose from the several hundred Thais and *farang* vacationers at the Promthiep Cape lighthouse who gathered for the show each evening.

It had been a pretty good day, all told. His first day ashore in several weeks, and it was in Phuket, Thailand, one of the US Navy's favorite destinations. Good food, great weather, cheap cold beer, pretty and willing girls, what could be better? David had gotten a late start, renting a motorcycle in Phuket Town, then riding over to Patong Beach. Technically, he should have a liberty buddy, but no one else wanted to go exploring by bike, so he had left alone. He had gotten a good massage on a beach mat right on the water by an older, heavyset lady named Nok. It had felt so good, he had extended the massage from one hour to two, then had wandered over to one of the open-air restaurants for some lunch. Many of the restaurants offered American or European fare, but he wanted Thai. He had learned to like Thai food while a ROTC student at Oregon State, but this was different. The Lard Na was thick with sauce (looking sort of like flat noodles covered with snot), and the Moo Ga Pow was bitingly spicy. Good, more authentic perhaps, but not what he had gotten used to at the Thai Thai Kitchen in Corvallis.

He had gotten back on his bike, fought through the traffic in Patong town, then started up the long hill to drive over to Karon and beaches south when he saw some elephants right at the side of the road. The elephants had benches on their backs, so he had stopped to look. These elephants, with no trees left to haul, made a living for themselves and their mahouts by giving rides. Then feeling like a million different levels of tourist, he had actually paid for a ride into the jungle. Surprisingly, a fighter pilot now used to being at sea, the animal's rolling gait had almost made him sick. As the elephant lurched up and down some washed-out jungle gullies, his stomach threatened to rebel, But the sun, the butterflies fluttering around, and the rubbery feel of the elephant's skin under the heels of his New Balances made the experience rather exotic. A man at the side of the road come out to take a photo of him on the back of the elephant, and after the ride, he was offered the photo for $10. Feeling even more like a tourist, he actually bought it. He knew it was kitschy, but still, he found out he really wanted it.

His guidebook had mentioned Rawai as a good place for seafood, (another taste he had acquired at school), so after getting lost only twice, he made it to the beach where open-air restaurants lined the shore. Walking into the closest, he picked out fish and crabs by pointing at them, then he sat on the pillows, which were offered instead of chairs. It surprised him that they did not offer beer. He ordered a cold coke and looked out over the turquoise waters until his food came. He hadn't told them how he wanted his fish and crabs prepared, but he liked what turned up. He had no idea what it was, but the crab was in some sort of curry sauce, and the fish steamed with vegetables. He slowly ate his meal, smiling at the young Thai toddler who came up to stare at him. The toddler did not smile back, but just stared at him.

After the meal, he got back on his small bike and puttered up to Promthiep Cape to watch the sunset. While sitting on the stone wall around the lighthouse, waiting for the sun to dip into the water, two Thai teenage boys came up to him, mentioning "India" amidst a torrent of Thai, pointing at him and mimicking shooting rifles. This rather surprised him. He didn't really think his Native American features were that pronounced, and for non-Americans to recognize those features seemed rather far-fetched. And for them to act out what must be the cowboy role seemed somewhat rude, something out-of-character to Thais. Feeling uncomfortable, he merely ignored them and looked out over the Andaman Sea.

The sun got large and red as it slowly dipped into the sea. Young Thai lovers, no more than schoolchildren really, sat leaning against each other, watching the sun set. Tourists of all stripes wandered around, cameras in hand, or sat on the stone wall quietly watching. He had heard that there was an audible snap and a flash of light as the sun slipped over the horizon, but he never saw nor heard anything like that. The sun merely slipped away. The only sound was the communal sigh from the gathered throng.

As the crowd slowly dispersed after the sun set into the sea, LT Littlehawk got back on his bike and started up the coast for Patong, anxious to sample the infamous Thai nightlife. He had planned on hooking up with a few guys from the squadron at a bar they had picked out at random from the internet.

He made his way up the coast, past several small beach towns and up the hill, then down the long grade into Patong. He drove up the beach road and was surprised not to see several thousand sailors taking over the place. He felt odd parking his motorcycle at the beach side of the walking street, then walked up towards Annabell's. The street was not deserted; just no sailors were in sight. There were the expected calls of "Welcome, sir," as the girls (and not a few guys looking like girls) gave their hopeful plugs to come in and sit down at the various bars lining the street.

Walking into Annabell's, he sat down and ordered a Singha from one of the short-skirted waitresses. As he waited, he scanned the bar for his compatriots. The bartender caught his eyes and motioned him over. She was an attractive woman, older than the average waitress, but with long black hair, a slender body, and a refined face. He shrugged and got up, walking over to her.

"You Loo tenna Little Hawk?" she asked pausing between the two parts of his name.

Somewhat surprised, he merely nodded. She reached under the bar and handed him a folded piece of paper.

Chickenhawk,

Get your ass back to the boat. We're pulling out at 2100.
Look at the news and you can figure out where.

Gopher

He read the note twice. He automatically looked up at the television over the bar, but it had a soccer game on. He glanced down at his watch. *Shit! It was 2030!*

He sprinted out the bar and down the street, knocking down one pot-bellied tourist who had already had a good start on the night's drinking. The man's challenges faded behind him as he ran to his bike. Fumbling with the key, he finally got the bike started and he tore down Beach Street, almost crashing head first into a taxi before he remembered that the Thais drove on the left side of the street. *Please let me make it on time!*

He held the throttle wide open as the bike huffed its way up the mountain behind Patong, trying to will it to make some speed. Cresting the rise, he tore down the other side, cutting inside pick-ups and buses, passing wherever he could find a few inches to spare. Trying to follow the signs in to Phuket Town, he made one wrong turn and had to double back. Near a shopping mall, there was a line of cars waiting o at the light—he worked his way to the front, then scooted across the 4-lane road in front of him against the red light.

Entering the town, he knew the port was off toward the right, but knowing that and navigating through the winding streets were two different things. Finally, he saw the bright lights of the port and drove up, blasting through the gate much to the consternation of the guard there who yelled Thai pleasantries as he sped through. Tearing around a group of warehouses, he looked up to see the *Reagan* moving out, several miles out to sea already.

His heart sank. Slowing down, he drove up to the landing where the liberty launches had been bringing in and taking back passengers. There was a knot of sailors there, perhaps ten or twelve, all in civies. Two sailors in uniform, a lieutenant (jg) and a third class petty officer were there as well, clipboards in hand.

He walked up to the two in uniform. "Name?"

"LT David Littlehawk."

The petty officer wrote it down. "OK, if you can wait here, sir. We're gathering everyone who missed the ship. We'll get you put up for the night, then we'll get word on what's going to happen with you next."

"What is going on, anyway? Why the sudden departure?"

"You haven't heard, sir? The Indians have taken over our embassy, and they've got the president prisoner. We've got to get him back." He turned away as another sailor asked him a question.

LT David Littlehawk, F-35C pilot, had missed movement when his training and skills might be needed. He stared at the *Reagan* and sat down on the edge of the pier, watching his future sail away.

Chapter 16

"Gunny, something is happening!" PFC Ramon stood with the major and the president, looking at the television. Gunny and Loralee rushed over to the screen too see for themselves. The satellite shot showed movement near the gate and what looked to be uniformed and armed men pushing back the crowd and then several of them climbing the wall.

"Finally, the Indian police. It's about time." The president sounded almost petulant. They watched as about half a dozen men made it over the gate, collected themselves, then started walking, not toward the embassy, but approaching the consulate building. The CNN talking heads were giving all sorts of reasons they might be doing this, but the group in the embassy ignored most of the commentary. Gunny McCardle sprinted out of the room and down the passage to Post 1, arriving just as the call from Post 2 came in.

"Gunny, the Indian Army is here, and they want to get in the consulate. What do I do?" asked SSgt Harwood over the landline.

"Hold them off for a second and get Ambassador Tilden there. I don't know who is actually senior for the foreign ambassadors, but get him anyway. And get the senior US State guy there. See what they want. The consulate is still US soil, but if the Indian government is finally moving to help, then we don't want to piss them off."

"Roger that!"

Major Defilice and PFC Ramon came down the passage together. The major looked at the gunny, eyebrows raised. "The Indian Army is here, but they want into the consulate. I don't know why they aren't coming here."

"Do you think we should meet them, Gunny? We've got the president here and our wounded."

"I don't think so, sir. You saw them on the screen. They walked right past the bodies in the courtyard. And they went right to the consulate. I told SSgt Norwood to get Ambassador Tilden there to find out what they want and what they are going to do." He turned and sat down on the jutting shelf that served as the post's desk.

They sat there staring at each other, wondering what was going on. The tension kept mounting. After five minutes or so, which seemed like an hour, the landline rang again.

"Gunny," came SSgt Harwood's hushed voice. "The Indians told Ambassador Tilden and Ms. Parker that they're going to evacuate the consulate. Ms. Parker told them they got to get rid of the mob, but the Indians say the situation is too delicate. Ms. Parker is pissed, and she asked about Ambassador Tankersly and the president, but the Indians keep telling them they need to evacuate first, then they can try to deal with the crowd. Oh, the Ambassador and Ms. Parker are going back inside now."

Gunny felt a sense of foreboding. He could see the photos of the Embassy takeover in Tehran in 1978, the photos of the blindfolded Marine security guard being led down the steps. The photos were part of a series of classes at the school, and all Marines had the images imbedded into their psyche.

If the consulate was vacated, that meant the embassy grounds would be empty, and except for Sgt Niimoto, the only thing between the president and a hostile crowd was his group of Marines, an army major, an elderly woman, and an Indian servant of unknown loyalties. The doors to the embassy building were pretty solid, as were the lower floor windows. Then he thought of the access tunnel. If he knew about it, then certainly some Indians knew about it. Feeling paranoid, he got back on the landline.

"SSgt Harwood. They don't have a choice, and neither do you. They are going to have to evacuate. Everyone. And it won't be long. I need you and Chen to go down to the access tunnel and block it somehow. Jam the hatch, then put some furniture or something in front of it. No need advertising where the hatch is. Do it quick, because they are going to want you to evacuate, too. When they tell you to leave, do it. Help keep everyone calm."

"What about the post? We can't leave it unmanned."

"Mark, the situation has radically changed. You're going to have to leave the post anyway, so do it now. Flash the computer, then lock it up and leave."

"Roger that, Gunny. We're on it."

"Give me a report when you're done, then get out with the rest. Wherever you end up, there will be somebody in charge. Get word back to Quantico where you are, then wait for further orders." Big Mac looked at Little Mac, gave a sigh, then turned around to go back down the passage and report to the president, with Defilice and Ramon in tow.

Chapter 17

Tuesday Morning, HQMC, Quantico

Colonel Lineau looked at his S3, Lieutenant Colonel Stephanie Cable. "You understand what I want, right?"

LtCol Cable hesitated a second. "Yes sir, but are you sure you want to do this?" LtCol Cable was a hard-as-nails triathlete and an outstanding operations officer, excelling at managing the training and operations of the far-flung Marines around the world. She was dual-hatted as the Staff Judge Advocate, and she was letting the conservative side of that billet make her urge caution.

"Yes, colonel, I am sure. It is my prerogative as the Commandant to place my Marines wherever I deem fit so they can best perform their duties. And I think that place right now is Thailand. And, if you can remember, we have dead Marines in India right now, and more in harm's way. You are to go to N3 and act as our liaison there. When I or the XO contact you and tell you to do something or cough up some assets, you are going to get it done. Period. I don't care how you get the Navy to play along, but that is what we pay you the big bucks for. Understood?"

"Yes sir."

"OK. Get going." As she turned around as started hurrying down the passage, he called out after her, "Stephanie, we are counting on you."

He turned to his S1, Captain Amir Mahmoud. "How are we doing on personnel?"

Capt Mahmoud immediately replied "We have 63 Marines and Doc Hollister on their way to Andrews in POVs. Captain Krieg is in charge. We're the only ones left here, and we've got the duty van ready to take us." Capt Mahmoud never seemed to use notes, but he always had figures at his beck and call, so Colonel Lineau took his words as gospel. "The detachments at Bangkok, Phnom Pehn, Hanoi, Jakarta, Kuala Lumpur, Vientianne, and Singapore had been told to quietly get available Marines to U-Tapao, but we don't yet know how many that will be."

"Well, keep me informed as those numbers come in. Four, is everyone armed?"

Major Jesus Roberto, the S4 answered up, "Sir, everyone who has left is armed, and we've got three mount-out cases of ammo, grenades, C4, and some extra weapons. I've got a list here of what we have." He handed it to the commanding officer. "All those weapons are going in the POVs like you directed. I just hope nobody gets stopped for speeding on the way up to Andrews. This is a major, major breach of regs. I know why we are doing it, sir, but the Maryland Highway Patrol might not be so understanding."

"You've got that right. I hope Master Guns Chung put the fear of God in them before they took off. He's in the lead vehicle, right?"

"Yes sir, and Captain Krieg is in the rear. Master Guns will probably blow out the tires of anyone who tries to pass him. When they get to Andrews, they'll go in Gate 4. I hope they've been cleared, sir."

Colonel Lineau glanced at the Sergeant Major who nodded slightly. "Yes, Four, they've been cleared." Actually, Colonel Lineau seemed perhaps most surprised by this than by any other of the wheeling and dealing that had occurred over the last couple hours. From his experience, the Air Force tended way to the right on standard procedures. But somehow, the Sergeant Major, in that weird brotherhood/mafia of E9s, had paved the way for his Marines to get on the base with POVs and personal weapons, park next to the ball field, then get on a bus to the tarmac to meet the incoming C17. Col Lineau had managed to wangle that from an Industrial College of the Armed Forces classmate who was now at TRANSCOM. Too much wheeling and dealing, too much going outside of channels. His career was almost certainly over after all of this, but he was due to get out in 52 days and a wake up anyway, so WTF? It was the right thing to do, even if he wasn't quite sure what they would do if they ever got that far.

The hatch opened and LtCol Saunders walked in. Col Lineau looked up at him expectantly and not without a little bit of dread. If Tye did not come through, then all the other rushed plans might turn out to be an exercise in futility.

A smile broke out on LtCol Saunders' broad face. "Sir, I've got them. Four Ospreys on loan to the Indonesian government for piracy interdiction. Don't ask me how, but they are on the way to U-Tapao. I've got two Coast Guard pilots on their way who are qualified, and I've got an old squadron mate of mine who's now flying for the DEA heading to LAX to catch a flight to meet us there, too. The Indonesian pilots can't fly further than Thailand, so I am still trying to scare up some co-pilots. But we've got the birds."

A tremendous feeling of relief swept over him. Nothing was for certain yet, and he hoped the situation would resolve itself. But at least the Marine Corps was not standing by when its own were in trouble.

"Good job, Tye. Great job, I should say. OK, we've got to move. We've got less than an hour to wheels up, and I still have a call to make."

A chorus of "Aye-aye's rang out as Marines started hurrying out of his office. Col Lineau picked up the secure phone and called a number that patched him through a series of com links before ringing in the stateroom of RADM Joshua Conners, Commander, Carrier Battle Group 31 aboard the *USS Reagan*.

"Josh, it's me. We're on. We've got the Ospreys."

"OK Jeff. Then let's do it."

"We're wheels up at 1000 local. We should arrive at U-Tapao around 1600 on the 4th. Give us an hour to get on the Ospreys, then 4 hours out to your pos. So you need to be less than 1,500 miles from Thailand by then. Can you swing it?"

"Well, I just reported that we are having a little shaft problem, which is slowing us down. I expect that we'll have it fixed in, say 23 hours or so?"

"Thanks Josh. You know, I really appreciate this."

"Yea, I know." There was a pause. "Well, I guess it's been a good career."

"You were slated for your third star. You had better places to go. I'm stuck at my terminal rank, and anyway, I'm out in 52 days and a wake-up. You're delaying a fucking carrier battle group for us. They could court martial you."

"Life's a bitch, then you die. So what? When we took an oath that July so many years ago at the Academy, we took an oath to the nation, but really also to our armed forces, and to each other." There was another pause. "Who would of thought it? Our Plebe Summer's two biggest shitbirds. You're the Commandant of the Marine Corps, and I've got two stars."

"Yea, who would have thunk it. Well, I've got a bird to catch. See you in a few!"

"God speed , Jeff, God speed."

Colonel Lineau hung up the phone. He picked up his body armor and put it on, then his deuce gear. Strapping on his 9 mm, he took a look around the office before a thought struck him. He walked over to the computer and quickly typed, then printed out a page. He left his office and went to the front hatch where he could see the duty van waiting for him. He walked out, closed the hatch and locked it. Turning around, he taped the paper he had printed to the hatch. He turned again and hurried to the van.

On the paper was the simple message, "Gone to fight the Indians."

Chapter 18

Tuesday Evening, US Embassy. New Delhi

Gunny McCardle sat in an overstuffed office chair, feeling he should be doing something, but not knowing right then just what that something was. He looked over at the president who was sitting with Major Defilice and Loralee, sipping the tea that Mr. Dravid had recovered from the ambassador's office, looking for all the world like British imperialists without a care in the world. Mr. Dravid stood attentively just behind the president.

LCpl Saad came up to the gunny and bent over to whisper, "What about him?" tilting his head towards Dravid.

Gunny knew what he meant, having some of the same thoughts himself. He looked over at Dravid, serving tea as if nothing had happened. A slight man in his early 50s, he had a touch of gray coloring his hair and dark, smooth skin. Gunny has seen him at various social functions serving the guests, and he knew that Dravid was a favorite of the ambassador, but other than that, he really knew nothing more about him. And now here he was, three feet from the president while a mob of his countrymen milled around outside having already killed and probably wanting to kill again.

He had considered restraining the man but hadn't decided it was necessary yet. But no use in taking chances. "Just keep an eye on him, OK?"

Saad nodded and moved around in back of the man and sat down.

"Steptoe, come here." LCpl Steptoe got up and came to stand in front of him. "Great job with the PDA, by-the-way. Everything still OK with it?"

LCpl Steptoe hesitated. "Uh, well, we are still connected. But I wonder how long the battery will last. The charge is half full now, but I don't have his charger here."

"Can we use anything else? Somebody has to have a charger in one of these desks."

"This is proprietary gear. It can only be charged with its designed charger. I can probably jury rig something to charge the battery, but I have to open this up and take out the battery to do that. And that means no com while I'm doing it, and I might not get it back together right without the right tools here."

Gunny McCardle took a second to digest that. "OK, well, watch it and let me know when it starts getting low."

The president stood up. "Sergeant! What the hell is going on? I want Washington back on the phone, now!" Gunny almost rolled his eyes but managed to stop the motion. He nodded to LCpl Steptoe who nodded back and went over the president to make the connection. Gunny chose not to listen in this time.

He called LCpl Kramer over. "Kramer, take Ramon," he hesitated and looked around the office, "no, take Saad and stay in the Cultural Affairs office across the passage."

PFC Ramon had grabbed her weapon upon hearing her name, but when Gunny changed his mind, she sat back down with a scowl.

"Stay back from the window so no one can see you, but look out and watch. I think the people at the consulate will be moving out shortly, but let me know when that happens. I don't want to be relying on CNN for this."

He sat back and half-listened to the president shouting angrily on the PDA. He was wondering just what he was missing, what he could be doing now. What he should be doing now. He was trained for this, but "this" was nothing he had really imagined would happen.

He looked over at SSgt Child lying on the desk and wondered for the umpteenth time if maybe Child would have been a better Marine for the situation. Well, there was no getting around it. He was in charge, and it was up to him to take care of things until someone else got there to relieve him.

PFC Rodriguez came into the office. "Gunny, it's SSgt Harwood. He wants to speak with you on the landline." Gunny got up and followed Rodriguez back to Post 1.

He picked up the phone. "Yea Mark. What's your status?"

"We've got the hatch secured. And they are calling for me now. I've got to go. But you need to go and open your end of the tunnel."

Why?"

"Well, I thought we better secure the hatch from the inside too. So Chen took this guy Drayton and did that, but now they need to get out of the tunnel, and that's up to you."

"Peyton?" he misheard. "Who the hell is that?"

"I gotta go Gunny. The Indian Army guy is motioning me to put down the phone and get in line."

"But... well, OK. Get out of there. Don't do anything stupid and make sure you get word when you can back to Battalion." There was no answer. SSgt Harwood had already hung up and left.

"Rodriguez, come with me." They went the closed hatch to the tunnel. Gunny McCardle pulled out his 9 mm and knocked on the hatch. There was an immediate pounding back. "Cover me," he told Rodriguez while he undid the locks and opened the hatch.

Sgt Greg Chen stepped up the last step and out into the passage followed by a thin young man in a suit coat with a red tie half-stuffed in the front breast pocket. Gunny had never seen the man before and instinctively kept his 9 mm at the ready.

The man handed Gunny a paper bag and stuck out his hand. Taking the bag, Gunny McCardle had to holster his 9 mm to take the proffered hand.

"Drayton Bajinski, USAID Dacca. Pleased to meet you. I though you might want some of that, so I brought it along." He pointed, indicating the bag.

Gunny looked in the bag and saw a mishmash of what might have been at some time some very nice reception finger food. He looked back up. "Sgt Chen, why is there a civilian with you?"

Sgt Chen replied, "Gunny, they were always asking for SSgt

Harwood, so we knew he had to leave with the rest. But I might need help in the tunnel, and Drayton here had already been helping, so he sort of came along."

"Gunny," with emphasis on the title as if he had just had the term explained to him, "Don't blame Greg here. I bulled my way here, no doubt. I don't want to sit in some sort of detention center while they figure out what to do with us, and it sounded more exciting to be here with you. So here I am." He positively beamed at Gunny McCardle.

"Exciting?"

"Yes sir! I think so, and I can help. I'm pretty resourceful."

"Well, you are here now. No getting around it. OK, let's get back. Rodriguez, you go back to Sgt McAllister." The gunny, Sgt Chen, and Drayton trooped back to the Admin Section's office.

Everyone else was gathered around the television when they entered, but Drayton immediately went up to the president and offered his hand. "Drayton Bajinksi, USAID Dacca. A pleasure to meet you sir."

Reflexes took charge, and the president shook the offered hand. "Pleasure to meet you, too." He looked perplexed. "Where did you come from?"

"From the reception, Mr. President, or what would have been the reception, at least."

"Were any of my detail there? Did any of them make it?"

Now it was Drayton's turn to look perplexed. "Your detail sir?"

"My secret service detail! Did any of them make it?"

Drayton looked over at Sgt Chen, who stepped up. "I think so sir. I know a couple ran out, and I think they got hit. But another one, he was going to try and run out, but his boss, I think, held him back. Wouldn't let him go."

A look of anger slowly spread over the President's face. He looked over at Sgt Chen. "I had secret service agents over there, and you didn't think of bringing them over here with you? These are trained professionals in this, not glorified security guards like you!"

Sgt Chen stepped back a pace and looked at Gunny Mac, arms splayed out with hands forward indicating confusion. "I... uh, sorry sir. Nobody told me nothing about bringing...."

Loralee interrupted while watching the television. "Looks like something is happening..."

LCpl Saad stuck his head in the door. "Gunny, they're on the move." Everyone started for the door.

"Saad, stay here with SSgt Child and Wynn." The rest moved across the hall and into the office. "Sir, please stand back from the window. Without the lights on in here, no one should be able to see us, and the windows are supposed to be one way, but no use giving anyone any ideas." The president nodded and they all stopped about ten feet back from the window and looked out across the courtyard.

The darkness made it a little hard to make out, but a long line of people were being escorted by Indian soldiers along the front of the consulate and over to the front gate. Many of the diplomats glanced fearfully at the bodies still lying on the ground. Apparently the army did not want to tempt the crowd, because they kept the gate closed. They had leaned what looked like a garden-variety stepladder up the face of the gate, and had another one going down the reverse side. Slowly, each well-dressed member of the diplomatic community made his or her way up the ladder where a soldier helped them reverse and back down the other side.

This took a long time, considering the number of people to make it over the gate and the lack of physical prowess most of them had. It was almost dark when SSgt Harwood, the last person, got to the top of the gate. He turned around and made a quick salute in the direction of the embassy and disappeared over the other side.

About a dozen soldiers climbed back into the compound and took down the ladder. They arrayed themselves along the edge of the fence, facing in toward the embassy with their backs to the crowd and coming to their best parade rest. They were on guard, but keeping the mob out or keeping them in was the question.

"Well, I guess that is it," intoned the president. "Looks like we are here for the night." He turned around and walked back to the Admin Section's office, the rest filing along behind him.

Chapter 19

Tuesday Evening, Phuket, Thailand

David Littlehawk sat on the couch in the suite at the Royal Phuket City Hotel, watching the BBC. He had been given a room, but he chose to sit in the suite which was serving as the Rear Party (or would the "Missing Movement Party" be more accurate?) headquarters. He and several other sailors were glued to the television, watching the same video clips over and over, listening to the commentators and the expert guests give their take on what was happening. Littlehawk was kind of partial to CNN, but the hotel did not carry it, so BBC it was.

Regardless of whatever legal trouble he might be in for missing movement, he had a hollow feeling in the pit of his stomach. He had trained extensively to be the best pilot he could be, and now that the nation might need his skills, he was sitting in a hotel suite in Phuket watching events unfold on the BBC. This was not supposed to be how things happened. He took a sip of his now-warm coke, then leaned back, hands behind his head, looking at the white ceiling.

The Rear Party OIC, LTJG Warren, hung up the phone. "Hey, listen up! It looks like we are going to get almost all of you back to the *Reagan*."

Lt. Littlehawk felt a jolt of adrenaline surge through his body as he jumped up off the couch. "We've got some Ospreys passing through, and the powers-that-be decided to order them to touch down and pick

97

up you guys and get you back onboard. Grab your trash, 'cause they are going to get here in about 50 mikes, and we've got to get you back to the dock where the birds will touch down, Thai clearance willing. We've got, um, let me see, 96 boat spaces, so that's almost everybody."

"Petty Officer Kent, did we prioritize the list yet?"

Kent shook his head.

"OK, well, then, we have to do it on the run. I want the first bus to leave in 5 mikes, so let's try to get the highest priority folks on it, but just get it filled and off to the port. You three sailors," he said, pointing at the three, "start pounding on hatches and getting people up out of the rack now and down to the lobby."

Littlehawk moved closer and grabbed the jg by the arm. "I am priority. I have to get on the flight."

"Sure lieutenant, sure. Just get down to the lobby and get Kent to manifest you."

Littlehawk rushed out of the room and pelted down the stairwell, ignoring the elevators. Bursting out into the lobby, he vaulted a couch in front of reception, thoroughly startling an elderly couple trying to check in as he rushed to get in position by the front door. By God he was going to be the first one manifested and the first one on the bird. As a fixed-wing jock, he had a fatalistic fascination with that whirly contraption that some people called an aircraft. That fascination did not extend to ever wanting to get onboard an Osprey. But at this stage of the game, he would strap a rocket to his butt if that was the only way to get back to the *Reagan*.

Down in the dumps five minutes ago, he was brimming with enthusiasm now. History was not going to pass him by. He was getting back to his ship.

Chapter 20

Tuesday Evening, US Embassy, New Delhi

PFC Ramon was pissed, plain and simple. She flounced to an empty desk and began to field strip her M18. Well, even if she couldn't shoot it very well, her weapon would be clean.

Everyone treated her with kid gloves, like she wasn't a real Marine. Gunny did it. The other Marines did it. She realized that she wasn't very strong and wasn't very tough, but that didn't mean she couldn't take her fair share of the load. Gunny wouldn't let her go get Cpl Crocker, and now he wouldn't even let her stand a simple watch. It just wasn't fair.

Ivy Ramon was born in East LA, the youngest of five children and the only girl. Her actual name was Haydee, but no one ever used that. As a toddler, she had a habit of holding tightly to her dad's leg, and he would even walk around the house with her clinging to his calf, sitting on his foot with her little legs wrapped around it. He would lift his leg for each step with exaggerated height and care, and she would shriek with laughter. He started calling her "Ivy," and the name stuck. Most people didn't even know her given name.

Her father had been a big jock in his day and had even played Double A ball before getting Ivy's mother pregnant with Arturo, her oldest brother. He quit playing ball, married her, and got a job in a local produce warehouse, but sports remained his passion. All four of Ivy's brothers were quite athletic, and both Arturo and Jorge, her number three brother, had received football scholarships to USC, and Jorge was now on the Seattle Seahawks practice squad (something she never told any of her fellow Marines.)

Ivy, on the other hand, was not a jock, by any stretch of the imagination. Oh, she tried. As a small girl, she used to follow her brothers out to the vacant lots where they played ball and tried to get them to let her play. One of her undying memories was when she convinced Jorge to throw her a football. Her six-year-old hands could not close on the ball to catch it, and it hit her in the face. She broke out in tears and ran home, the boys' laughter chasing her. When she got there, her father pulled her in his lap and laughed, telling here that she was a girl. All she had to do was be pretty. She should not be trying to be a boy.

Later, she tried track and field, she tried softball. She couldn't make either high school team. Her mother had suggested that she do a nice girls' activity like cheerleading, so for three weeks she practiced that with abandon only to not make even the first cut at tryouts.

Ivy saw how much her father loved sports, and she felt this was the only way to get his approval. And not to get it gnawed at her.

But despite this, Ivy was a happy girl. Growing up, she loved her dolls and could spend hours upon hours dressing them up and playing make-believe. Her mother gave her a fashion cutout book, and she lost herself in it, imagining herself as a fashion diva. She pranced up and down her bed-turned catwalk. She loved ribbons and Barbie and Prancing Pony and all things little girl.

Ivy was a short girl with a slightly chunky body. Then, after her twelfth birthday, she started developing. Not in height, but in her chest. Her breasts started to swell, and they didn't seem to want to stop. She started to get noticed, and at first, she enjoyed the attention. But as her breasts got bigger and bigger, some of the attention started taking a nasty turn, so Ivy pulled away from people and spent more time at home.

Her mother kept telling her that this was a normal part of growing up, and she should use them for any advantage she could. Ivy's mother was also short and had rather large breasts. But she was also quite fat, and Ivy feared that she was going to follow her in that way, too. She put a mirror up in her room daily stood in front of it naked, examining her body for any change. He thought her hips were getting too big, her belly too pronounced.

She thought about breast reduction surgery. It was not so much that she really thought they were too large, but rather that she did not like the suit-of-armor bras she had to wear to support them. She thought the frilly, lacey things she saw in the fashion magazines were so pretty, but it seemed they didn't make them in industrial sizes.

She often confided in Victor, a gay boy in class who was her sometimes confidant. When she expressed concern on her growing width, he told her that his brother, in a desperate and concerned "man-to-man, see-you-are-not-really-gay" talk, had told him a woman's body was fine if in the noon sun, her stomach was in the shadow of her tits. Ivy laughed out loud at this and took this as her personal boundary. As long as her belly was in the shadow, and it looked like it would be in the shadow for a quite some time yet, she was OK.

Ivy never really had a steady boyfriend. She played with Victor, teaching each other how to kiss, and she went to her junior and senior prom, but there was nothing too serious. Truth be told, her opinion of men was somewhat shaped by the men in her life. Her father and brothers were fit, well-muscled men, rather masculine, and rather appealing. None of the boys in high school fit that mold, so she never really felt a pull toward any of them.

After graduating from high school, her parents expected her to settle down and start producing grandkids to add to their growing count. But Ivy still wanted to do something more, to achieve something. When her friend Teresa needed to get a marriage license, she went down with her to the county building. Waiting on the bench, she looked up at a poster for the Marines. On it was a handsome black Marine, broad-shouldered and obviously fit. In other words, he was the kind of man who appealed to her sense of what a man was supposed to be.

She snuck off to the recruiting office where a Marine told her about the adventure of the Corps, all the while trying not to stare at her breasts pushing out against her designer t-shirt. Ivy listened and wondered if she could succeed in this man's game or not. She promised to bring her school records back, thought about it overnight, then came back on the next day when she signed on the dotted line.

Her mother cried when she left for boot camp, but her father gave her a crushing hug and told her how proud he was. As he let her go, Ivy could see a tear rolling down his face.

It was that tear that kept Ivy going in boot. As soon as she arrived, she thought she had made a huge mistake. The yelling, the shapeless cammies, the lack of proper skin care, the food. One DI, Sgt Contreras (known as the "Dragon Queen" to the other recruits) seemed to particularly take pleasure in tormenting her. Ivy, as in her attempts at sports, did not excel, and Sgt Contreras took great delight in pointing out all her faults, putting her through "extra instruction." Three times Ivy was called before a review board, the third time before the company commander. But each time, she squeaked through, the image of her father's tear pushing her forward.

The company commander seemed to take a personal interest in her progress. Ivy did not know exactly why, but she was willing to grab at any lifeline. And somehow, by some miracle, she made past all the obstacles thrown in her path. The O-course, the PFT, Range Week, all the hours of EI, even Mount Motherfucker. She defeated them all and graduated. Last in her class, to be sure, but she graduated.

She was amazed that before the graduation parade, the Dragon Queen came up and hugged her. Yes, physically hugged her. And said, "I knew you could make it *màna*, I knew you would." Ivy was flat-out astounded.

But more important than Sgt Contreras' opinion was that of her family. Her parents and all four of her brothers (and two of their families) flew to Quantico to see her graduate. This was the proudest moment in her life. She had made her father proud.

She went through the rest of her training without too much problem. She was certainly glad that she could wear regular clothes when not on duty, she could read *Seventeen*, and she was allowed to wear at least a little make-up again.

And when she reported for duty in New Delhi, she was surprised to see that the Marine on the poster, the one she saw in LA, was there, SSgt Child. He still was a pretty hot piece of man-meat, one who Ivy could really appreciate, but he was a Marine, and to Ivy, that now meant family. She didn't date her brothers.

She had caught MAJ Defilice checking her out, and during the day, they had spent time talking. He wasn't such a bad piece of man-meat himself, and she thought he was rather interesting. A bad boy with a heart. He was Army, so he wasn't a brother, was he now. But he was an officer. She would have to think about that.

Oh, she knew her fellow Marines looked at her and some were interested. She chuckled as she thought of tough SSgt Child not knowing where to look at the inspection early that morning (was in only this morning?), then she looked up guiltily at his prone body on the desk. Tears welled in her eyes.

She may not be the strongest or toughest Marine here, but she was going to give out some payback. Gunny Mac or not, she was going to whup some ass.

Chapter 21

Tuesday Evening, US Embassy, New Delhi

High in the bell tower, Sgt Niimoto watched the procession of diplomats climb over the fence. He kept his rifle at the ready, scanning the crowd, not having orders to fire, but knowing he would if the diplomats got in trouble.

Hungry and thirsty, he wished he had thought to bring some food with him. He had talked with Little Mac on the landline, and he knew the tunnels were secure now. So he was just going to have cope. He had gone through an extremely uncomfortable period when he thought his bladder was going to burst, so he had finally sidled over to the far side of the cupola and peed right there on the floor against the bulkhead. He had considered peeing over the side, but that might draw attention to him, so he was just putting up with the stench, even if it had since faded in the Indian heat. He was somewhat perversely fascinated but the ever growing Rorschach-stain his urine made on the plaster of the wall of the tower. He wondered how much more the plaster was going to wick up the urine, and how much larger the stain would get. Oh well, thank God for small miracles that he hadn't had to take a crap yet.

Concerned about exposing his head and rifle barrel over the edge of the railing, he had taken out the cleaning rod for his rifle and tried to push it through the side of the wall. But once the plaster was removed, the wall proved to be some very heavy gauge steel or something, he couldn't tell what. He couldn't even scratch it. Whatever this tower really was, that was more evidence that it wasn't a bell tower. Niimoto couldn't even guess as to what needed this kind of construction.

In the growing darkness, he felt more secure in peering over the wall and down to the antline of diplomats climbing over the ladders and down the other side. The Indian soldiers had a nice cordon going on the other side and up to the waiting buses, but the mob, while looking on with evident interest, did not seem to be agitated or trying to get at the diplomats. So Niimoto just watched, ready to take action if needed.

As the line finally started to peter out, Niimoto saw SSgt Harwood approach the ladder and hurry up. Once at the top of the wall, he turned and gave a salute back to the embassy. Niimoto laughed out loud. "Get some, Harwood!" he whispered.

SSgt Harwood climbed down the other side and sauntered over to a waiting bus, not even glancing at the mob. He looked like he didn't have a care in the world. He got onboard and an Indian soldier pounded on the side of the bus. The driver closed the door, and the bus pulled slowly out and disappeared down the road. The mob slowly closed in on the space left by the bus until it was packed up against the embassy wall again. They seemed strangely subdued now somehow, without the chanting and gesturing that had been so evident before. Some soldiers climbed back into the compound and took positions along the wall, facing in toward the embassy building.

Still wishing he had something to drink, Sgt Niimoto settled back to watch. Just what he expected to see, he really didn't know.

Chapter 22

Tuesday Afternoon, The White house, Washington, DC

Vice-President Wright looked over her desk at the two men sitting there. She had briefly thought about taking over the oval office, but she knew that was pretty crass, and she was an astute politician, if nothing else.

David waited expectantly, and the vice-president could see him trying to maintain professionalism when excitement was trying to take over. General Litz was different, with a look of apprehension as he sat on the front third of his seat, back straight, hands in his lap.

The vice-president considered him. She had known the general for years as he climbed the general officer hierarchy. While not a close friend, her stand on military issues certainly put them in the same camp. He was known to be an efficient administrator with a prickly demeanor, and he was very concerned on how others perceived him. She decided the personal approach was the right choice here. David had given her the general's pilot nickname of "Coptic," but at the last second, she thought that would sound too patronizing.

"Hank, thank you for coming here. I wanted to talk to you privately to get a better feel for what's going on. Secretary Pitt is dedicated, but he can be a big distraction at a time like this."

The general's almost imperceptible easing of his back and the slight slide back into his seat confirmed her guess that this was the way to go. "What is the situation now? Where do we stand?"

The general cleared his throat. "Well, ma'am, as I briefed before, we have the Reagan Battle Group heading out from Thailand. There has been a slight delay as the Reagan is undergoing some repairs while underway, but it should be back up to full speed in about ten hours or so, and it should be off the coast of India by Thursday afternoon local. The *Honolulu*, though, a missile sub in the group, should be off the coast near Calcutta Wednesday night."

"Can the carrier really do anything about the situation?"

"No ma'am. Not really. It is there to show the flag. That's about it. Or, if the president is released, it can serve as a receiving station. We also have various air assets arriving at Diego Garcia, and the Quick Reaction Brigade is still on alert in Korea. But once again, ma'am, we can bomb the hell out of New Delhi, pardon my French, but I'm not sure we can go in and secure the embassy safely and without collateral damage." He paused. "Do you want us to transport the Quick Reaction Brigade? We are just waiting for your OK on that."

She caught David's upraised eyebrows and short shake of his head. David was valuable to her, but goodness, he could be such a pain. She didn't need him to remind her of what was her own decision in the first place.

"Hank, don't move them. The situation is precarious in India now. Pitt is right about that, and moving the brigade might provoke the mob into rash action" (as if attacking the embassy wasn't already rash enough, she thought). "Keep the *Reagan* moving, but I want no action taken at all, none, that can be taken as offensive action. Keep everyone else out of the region. Understood?"

"Yes ma'am. Understood."

The vice-president smiled as she stood up and came around the desk, offering her hand. "I appreciate your efforts, Hank. I am glad you are chairman during this crisis. We'll get through it."

"Thank you ma'am for your confidence. We're going to do our best." The vice-president almost burst out laughing while he came to attention, saluted, then did a smart about face and strode out of the office.

Once the door closed, she waited a second, then turned to look at

David and did laugh. "What a character!" She paused a few seconds. "Well, I think that went well."

"Yes ma'am. Great job playing both sides. Not sending the brigade will appease Pitt and be taken as judicious restraint. Sending the *Reagan* will show resolve and strength. And since the *Reagan* can't really do anything, we'll just let things…"

She quickly raised her hand stopping him. Some things were better left unsaid, even among the closest of confidants.

He looked awkwardly about for a second before pulling himself together. "Are you ready for Pitt now?"

"No, give me a few minutes. Then send him in." He nodded and left. It had been a long night and morning, and the afternoon offered no relief. She walked back over to her desk and sat down, looking out the window though the leafy trees to the White House. Would that be her new address in the very near future?

Chapter 23

Late Tuesday Night, US Embassy, New Delhi

Gunny Mac woke with a start, wondering what he was doing and what he should be doing with a sense of panic until his brain came online. He looked around the room. The president was asleep on one couch. Major Defilice and the off-watch Marines were asleep either in chairs or on the floor. LCpl Saad was alert watching SSgt Childs and LCpl Wynn. He had the PDA in front of him, which had been turned off to save power. A schedule had been made for it to be powered up and contact established. He nodded to Gunny.

It was fairly dark in the room with only the emergency lights on. These battery powered lights did well enough in enabling people to move back and forth and get along with what had to be done, but they weren't the same as regular lighting. When the power was cut off an hour after the diplomats from the consulate were evacuated, there had been a momentary panic setting in until the emergency lights kicked on. Now, at least they had some lighting.

Gunny Mac slowly got up and stretched. It seems a little surreal to be in the darkened room with people sleeping, considering the situation. He felt they should be doing something, but intellectually, he knew there wasn't much to do at the moment, and keeping everyone awake would only hinder their effectiveness later.

He only noticed then that Loralee Howard wasn't in the room.

Maybe she had gone to the head, he thought. He got to his feet and walked out the door to go down to Post 1, but as he turned the corner into the passage, he almost stumbled on Loralee, sitting huddled on the floor, back against the bulkhead.

She gasped and sniffled, then pulled herself together. "Gunny Mac, joining the nightowls here tonight?" She rubbed her sleeve across her eyes.

Gunny looked down at her, feeling a lump form in his throat. He put his back to the wall and slid down until he was sitting along side of her, their legs touching.

"I haven't said anything to you yet, Loralee, because I don't know what to say. And you seem so strong. But I am very, very sorry for your husband. He seemed like a real good man."

She was quiet for a moment, head back, staring up at the dim reaches of the passage. Suddenly, she put her head down in her arms, and Gunny could hear her quiet sobs. Not knowing what else to do, he put his arm around her shoulders. She tensed for a moment, then relaxed into his embrace, letting him support her while she finally let out the tears. They sat like that for several minutes, alone in the dark passage, her quietly crying and him just supporting her by being there.

Finally, the sobs slowed, then stilled. She sniffed and rubbed her nose on her forearm. "Yes, he was a good man, and I'm sure going to miss him." She paused for a few moments. "He was my second husband, you know? I married for the first time when I was 17, way, way too young. And when we lost our little girl, well, we were just kids ourselves, and we couldn't handle it. John, my ex, left me, and I just puttered along through life, not really caring about anything else. Then I met Stan, and he was so, well, so mature, so rock solid. I can be a little crazy sometimes, if you haven't noticed…"

"Oh no, never, not me ma'am," he responded with mock sincerity, and they both chuckled softly.

"Thanks for that, Gunny. You know how to sweet talk an old lady. But Stan, he was my governor, he kept me on an even keel. He was good for me, and I loved him for that. He wasn't the best looking man, the most exciting man, but he was right for me. And now, I am going to miss that man so much."

"You know, Loralee, it is OK to show your emotions. When we dragged you through the door today, well, I thought I must have heard wrong, that your husband wasn't even out there. You seemed so calm and collected."

"Oh, I am not one for much emotion. And I have to keep control now, do you understand? I can break down later, after we are out of here. But if I break down now, well, I'm not sure I can come back from that. And you don't need a hysterical old woman dragging everyone down. So, help me keep it together, OK? Help me keep strong. I will mourn my Stan later, when I can afford to do it right."

"Sure thing, but I kind of doubt that you really need me for that. You are an iron lady, Ms. Howard, if I may be so bold as to say that."

"Ah, once again, my dear Gunny, you sure know how to sweet talk a lady." The sat like that in silence for several more minutes. Slowly, Loralee took a hold of Gunny's hand and removed his arm from around his shoulders and struggled to her feet.

"No more copping a free feel for you, and I think you have kept me from my beauty sleep long enough." She turned to stand over him, looking down.

"Thank you, Gunny Mac." She leaned over, taking his face in her hands, and kissed his forehead, then turned and walked back into the Admin office. Gunny Mac sat there and watched her disappear inside the doors.

With a sigh, he stood up and walked down to down to Post 1. Sgt Chen was at the post along with PFC Van Slyke.

"Anything?"

"No Gunny. Quieter than a witch's tit out there."

"A what? And just how quiet is a witch's tit?"

"I don't know Gunny. Pretty quiet, I guess. I mean, who wants to go and grab a witch's tit. All ugly like that?" Listening in, Van Slyke laughed, then groaned and put his hand up to his face as the pain hit him.

"You OK?" He looked closely at the bandages on Van Slyke's face.

"Sure Gunny. It only hurts when I laugh."

"Well then--"

Both Chen and Van Slyke chorused in before Gunny Mac could finish, "DON'T LAUGH!"

Gunny Mac smiled and turned back, going to the Cultural Affairs office where Steptoe and the USAID guy, Drayton were posted. Gunny had a problem with putting Drayton there, but the guy insisted, and he knew he should get his Marines as much rest as possible. There was no telling what was coming down the pike, and he wanted everyone in the best condition possible.

Drayton spun around nervously, weapon in hand, as Gunny Mac entered. He saw it was the Gunny, and he sheepishly lowered his M18. Gunny Mac almost said something, then decided to ignore it.

"Anything at all out there? Any movement?"

"No Gunny," answered Steptoe. "It's been real quiet. After the Indian soldiers went back over the wall, there hasn't been much. We've seen a couple heads poke over the wall to take a look, and we can see people peering in through the gate, but nothing else."

"Well, OK. Let me know if you see anything. You've got another hour and Ramon and Kramer will relieve you. Try to get some sleep then."

"Aye-aye, Gunny," they both replied in unison. For a civilian, Drayton was picking up the Corps lingo pretty quickly.

Gunny Mac walked back to the Admin office and lay down on the newspapers with which he had staked out his claim on the floor. He tried to get some sleep, but it kept eluding him as his mind filled with thoughts on what he was missing, what he should be doing. He heard the ongoing watch get up and leave, then the off-going watch come back and lie down. Soon, snores were emanating from LCpl Steptoe, but Gunny Mac could not drift off himself. Finally, he gave up and went to join Ramon and Kramer where he watched the dawn slowly lighten up the embassy courtyard. He wondered what the day would bring.

Chapter 24

Wednesday Morning, U-Tapao Air Base, Thailand

LT Littlehawk stood anxiously in the old hangar at U-Tapao. He had flown up the night before with the rest of the *Reagan* stay-behinds aboard one of the four Ospreys, but now they were just in hurry-up-and-wait mode. He knew that with each passing moment, the *Reagan* was getting further and further away, and he wasn't sure about the legs on the Ospreys. The Indonesian crews had landed the birds, taxied them into the hangar, then drove away in two waiting vans, leaving them alone except for two Thai airmen guards who didn't seem to speak any English.

He stared across the runway to the nondescript terminal and the one commuter-sized plane parked there. The terminal seemed to shimmer through the heat waves radiating off the runway. The airport was obviously dual-purpose with both civilian and military aircraft, but the civilian side seemed a little light. A few old F16s with Thai markings were parked further down from the terminal near some somewhat newer-looking buildings, and a number of helos were out on the aprons. On this side of the runway, however, there was not much. Three old hangars and a beat-up one-story building seemed to make up the bulk of the facilities. The sailors and Ospreys were obviously being kept as out-of-sight as possible.

The heat was getting a little oppressive as the sun beat down on the tarmac and radiated inside the hangar. Littlehawk looked back into the hangar where most of the sailors were sleeping wherever they could find a free space on the concrete. Another group was playing spades. No matter the situation, probably since time immemorial, sailor always seemed to find the will and the way for a game of spades.

An approaching van, coming from out of the dense forest in back of the small facility, pulled in front of the hangar, and eight Marines in cammies and full battle gear got out. One, a Staff Sergeant, Littlehawk thought, came up to him.

"Can you tell me who is senior here?"

"I am Lieutenant Littlehawk. I guess it might be me."

The Marine snapped off a salute, which Littlehawk instinctively returned despite not being in uniform. "Sir, Staff Sergeant Montrose here. I'm afraid there has been some mistake. We are from the embassy in Bangkok, and these Ospreys are for an incoming group of Marines. Someone doing the air schedules thought it would be perfect to get you back out to your ship, but he didn't know these birds will be full. So, I'm going to have to ask you to let your people know you are going to have to stay here until the JUSMAG can figure out what to do with you."

Littlehawk's heart dropped. He had thought he was going to get back onboard the *Reagan*, but now it looked like this was getting snatched away from him.

"What do you mean these birds are going to be full? Who is getting on them?"

"Sir, I am not at liberty to tell you that. Please, just inform your people and move them back out of the way. We'll be using the front of this hangar as an assembly point. Someone from the JUSMAG will get here soon and figure out what to do with you all."

He started to protest but realized this Marine was not in the position to change anything. He would wait until someone from the Joint US Military Assistance Group arrived, or whoever arrived to fly in these birds showed up. By hook or by crook, he was going to get onboard.

Chapter 25

Wednesday Morning, US Embassy, New Delhi

The president was antsy. He had barely eaten any of the somewhat smashed reception food or the fruit and crackers Mr. Dravid had gleaned from the ambassador's refrigerator. Now he was pacing while methodically cleaning each fingernail with the nail from the opposites hand's forefinger. He had just been briefed on the *Reagan's* movement and the progress (or lack thereof) on the diplomatic scene. Now the PDA had been turned back off, and the president had commenced pacing.

Gunny Mac understood the feeling. He knew he should be doing something, but he really could not determine exactly what he should be doing. Twenty-four hours ago, he was in his element, getting ready for a pain-in-the-ass presidential visit. He understood that. Pain-in-the-ass VIP visits were part of the Marine Corps' stock in trade. Now, he had dead Marines, Marines in his charge. And he had the President of the United States sitting in an office in a hostile, life-threatening situation. But it was jarringly quiet now. In fact, nothing much had happened since early in the morning when some Indian police had entered the courtyard and removed the bodies there. Gunny thought someone in the Indian government finally must have realized that the CNN satellite could easily see them, and those images were perhaps not in India's best interest. Still, no one had attempted to contact them in the embassy building itself, not even to ask as to the president's condition.

He heard a quiet laugh and looked over to see PFC Ramon sitting alongside MAJ Defilice, while he grabbed her arm and tried to say something more. PFC Ramon threw her head back and laughed louder. Gunny felt a little pang of, of, well he wasn't sure what it was. It couldn't be jealousy, right? There was no reason for that. But it was a pang of something, never-the-less.

He heard steps and looked up to see LCpl Steptoe with Mr. Dravid in tandem approach him. "Um Gunny? Mr. Dravid has been in the ambassador's office, and well, Cpl Croker and Cpl Ashley, well, they aren't doing that well in the heat. Mr. Dravid wonders if we should put them in the reefer in the ambassador's pantry. We can take out the shelves, and they should fit. There is still ice in there, so it should stay cooler in there than out in the office." Mr. Dravid stood behind Steptoe, looking over his shoulder at Gunny anxiously.

He felt the eyes of the others swing to him. "Yes, I think that is a good idea. Go do it." He felt a little guilty watching the two of them move off, but frankly, he didn't want to help move them, to see their dead bodies. The office returned to quiet.

"Sergeant, when do you think something is going to happen?" Gunny Mac looked over to see the president watching him expectantly.

"I don't know sir. It's been pretty quiet, but you know people are working on this."

"I know they are. I just got off the PDA with the vice-president. We've got the *Reagan* on the way, but it won't get offshore near Calcutta for another 14 or 16 hours. But what do *you* think. What does your gut tell you?" The president was speaking normally to him, man-to-man, perhaps for the first time since his arrival. Gunny couldn't be sure, but the look in the president's eyes might have even been a little hopeful.

"Well sir, I don't know. I think this is going to break one way or the other before the *Reagan* gets offshore. Marines have been through this before. Tehran. Beirut. Nairobi. Caracas. Lima." He gestured to SSgt Child, still prone on the desk, chest slowly rising and falling. "I am surprised, to be honest, that the crowd did not storm the place immediately, when they were riled up like that. I don't know why they didn't. Maybe it was Sgt Niimoto taking out those guys. Maybe they were as surprised as everyone else things escalated. What you told us about the government participation in all of this might mean the mob out there isn't really wired into all of this."

He paused for a moment. "But the fact that it has been so long, almost 24 hours now, well, that could be a good sign. That means if the government is involved, that they don't want something drastic to happen, or that our diplomatic efforts are doing some good. The longer this drags on the better, but that crowd out there, I don't think it is going to wait. Sgt Niimoto says there are guys with bullhorns taking turns speaking to them, and the crowd is agitated. Either they are going to get bored and go home, or they are going to come into the grounds."

The president walked over and sat down on an office chair, slowly rotating it back and forth. "If they come, can we do anything about it? Can we protect ourselves?"

"Well sir, to be honest, no. We can delay them, and we'll get you into the vault. But if they are here, given enough time, they can cut into even that. But I promise you sir, if they do that, it's going to cost those bastards."

The president leaned back, looked up at the overhead, and locked his hands behind his neck. He was quiet for a few moments. "How long have you been a Marine?"

"I came in during Iraq, sir, before the drawdown. I was here for the Diss... for the reduction of the Corps mission."

"Why did you stay in the Marines? The Army still needed good soldiers."

Gunny paused. "With no disrespect to the Army, sir," he glanced over to where MAJ Defilice was still chatting up PFC Ramon, "the Army is a job. I mean, they are patriotic and everything, and they're good people. But being a soldier is doing a job. The Corps, well the Corps is a lifestyle. It is what we are. You can't change that. I'd just as soon cut off my balls and become a fucking eunuch before...." He stopped, reddening after realizing what he has just said in front of his Commander-in-Chief.

The president seemed non-plussed. "So you'd rather work as a member of a glorified security guard rather than be a member of the US Army? Or Navy or Air Force, for that matter?"

"Yes sir, I would. No 'bout adoubt it.'" His fervent feelings were undermining his normal this-is-how-you-speak-with-officers-and-bigwigs speech patterns.

The president took a longer pause. "Since it seems like it may certainly be a possibility, would you die for your country?"

Gunny hesitated, took a deep breath, and replied "Don't take this wrong, sir, but I don't think I would willingly die for my country, as much as I love it. But I would die for my mission if that was necessary. I would die for Loralee over there, for Drayton, and for you." He seemed to consider that for a moment. "Yes, I'd die to protect you. But most of all, I would die for my fellow Marines. Without question, without hesitation. He gestured to Ramon. " I'd give my life for PFC Ramon, and you know what sir? I know she would do the same for me. Maybe that is what it means to be a Marine. Whatever your background, whatever your situation, you are part of something bigger, something far greater than yourself. And so yes, I'd die for the Corps and my brother Marines."

The president looked down at his fingers splayed before them, absent-mindedly checking the nails. "I've read my history. I know Marines have fought and bled for this country, and I know about Marines dying in combat. But so has the Army. When I was a kid, we were taught a song about a soldier named Roger Young, a nearsighted young soldier who willingly went to his death in the Solomons to take out a Japanese machine gun nest. Isn't that the same thing?"

"Well sir, I don't know this Roger Young guy, but there are plenty of brave men in the Army. Look at all the Army Air Corps bomber crews who died in that war. Hell, look at all the Navy sailors who died when their ships were kamikaze'ed. The Army, the Navy, the Air Force, well, they all have good people, brave people. And I respect them. But for most of them, especially now in peacetime, it seems to me that it is a job for them. It gives them a skill or money for college. And there's nothing wrong with that. But Marines? This is our life. Other Marines are our family. Marines are warriors, not people just looking for a way to pay for school."

"But there we go back to one of my original questions. The Marines are pretty much now glorified security guards. If you were a 'warrior,' why not join the Rangers, the SEALS? They fight, even now in this so-called peacetime?"

"Sir, you may have made our jobs into being guards," he replied, with a slight emphasis on the "you," but every Marine in a rifleman. We are warriors, by a long tradition earned in blood. And I am sorry, but with all due respect, no politician can change that."

Gunny was surprised and a little embarrassed to feel a small lump form in his throat while he said that. "I am sorry sir, but I need to check on the watch." He turned away and walked out of the office.

The president just watched him go.

Chapter 26

Wednesday Afternoon, Ministry of External Affairs, New Delhi

Dr. Amarin Suphantarida, Thailand's ambassador to India, waited outside the office of the Indian External Affairs Minister. Dr. Amarin, or "Pui" as he was known by his friends, had been in Thailand for a family matter and was returning aboard the daily Thai Air flight between Bangkok and New Delhi when the embassy was attacked. Given that he wasn't part of the diplomatic corps at the embassy, given Thailand and India's close economic relationship, and given Thailand's good relations with the US, others, within ASEAN in particular, and the UN in general, thought he might be a good choice to try and jump start some action to rectify the situation.

Pui wondered now if he was such a good choice. Shortly before arriving, he had taken a call from Richard Case, the US ambassador to Thailand and a good friend. Pui and Rick had served with their respective missions at the same time in Cairo and London, and they had formed a close relationship based on mutual respect and a similar taste in sports, food, and movies. Now, both were ambassadors, and Rick was even assigned to Thailand. Rick's call was short and sweet and probably unauthorized. Rick told him that Thailand was being used as a staging area for a small number of US combat troops who may or may not be going to the region. Pui had known about the *Reagan* already. At a dinner with Rick and his wife two nights earlier, they had mentioned the carrier group and talked about 10,000 young men taking liberty in Phuket and the potential for incidents neither government wanted. But combat troops being transported via Thai soil? And why hadn't his own government informed him of this?

He made a sort of mental sigh, with nothing showing on his face as he sat on the hard seat. For perhaps the first time in years, he wondered if he had made the right choice in joining the Ministry of Foreign Affairs. It would have been so easy, as the eldest son, to take over his family's sprawling industrial complex in Chonburi, making auto parts for Toyota. But that fateful day upon his graduation from Chulalongkorn had sealed his fate.

Even now, so many years later, a feeling of awe flowed through him as he remembered that moment, that turning point in his life. Pui had sort of expected he would in fact take over the family business, and he had gone to Chulalongkorn without any different aspirations. As one of Thailand's "hisos," (short for High Society), he had his life mapped out for hard work and even harder play. He studied, managed to achieve passable grades, and was ready to move on. At his commencement, though, the King himself gave the commencement speech and presented the diplomas. The King spoke about the importance of serving society, serving Thailand, not just serving oneself. Pui was pondering the King's message when he was in line, waiting to receive his diploma. As he walked down the stage, both excited and nervous on being so close to the King, he concentrated on not tripping or looking like a fool. He made it to the King and went into a deep wai. As he came up and reached for his diploma, he caught the King's eye. The King smiled and simply said "Thailand needs you." Taken aback at actually being addressed, he paused a moment, then deeply wai'ed again before hurriedly walking off the stage.

Oddly, he felt a sort of rapture, a sort of spiritual uplifting. Some casual questions with other graduates seemed to indicate that the King hadn't spoken directly with others. Pui wondered if he was somehow being singled out. The more he thought about it, the more he was sure this had to be the case. So right then and there, he dedicated himself to the public service.

With the typical Thai respect for education, he was able to convince his father that he needed to get some higher degrees. His father was willing to let him delay his entry into the world of business for that, so Pui earned his masters at Boston University and his doctorate at Oxford. It was after his doctorate that he told his father he was joining the government. And not only that, he was not joining one of the revolving parties of power and becoming a member of Parliament or the Senate, but he was joining the Ministry of Foreign Affairs. His father at first actually forbade it, but when Pui told him about the King's words, he relented. He had two more sons, after all, who seemed more than eager to make money for the family.

So Pui, as a rich mid-level bureaucrat with an actual talent for the job, rose up through the ranks despite no real party affiliation. He earned a reputation as an honest broker. Now he wondered how honest he was going to be with the Minister. Should he or should he not mention the combat troops?

"Mr. Ambassador? The Minister will see you now." A young woman in a conservative brown suit held open the door for him.

Pui sighed a little once more before standing up and walking into the Minister's office.

Chapter 27

Sgt Niimoto was thirsty, real thirsty. He could smell the street stalls that some enterprising entrepreneurs had set up to feed the mob, and his stomach rumbled, but his thirst was becoming overpowering. He had once read where shipwrecked people sometimes drank their own urine, but he was not quite to that point yet. Give him time, he chuckled to himself, and he might be there.

Thinking back to his Psych 101 class and old Maslow and his Hierarchy of Needs, Niimoto now understood it on a more base level. Given the choice of Astral Humphrey, last year's Playmate of the Year, naked and willing, right there with him, or a tall, cold glass of water, he thought he might take the water, although maybe Astral would hang around a little, too, given the present situation. He sure wouldn't mind both.

The crowd's undercurrent of noise changed up some, so Niimoto peeked over the edge again. A group of civilians were coming over the ladder and into the courtyard. He grabbed the phone and rang up the embassy, getting Little Mac. "Hey, we've got some activity here. It looks like 10 or 12 men are coming in. What do you want me to do?"

"Wait one. Let me get Gunny." He could hear her tell someone to go get Gunny , then the sound of running footsteps fading away. He watched the men mill around for a few moments until Gunny Mac got on the phone.

"Sgt Niimoto, what do you got there?"

"Hey Gunny. There're about twelve guys over the wall. All civies. None look armed, but wait, there is one soldier coming over now too. What do you want me to do?"

"Hold off right now. Just watch them. I'm getting the rest ready." He paused and Sgt Niimoto could here him tell someone to get the rest of the Marines there ASAP. He came back on the phone. "If they start shooting or something, or if you see us shooting, then take them out. Take the soldier out first, then anyone else. If they don't do anything, then you don't do anything."

"Aye-aye, Gunny." Sgt Niimoto settled down to watch them.

The group seemed to confer for a few moments, then most of them started for the embassy. Sgt Niimoto brought up his weapon and tracked them through the scope. The Indians walked up to the main hatch first and seemed to be inspecting it, touching it and obviously pacing its width. A few other men started walking alongside the walls of the embassy, trying to look into windows. The soldier hung back, sort of covering the others, although his weapon was still at sling arms.

This took about fifteen minutes before one man called the others back together. They conferred for a few moments, gesturing at the hatch a few times, before they started to move back to the wall. One by one, they climbed the ladder up and over the wall and moved out into the crowd. The soldier was the last one over.

The phone's light flashed (he had disconnected the ringer). "This is Gunny. Did they all leave?"

"Yes Gunny. They've all left. They cased the place out pretty well. It looks to me like they are trying to see what it will take to blow the emergency doors."

"Yes, to me, too. I sent Kramer to the Cultural Affairs' office windows, but he couldn't see much from his angle. But that is what is seems like to him, too. Oh well, I guess we don't need a crystal ball to see what's happening." He paused. "How are you doing, Tony? You OK up there?"

"Well, I sure wouldn't mind some water here. Hell, I would even drink one of those Thums Up piss-water cola things things you like so much." He laughed. "But I'm doing OK."

"OK, I'll run one up to you next chance I get. All you have to do is clear all those Indians away from the embassy. You want diet or regular?"

"Well, gaining weight might be the least of my worries now, so let's go with regular."

"You've got it, Tony. Take care up there, and keep your eyes on things. We can't see much from our vantage, so we are counting on you."

"Any word on some sort of rescue here?"

"I wouldn't count on it. If the Indians are planning anything, I don't see how we can do anything about it in time."

"OK, then, it will just be up to us. Semper fi, Gunny,"

"Semper fi, Tony, semper fi."

Chapter 28

Wednesday Afternoon, U-Tapao Air Base, Thailand

The C-17 slowly turned off the taxiway and onto the runway to leave U-Tapao. It had barely taken on enough fuel to reach Okinawa before starting its departure. Col Lineau shaded his eyes with his hand against the setting sun to watch it leave. The Globemaster had done its job in getting them there and could really do nothing else, but he still felt a small pang of abandonment. Well, he was pretty well committed now, so it was time to march forward.

He had spent the time aboard the C-17 with his principal staff trying to make contingency plans, which was difficult as they had no idea of what they might possibly face. But it seemed to make sense that the unit be broken into platoons and a headquarters section, sort of an old rifle company, albeit smaller. With the staff he had on hand, he decided that LtCol Norm Ricapito, the Camp David Det CO, would be the platoon commander of 1st, Maj Roberto the 2d, Capt Dave Kreig (the S-3 A) the 3d, Capt Mahmoud the 4th, and 1stLt Stacy Hoins the security force/reserve. Stacy was kind of a sports stud, an All-American at Princeton in field hockey and track, but she was so new and young! He thought about using Major Kristen Rogers, Norm's XO as a platoon commander, freeing up one of the other captains to take the security force, but he thought he would need someone of some rank to stay behind on the *Reagan* should something actually take place. Norm also had a Captain Steve Kyser as his training officer, and Steve was one of the up-and-comers in the Corps. He would have given Steve a platoon without hesitation, but the young captain was off to Cancun on his honeymoon. So it was 1st Lt Hoins into the breach. He had assigned Master Guns Chung to be her platoon sergeant. He kept the Sergeant Major, Doc Hollister, LCpl Luc as a radio operator, and PFC McNair as a runner with him in the headquarters section.

If LtCol Tammy Dews, his Security Battalion CO, made it from Nairobi, he would put her in charge of the second team, sliding the other commanders over one and Stacy out of a position. But the commercial flight schedules didn't match up well, and as he stood here at U-Tapao, it didn't look like she was going to make it in time.

The Marines were lined up in sticks at the front of the hangar, getting used to their new organization. And the Ospreys, four of those beautiful birds, were sitting there, ready to go. Tye Saunders was there, going over a checklist with what looked to be two Coastguardsmen and a civilian, so he figured those must be the pilots. There were several groups of Marines from the regional embassies—he recognized Gunny Jasper from the Singapore embassy and Sgt Williams from the Malaysian embassy, among others. But there were also about a hundred or so military men in civies lounging around, with a couple of them up and talking with his Marines. One seemed to be rather adamantly arguing with Capt Mahmoud who seemed to be equally as adamant in trying to ignore him. Col Lineau shouldered his pack and marched over the tarmac to see what was going on.

Capt Mahmoud was asking SSgt Boyles for a separate manifest for each bird, trying hard to ignore the tall gent who was attempting to get a word in edgewise. Col Lineau stepped up and grabbed the man by the upper arm. "May I help you?"

The man spun around and took in the eagles on his collar. He came to attention. "LT David Littlehawk, sir. I am from the *Reagan*, with VFA 41. If you are going to her, I really need to get back to her."

He looked at the young man and could see the eager hope in his eyes, but also the fear of being left behind. Jeff could understand that, but he didn't see how he could help. "I am sorry Lieutenant, but we are full on boat spaces. I'll have to leave some Marines behind as it is, so I don't think I can drop one of them so you can make it back to your ship."

"You don't understand sir, I am a fighter pilot. I have to get back." He was getting desperate.

"And my Marines are riflemen. Your point is?" He felt some sympathy for the young man, but to infer that fighter pilots were somehow more important than others was something he had hated since his Academy days.

"You are a pilot?" Jeff turned to see Tye Saunders had walked up.

"Yes sir!"

"What do you fly?"

"The Lighting II, sir."

"Have you ever flown an Osprey, by chance?"

The lieutenant's face fell. "No sir. But I did fly the simulation at Pensacola in our platform orientation package." He looked up hopefully.

"Any other pilots with you here?"

"One sir. LT Shefield. He's a Viking pilot."

The XO looked to the CO. "Sir, we don't have any co-pilots. I sure would rather have someone in the right seat who has actually flown something than leave the seat empty."

Jeff turned back to the Navy lieutenant. "Well son, today is your lucky day it seems. Go get that other pilot, if you please, and report back to LtCol Saunders. We're leaving here in less than fifteen minutes, so make it snappy."

A huge smile broke out on LT Littlehawk's face as he came to an even straighter position of attention, then he shouted "Aye-aye, sir!" before wheeling around and running off to the back of the hangar.

"Everything look OK, Tye?"

"Yes, sir. The birds look fine. Those Indonesians take care of their war toys. We are still short two co-pilots, but on a straight flight to the ship, I hope it won't matter."

Master Gunnery Sergeant Chung walked by with Sergeant Lipsz in tow. "Master Guns, any confirmed location on the *Reagan* yet?"

The Master Guns gave his clipboard to Sgt Lipsz and pointed him toward the Ospreys. "Yes sir. I just confirmed it with the Air Force major from JUSMAG there. The *Reagan* is more than halfway to

India, about 900 miles from here. She's steaming at 25 knots with her 'mechanical problem.' " He raised his hands and used the double finger quotation hook as he said the words "mechanical problem."

"OK, that is good. That is what, about two-and-a-half hours from here?" He looked up at the XO.

"Maybe closer to three hours, sir."

"OK, three hours. " He turned back to his Ops Chief. "Master Guns, please ask the JUSMAG major to see me."

Master Gunnery Sergeant Chung nodded and moved off. "What are you pussies waiting for? I told you to be on those goddamn birds in five minutes, what, seven minutes ago? What the fuck are you waiting for, a fucking invitation?"

The XO suppressed a smile. "That's our Master Guns!"

Yes it is. I'm just glad he is on our side." They both chuckled. "You better get to your birds. I really do want to be off the ground in ten minutes, if at all humanly possible."

"Aye-aye, sir." LtCol Saunders came to attention and rendered a salute. Col Lineau returned it just as smartly.

Jeff watched the Marines start to file into the Ospreys as a major in Air Force fatigues walked up to him. "Sir, I am Maj Paulson with the JUSMAG." He held out his hand. Jeff had automatically started the move for a salute, but he stopped it and took the proffered hand instead.

"Col Jeff Lineau."

"Uh yes, sir, we know. Admiral Conners personally called our boss, COL Smith, and told us to help you as well as babysit his lost sailors. You are going to the *Reagan*, right?" he positively beamed with excitement.

"Major, I hope you understand that I am not at a liberty to tell you anything right now."

"Oh I know sir, we can't tell anyone. But what with the president and everything, you are going over there, right?"

"Once again Major, while we appreciate your help here, I really can't say anything."

"OK, I understand sir." Then he gave Col Lineau a wink, an actual, drawn-out wink. Jeff didn't really know what to do, it was so out of his comfort zone. So he ignored it.

"I just wanted to ask you to help some of our Marines get back to their stations. Capt Mahmoud, my S1, he's the short guy over there by the first Osprey, has the list, but I think it's about twelve Marines who have to be left behind." He hesitated before adding "And Major, needless to say, this whole evolution is rather sensitive. This has all been done back channels, so-to-speak, so we would like to keep it quiet. I'm sure you understand."

"No problem with your Marines. We'll take care of them. Your captain has already given me the list. And we'll keep all of this hush hush. But you do know the ambassador knows all about this, right?"

Jeff's heart jumped. He really did not want anyone at State to know exactly what was going on. He did not want anyone to be able to counter any possible action. Better to act first and apologize later. "How did he find out? I was to understand that Admiral Conners directed that as few people as possible be brought online for this, just the JUSMAG and whoever from the Thai military has to know to approve air clearance and landing rights?"

"Well, sure. We kept most people in the dark. But the ambassador, he is the head honcho here. COL Smith told him right away."

Well, there was no getting around that now. He hoped nothing would come of it.

"Col Lineau? We are waiting for you to get onboard now sir." He looked up to see Sgt Lipsz waiting expectantly by the first Osprey. He could see one of the Coast Guard pilots looking out the window at him, waiting for him to board.

"Well, thanks again, Major. I guess I've got to get going." He shouldered his pack and loped over the tarmac and up the ramp of the waiting Osprey.

Chapter 29

Late Wednesday Afternoon, US Embassy, New Delhi

"You've got that all wired, Steptoe?"

"Yes Gunny. We can talk to Post 1, Sgt Nimitz, and the post in the Cultural Affair's office." LCpl Steptoe got off his knees where he had been jury-rigging a wire to one of the office phones. "It's connecting through the switchboard, so it'll act like a regular phone. I've assigned 2002 for bell tower, 2003 for the Cultural Affairs office. This one is 2000, and Post 1 is 2001. Just hit pound and dial the number."

"And the vault?"

I am getting that now, Gunny. But you know, if anyone closed the hatch there, it is going to cut right through this wire, and phones won't work."

"Can't you hook it up to the intercom there?"

"Uh-uh." He shook his head. "I'd have to drill a hole right through the vault, and that's pretty tough steel. I don't even have a drill here to try it." He picked up the spool of wire he had scrounged and started out the hatch to connect the vault with the rest of the Marines.

Gunny Mac looked around the office. With the main power out, only the "green" lighting tube from the roof funneled enough light into the room to read. The emergency lights provided enough to move around and talk to each other, but they really weren't that bright. Loralee had found a magazine and was leafing through it, sitting directly under the tube's main dispersal globe. The president was sitting on one of the office chairs, head back, apparently sleeping. SSgt Child looked no different, but LCpl Wynn's breathing was becoming more labored. Mr. Dravid sat on the couch, watching him. Their eyes met, and Dravid gave a slight nod. MAJ Defilice was on one couch, head back and slightly snoring. It somewhat bothered Gunny that PFC Ramon was asleep as well, leaning up against the major's side. LCpl Saad was in the huge corner desk eating a very mushed what might have once been a finger sandwich. PFC Van Slyke had stripped his M18 and was cleaning it for the umpteenth time.

Gunny walked over to Van Slyke and put his hand on the young Marine's shoulder. "You hanging in there Peter?" Van Slyke looked up, and the damage to his face made Gunny Mac give an involuntary shudder. He looked like one of those zombies in a Hollywood gorefest.

"I'm OK," he managed to sputter out, the words garbled by the fact that half of his face was not functioning. "My face feels like shit, but what are you going to do?"

Gunny gave Van Slyke's shoulder a squeeze. "Good man. Put your weapon back together. I want you to go relieve Kramer. Give him a chance to hit the head and get some chow."

"You call this chow, Gunny?" Van Slyke laughed, then groaned as the pain intensified. "I've got to stop doing that."

"What are you complaining about? Good US embassy chow like this? It couldn't be better." Gunny laughed himself, gave Van Slyke's shoulder another squeeze, then turned around. He was pondering his next move when Loralee walked over.

"You kidding me, PFC Van Slyke? Good chow like this is heaven-sent. No Marine galley could match it," she laughed.

Gunny looked at her for a moment. "Loralee, I have to ask you, you certainly seem to know your way around the Corps. You were never a Marine, were you?"

She laughed again. "Oh no, not me. I don't have enough discipline to last as a Marine. But my kid brother is a Marine. Ian Cannon. He lost his legs to an IED in Afghanistan as a Staff Sergeant and retired, and he lived with Stan and me while he was at Bethesda. I guess I spent enough time with him and with the Wounded Warrior Detachment to get a feel for the Corps."

"I thought you said he 'is' a Marine." The President had walked over to listen in.

"Yes, I did."

"But then you said he retired." He looked perplexed.

"Once a Marine, always a Marine, right Gunny?"

Gunny nodded.

"Ian may not be on active duty anymore, but he is still a Marine. And president or not, he'd kick your butt if you tried to tell him different. His home is a homage to the Corps, like a Marine Corps Museum, and his buddies from the 'Stan drop in to see him all the time."

"You know Gunny Pyle, from Camp David?" she turned back to Gunny Mac.

It was a small Corps, especially within a pay-grade, so Gunny nodded. He knew Randy well.

"Well, Lance Corporal Pyle pulled Ian from the HUMVEE and helped hoof him to the aid station. Gunny Pyle stops in to see Ian whenever he can make it down LeJeune way."

"It was the saddest day in his life when his request to stay on active duty was denied." She looked thoughtful for a moment. "But he is a resilient old bastard, and he is doing fine." Her face broke out into a smile.

"So being a Marine was that important to him?" The president sat down and looked up at Loralee.

"That's what you don't get yet, even after being with these Marines here. It is not that it 'was that important,' as you put it, but that it IS that important," she replied, with a heavy emphasis on the "is."

PFC Ramon nodded in silence behind her from where she had woken up and listened in on the discussion.

The president started to respond when he was interrupted by the phone. Gunny pounced on it as everyone in the room swiveled his or her attention on it.

"Gunny, this is Fallgatter. We've got Indians inside again."

"I'll be right there." Gunny rushed out and down the passage to the Cultural Affairs office, followed by the rest. He went up to Sgt Chen and LCpl Kramer who were mindful of their previous instructions and were hanging back about five feet from the windows. Everyone else rushed up as well, until there was a line abreast looking out the window. In the afternoon light, Gunny could see that about ten men had made it over the wall so far. The first of these started moving toward the consular building.

Gunny looked around to where PFC Fallgatter was still holding the phone. "Hang up and then get me Niimoto." He went over to get it.

"Gunny, I've been trying to get you," he whispered loudly, "but the phone was busy." Gunny took a second to glare at Fallgatter who looked back perplexed and shrugged his lack of understanding.

"We've got about a dozen guys inside now, and more are coming. What do you want me to do?"

Gunny Mac turned back around so he could see out the window and talk on the phone at the same time. "Same thing as before. Hold your fire unless you or we are attacked. But keep on eye on things. We're almost one story high, so we can't see what's happening right below us. I'll keep this line open for now." He handed the phone back to PFC Fallgatter.

"Keep this glued to your ear!"

Fallgatter just nodded and took the receiver.

Gunny rejoined the line of people looking out the window. "What do you think is happening?" asked the president. Several sets of eyes looked at Gunny Mac expectantly.

"Well sir, it is kind of hard to say. It looks like these people are checking out the consular building. We've got Sgt Niimoto in the bell tower watching them, too, and he can see a lot more than we can in here." They all watched for a few more minutes.

"You know, this is bullshit!" The president turned and folded his arms across his chest belligerently. "I'm sick and tired of this. The Indian government should have taken action long before this. What the hell are they waiting for?" He turned to Gunny Mac. "I want the vice-president on the phone again. "

"Mr. President, I'm not sure that's a good idea. We are scheduled to contact them again in," he glanced at his watch, " uh, an hour and 36 minutes. The more often we call them, the sooner the PDA is going to be out of juice."

"I am not making a suggestion, sergeant. I am giving you an

order. Get the vice-president." He glared, almost daring any further comment.

Gunny didn't hesitate. "PFC Ramon, go get LCpl Steptoe. He's down in the vault." As Princess ran off, he turned back to the president. "It'll be just a moment, sir." They stared at each other for a moment, the president glaring, Gunny Mac keeping as neutral an expression as possible.

"Uh, Gunny? It's Sgt Niimoto. He wants to talk to you." PFC Fallgatter nervously looked at the two men, holding out the phone to the Gunny.

"Yea, this is Gunny."

"Gunny, most of the Indians are in the consular, but about four are back at the security doors, and there are two walking alongside your building again."

"What are the guys at the security door doing?"

"Well, one guy looks like he is explaining something to the others. He keeps pointing at different parts of the doors, then saying something. One of the other guys looks like he is taking notes."

"Well, that can't be a good thing," Gunny Mac harrumphed. "OK, keep watching them and let me know if anything changes." He gave the phone back to Fallgatter and moved back in line.

Everyone was intently watching what they could see of the courtyard when there as a thump on the window as a pair of hands appeared on the ledge. Everyone there took and involuntary hop back. Slowly, a face appeared in the window, and with a lurch, the man there managed to get his elbows on the ledge. He used his hands to form a tunnel between his eyes and the window to try and see into the room.

"Can he see us?" asked Loralee.

"No ma'am," offered Sgt Chen. "This is one-way glass." Everyone froze, though, and after a few moments, the man stopped trying to see in, and dropped out of sight. There was a collective outtake of breath.

LCpl Saad sidled up to the far side of the window and tried to look down. "How did he get up here? He must have been standing on someone's shoulders."

LCpl Steptoe, PFC Ramon, and Drayton Bajinski came into the office and everyone jumped. A nervous laugh followed, much to the three's confusion. "Gunny?" asked Steptoe.

"LCpl Steptoe, the President wishes to speak with the vice-president now." He saw the beginnings of an objection form on Steptoe's broad face. "And that is a direct order."

LCpl Steptoe grabbed a hold of his objection and smothered it. "You've got it, Gunny." He took the PDA out of his pocket and began the process of powering up. The president had wanted some degree of privacy, so after a search of the offices, an earbud had been found which was compatible. He held it up to his ear without actually clipping it on. A series of beeps and tone sounded, signaling when it was ready. LCpl Steptoe retrieved the number, then requested the connection. "This is LCpl Steptoe. The president wants the vice-president." There was a pause. "Yes, we know this is early, but you need to get her now. And hurry up please, our power is getting low on this thing." He looked up at the president. "It'll be a moment, sir; they have to go get her." Everyone except for LCpl Saad watched Steptoe expectantly. And waited. And waited.

Gunny Mac saw Mr. Dravid watching Steptoe along with everyone else. No use taking chances, he thought. "LCpl Kramer, please escort Mr. Dravid back to the Admin office. " Dravid started to object, but he obviously thought better of it and followed Kramer out of the room.

Finally LCpl Steptoe spoke up. "No ma'am, this is LCpl Steptoe. Here, let me give you the president." He handed the PDA to him and stepped back. The president clipped the earbud around his right ear and held the PDA up to his mouth despite the omni-directional mic, which could clearly pick up his voice from fifteen feet away.

"Jennifer, this is the president. You know, we are rather tired of sitting around here. Tell me you have some good news for us." He put his right hand up to his ear, pushing the earbud firmer into place. He nodded a few times before his face contorted. "No, that is not good enough! What do you mean you can't speak to any of them?" Another pause. "In case they haven't noticed, this is pretty much a crisis. I'm sure they want a peaceful solution, so why the stonewalling?" He glanced at the others in the room before leaning forward in his chair, as if to exclude them.

"What does she say about that?" He pulled at the collar of his shirt. With the power out, the air conditioning wasn't working, and it was pretty warm in the office. "Really? That's pretty hard to believe, but if she says so, then I have to trust her. OK, where does that leave us? Where is the *Reagan*?"

PFC Ramon nudged MAJ Defilice at the mention of the *Reagan*, and he looked down at her and nodded. Gunny wondered what that was all about.

"And Paul Lefever and General Litz both agree about keeping the Rangers in Korea?" He looked up at the ceiling. "Well, I am not sure I agree, but unfortunately, I am sort of out–of–the–loop here, so I will defer. If their ambassador is being kept out of the loop, so be it. But keep Pitt working it so..." another short pause "he what? When were you going to give me that gem of information?" He stretched out his legs and let his hand drop for a moment before bringing the PDA back up to his mouth. "OK, OK, it may do some good. This is his environment, let him earn his pay today. When does he arrive?" He looked at his watch. "Will he have an audience with the PM?"

LCpl Steptoe was watching the PDA, and as a red light started flashing, he frantically tried to signal the Gunny. He caught the Gunny's attention and pointed at the PDA, drawing his other hand across his throat. Gunny Mac stepped up. "Mr. President, the power on the PDA is failing. I strongly advise you to close this call now."

The president looked up at Gunny with annoyance clear on his face. Then he sighed. "Jennifer, I need to go now. We are running out of power for this thing. Let's skip the next scheduled call and pick it up again on the next one, OK? But if anything happens between now and then, we will initiate a call at that time." He took the earbud off his ear and handed the PDA back to LCpl Steptoe who hurriedly powered it down.

He sat there for a moment in thought. "Well. Are you going to keep us in the dark?" Loralee asked. When there wasn't an immediate response, she added "It is not like anyone here is a security risk."

At that, the president actually smiled. "I guess you're right. Well, the Indian ambassador seems to know nothing and can't speak to anyone back here. Secretary Pitt decided that he needs to come to defuse the situation. He should arrive here in another four hours or so. The *USS Reagan* will be off the coast in another ten hours as well. We have a Ranger battalion Quick Reaction Force in Korea, and I thought it was going to move to Diego Garcia, but it seems our friends in DC think that would put on a too aggressive face on us. Don't want to upset the Indians, after all." He chuckled wryly, and the others joined in. "No one of any weight is talking to anyone of us, nor to the UN, nor NATO. So it looks like we wait it out for a while longer. And pray for Secretary Pitt."

He slowly got up and walked out of the office. No one followed him. They turned around to watch the line of men going back and forth between the embassy wall and the consular building, each lost in his or her own thoughts.

Chapter 30

Wednesday Morning, The White house, Washington, DC

"Well, if the president doesn't make it, do you think we can use that to leverage the Indians to open up their financial markets?" Secretary of Commerce Ron Mason looked around the room.

General Mark Kantres, the Army Chief of Staff, broke his pen in half and threw it on the conference table while the Secretary for Homeland Security, Phil Mitchell, leaned forward on his elbows to stare at Mason with a look of incredulity.

"Oh come on, people! Don't tell me you haven't been thinking of what we can do if this all plays out poorly. We've been trying to get our banks into the Indian market for decades, and they keep blocking us. That means American jobs and American profits. Of course I hope things work out well, but if..."

Vice President Wright looked carefully around the table, noting reactions to Mason's comments. General Kantres was a man of action, so his reaction was not surprising. Same with Kai Yen Lin. She was the president's woman, after all. Phill Mitchell was somewhat of a surprise to her. She had rather thought he was not a strong supporter of the president. Paul Lefever was stoic, no expression on his face. But it was surprising that so many others were either stone-faced like Paul or actually seemed to be listening to the Commerce Secretary. Was there an opportunity here?

Ron Mason was a florid-faced man, and Jennifer Wright often thought his soft, pudgy body would be far better suited to sitting around a double-wide in his underwear, drinking beer, and complaining about how the refs stole the game on Sunday. The fat rolls around his eyes gave him a squinty look, as if he was rather dense. But his grooming and clothing were impeccable. His full grey hair was flowing and precise, his fingernails manicured, and his suits were superbly made and matched with the finest silk ties and gold cufflinks. Many people could not get beyond the seeming disparity between his unremarkable physical appearance and his fashion-conscious attire, and they often underestimated him. The vice-president did not. She knew that Ron Mason was an inordinately crafty, manipulative, intelligent, and possibly dangerous man. She hadn't had too much contact with him before, but as she thought about it, perhaps it was time to cultivate a somewhat closer relationship with him.

"Gentlemen! Ladies! As I just briefed you, President Eduardo is doing fine, at least as good as can be expected. And with Secretary Pitt due to arrive within a few hours, I am sure this whole situation will be defused." The vice-president had initially balked at letting Pitt go to India, and she used his security as an excuse. But the secretary could be quite persuasive, and it occurred to her that this could be a win-win for her. If the secretary could somehow find an ending to the stalemate and get the president home, well, she was the one in charge, and she would get the credit for guiding the nation through the crises. And if things did not turn out so well for the president, well, at least she could show she was a woman of action, and she had spared nothing in her attempts. And it would discredit Pitt, one of her rivals in the game of White House power mongering. Of course, if it came to that, she would have already won that game. And it would be now her task to lead the nation forward, forward in the right direction.

"Dr. Ryan, you had mentioned that several other nations and the Vatican have been able to get audiences with the External Affairs Minister. What have we had reported back to us from these meetings?" She looked expectantly towards Kathleen Ryan, the Deputy Secretary of State.

"Yes Madam Vice-President. As you know, we haven't been able to get an audience, nor any of our principal allies, nor the UN. The Arab League evidently met with the PM, but we have heard nothing back on that yet. The assistant secretary for the league has promised to give us a report. The Vatican and a few national representatives have been able to meet with the Minister..."

As the good doctor droned on, the vice-president smiled inwardly while keeping her face attentive to what was being said. Yes, this was turning into being a win-win.

Chapter 31

The last Osprey was being towed to the elevator as Col Jeff Lineau shouldered his pack and started walking over to the base of the island where he could see Josh Conners waiting for him. The surprisingly stiff breeze blew across the deck with the tang of salt giving it a clean sort of smell. Sailors in various brightly colored vests ran back and forth while directing the Ospreys and the Marines. One sailor in a red vest almost ran him down as he approached his old roommate.

He rendered a crisp salute, which was returned, then put out his hand and shook the admiral's offered hand. "Good to see you Josh."

"Welcome to my little kingdom." He turned to a waiting captain, a slight, trim man with only a hint of grey around his temples. "Jeff, this is Mike Carter, this tub's skipper. He's a ROTC guy." He laughed, pronouncing the acronym as "rotzy," "but OK for all of that."

The captain stuck out his hand. "I don't hold it against the Admiral that he decided to go to a trade school instead of a university, so I guess I can't hold it against you," he smiled.

Jeff took the hand and was surprised by the particularly strong grip.

"And you went to...?"

"THE Ohio State University, thank you very much," he replied, with an emphasis on the "The."

"I thought you said you went to a university? Last thing I knew, 'THE' Ohio State University was just a football trade school."

All three laughed. "I've been telling him that for the last five months, but it doesn't seem to sink in."

"Begging the admiral's pardon, and with utmost respect, of course," he said with faux humility, "but at least we can field a competitive team, a national championship team at that. And I can't even bet with you during March Madness because some school I know can't even get invited to the dance." The twinkle in his eyes and easy smile showed this was an ongoing jibe.

And without a real comeback, the admiral clapped the skipper on the shoulder. "Some day, Mike, some day! You just wait. Our turn will come."

Rear Admiral Conners looked out at the Marines gathering alongside the edge of the flight deck. He turned to Col Lineau. "Jeff, why don't you get your men below for a few minutes and have your staff meet up in the ship's CIC conference room. We've been going over a few possible scenarios, but we really need to run these by your guys."

"Yes sir. I'd like to get my men fed, but we really need to do some egress drills. Most of my Marines have never seen any military tactical bird, much less an Osprey."

"Sounds good. Mike, please have the Chief take care of the colonel's men. Then meet us up in the conference room."

"Yes sir. I've got a boat to run." He moved off while Jeff motioned Norm Ricapito over.

"Admiral, this is LtCol Norm Ricapito. With my XO flying, Norm will be my second-in-command for our ground task force." The two men shook hands. "Norm, tell the Sergeant Major to get the men below decks and fed." He paused. "No belay that. I am going to need Mike up with me. Have the Master Guns get them below deck, have a piss call, get fed, and then go to the hangar deck and practice getting on and off the Ospreys. I want this to be second nature to them. Then get my staff up to the conference room."

He looked up at the admiral as LtCol Ricapito walked off to relay the orders. "What's the situation?"

"Same as before. Basically nothing. No one is doing anything. One of your Marines has been released, I've been told. He went out with the diplomats and is on his way to Cairo if he isn't already there."

"Are we still getting the sitreps?" He looked up at his old friend.

The admiral smiled. "Yes, your Gunny Cassel seems quite adept at making sure there are Marines providing "security" for the com. I guess the powers that be decided to keep everything at that young man's apartment. But your Gunny seems to hear everything, and within a few minutes, she sends us a pretty detailed summary of what's happening. Then a couple hours later, we get a sanitized version of the same through DoD."

"Well, I'm glad it is Gunny Cassel there. She has a way about her. If she wasn't a Marine, I'm sure she would be doing hard time somewhere." They both laughed.

He changed tack. "Any chance we're going to get an OK to do anything? An official OK?"

"Doubt it. The Army Rangers are not being allowed to play, so it looks like we'll have to wait and see." Both men stared over the bow. There was a subtle change in the feel of the ship, almost a sense of urgency. The wind across Col Lineau's face started to pick up. He looked back, and he could begin to see a huge rooster tail in back of the mammoth vessel. The flight deck had to be seven or eight stories high, so how could he possibly see a rooster tail? The wind across the deck started to buffet him. He looked back at the Admiral.

Josh Conners leaned in so he could be heard. "This is one fast bitch when she wants to be."

"I guess so!" The group commander turned to walk though a hatch into the bridge tower as the Commandant of the Marines followed.

Chapter 32

Late Wednesday Afternoon, US Embassy, New Delhi

Sergeant Anthony Niimoto was thirsty, very, very thirsty. Drinking was pretty much all he could think about. He had even unlocked the access to the cupola and climbed down into the bell tower's base to try and find something to drink. He had found a first aid kit which had some cough syrup, and he had drunk that, but that seemed to make him even thirstier. He was still searching when voices inside the tower somewhere below him made him scurry back up the ladder and securing the cupola hatch with a piece of rebar.

It came to the point that he was dreading, but finally, he took the empty cough syrup bottle and peed in it. The urine looked dark and foreboding, but with surprisingly little hesitation, he drank it. The warm, bitter liquid going down his throat did little to assuage his thirst, but the logical part of his mind told him all liquid was good for him. He was surprised that he didn't gag it right back up.

He peeked over the wall again to the huge group of Indians who seemed camped outside the wall. He wondered what would happen if he just walked down the tower and into the crowd. Would they even know who he was? Would they assume he was an American, or could he pass himself off as from an Asian country? Could he make it to the Japanese or British embassies, and would they even let him in the gates considering they were most likely on high alert as well?

He settled back and looked up, lost in his thoughts. The bell was actually quite pretty in the late afternoon sun. It had a deep burnished gold hue. He wondered for the thousandth time just what its purpose was, why it was even there. When the power was cut off to the embassy and consulate the night before, the bell tower stayed powered up, so obviously, it has its own power source. Why would a simple bell tower have its own power? It didn't make sense.

At the very apex of the tower was a small rubber-looking pulley contraption. Sgt Niimoto sat up to get a better view. From that wheel-like piece of equipment hung a cable, which came straight down to the bell. Sgt Niimoto moved over for a better look. Now he could see a small cable running from the apex down along the curved ceiling of the belfry to one of the many boxes adorning one side of the wall. He hadn't noticed this before as it was painted with the same paint as the tower walls. In bright daylight, it would have been rendered practically invisible. But in the fading afternoon light, the shadows made it stand out some.

He followed the cable down to one small box, a non-descript grey metal compartment. Alongside the box was a red-handled lever, like a large switch. He knew he should leave it alone, but curiosity overcame him. He sidled up to the box, put his hand on the lever, and slowly pulled it.

There was a click and the bell started to lower with some groans and squeaks. Sgt Niimoto slammed the handle back up and the bell stopped with a jerk, slowly swaying from side to side. He waited for some hue or cry to show that the bell's moving had been seen or heard by someone. Nothing changed. Everything remained quiet.

He grinned. Well, he had figured out one thing about the tower. If he ever got back up here with any of the other Marines, he would have fun showing them that.

He crawled back to his position and settled in for the long night.

Chapter 33

Early Wednesday Evening, US Embassy, New Delhi

"Thank you, Mr. President for taking the time for this."
It had taken a little convincing, but finally the president had agreed to rehearse a quick movement from the Admin office to the vault below decks. Gunny had actually wanted to move the president there now, but he had declined to move. So at least in three tries, they had been able to rehearse a move and had gotten it down to a minute-and-a-half before the president thought that had been enough rehearsing. Gunny wanted to go through the whole thing again after dark, but he doubted the president would be up for it. Besides, there was no natural light going down the stairwell or on this level, only the emergency lighting, so doing it at night wouldn't make that much of a difference.

The president merely grunted and walked down the passage to the stairwell going up. Gunny motioned to Sgt Chen and LCpl Steptoe, who hurried to catch up and accompany the president back to the admin office. He wiped his brow. Without the air conditioning going, it was getting pretty hot and sticky in the building. He could feel his t-shirt sticking to his back. Like most of the others, he had taken off his uniform blouse and left it above decks.

PFC Ramon was another Marine who has taken off her blouse, and her sweat was soaking her t-shirt. She was still in the vault, and as what seemed to be the norm now, she was talking to MAJ Defilice.

Her damp t-shirt did little to conceal her compact torso and the rather significant bra that served to support her breasts. While speaking, she absent-mindedly reached to pull at the edge of the left bra cup, pulling it out slightly while shrugging her shoulders as if to settle things better. Gunny looked away guiltily.

Gunny looked back to check on the progress of Loralee down the passageway, but Drayton had her arm and seemed in earnest conversation. He followed them and made his way up the stairwell, around the corner, and back down toward the admin office.

The president had already sat down on the couch to which he had laid claim and was making some notes on a pad of paper. Gunny slung his weapon and started to sit down when he caught eyes with PFC Van Slyke, who had been left behind in the office during the movement rehearsal and who was now standing behind LCpl Wynn. Van Slyke slowly shook his head as a lump formed in Gunny's throat. He hesitantly walked over to the desk on which Wynn lay and looked down on her. There was no doubt that she was dead. The labored look on her face while she fought for life was now relaxed and pallid. Her fight was over. Gunny reached over and took her hand.

"Gunny, shouldn't we stage some of this food in the vault? MAJ Defilice thinks it might save some time if it comes to that." It was PFC Ramon crowding up behind him.

"There isn't any air circulation in there, and it is hot, so any of this we bring down there, if it starts to spoil, it'll be pretty ripe," he responded flatly, still holding LCpl Wynn's hand.

"But what if we take some now and…" she came around him and saw LCpl Wynn. As she stopped talking, the others seemed to notice for the first time and came around to stand around the desk.

"Is she, you know…" The president had walked over and now looked over PFC Van Slyke's shoulder.

"Yes sir, she's dead. She couldn't fight anymore. If we could have gotten her to a hospital, I think they could have saved her. Keeping her here, we killed her."

Loralee spoke up. "You know that wasn't possible, Gunny. We've been trapped in here, and we couldn't have gotten her out. They killed her, not anyone in here."

"But what if we had just taken her outside and left her there. I bet they'd have taken her and got her to a hospital." Gunny Mac barely even knew LCpl Wynn. He didn't know her parents' name, if she had a boyfriend, what she liked to eat, how she felt about things. But she was in his unit, and he felt an overpowering sense of responsibility for her. She was part of his family, part of his very essence.

"Bullshit. They were the ones who shot her, after all. No telling what they might have done to her or if she'd be held hostage at another place. You did what you had to do, and any blame lies on them. Not you. You know that, and we don't need you wallowing in self-pity now. You need to do your job." Loralee looked at him with piercing eyes.

Gunny Mac looked back at those eyes. She was right, and his intellect knew that even if his heart did not.

"Chen, Van Slyke, go relieve McAllister and Rodriguez. Steptoe and Kramer, go relieve Saad. Mr Dravid, if you can lead the way to the reefer?" He reached down and put his arms around LCpl Wynn's still body and lifted her up. He had always heard that dead bodies seemed heavy, but she seemed very light in his arms.

Chapter 34

Wednesday Night, US Embassy, New Delhi

Sgt Anthony Niimoto was dreaming of lemonade, ice cold, in pitchers. He could feel the cold cascade down his throat, fill his stomach. He could feel the very cells of his body swell up as the lemonade poured directly into them.

A commotion beneath him finally broke though his consciousness. He slowly dragged himself up and peered over the edge of the cupola wall to see four men dragging some sort of pressurized tank over the embassy wall as the crowd watched and buzzed in anticipation. Two men made it over and sat waiting as two others straddled the wall and slowly lowered the tank into the other's waiting arms. The waiting men grunted and almost dropped the cylinder before setting it on the deck. The other two climbed down and together, the four men walked over the main doors of the embassy, pulling the cylinder in a small wheeled stand.

Sgt Niimoto dialed the embassy. PFC Fallgatter picked up the other end. "Fallgatter, get me Gunny." As he waited for the Gunny, he watched three of the men point and gesture at the door while one seemed to work on the cylinder. With only the running lights providing illumination, it was hard to make things out clearly.

"This is Gunny, what do you got, Tony?"

"Gunny, there are four men with a cylinder at the main doors. It

150

looks like some sort of welding or cutting set-up. I think you need to get over there."

"Shit! Really? Can you see what they are actually doing?"

"I can't see yet, but it doesn't look good."

"OK, I am going now. Pick me up on the Post 1 phone. Gunny, out."

He shifted to where he could maintain a better view. The men had brought the cylinder right up to the doors. There was a barely visible spark and then a tongue of flame shot out. He could hear the hiss all the way across the courtyard. He glanced back and could see a line of eyes peering over the wall and intent on the men at the doors.

There was a dull glow as the flame touched the door. In the glare, Sgt Niimoto could see the man holding a piece of dark plastic or something in front of his eyes. Sgt. Niimoto guessed they didn't have real goggles available.

The phone flashed and Sgt Niimoto snatched up the handset. "Tony, what is happening out there?"

"It looks like they are trying to cut through the door. But there is no one else there. Do you want me to take them out?"

There was a pause. "No, they'll know then that you are there. Let's stand by and watch. These doors are pretty solid. I am going to give the phone to PFC Rodriguez. Let him know what is happening."

The flame kept going, and there was a dull glow on the metal of the right door where the flame was torching, but not much else. Sgt Niimoto kept watching. The heat of the night seemed even hotter from the direction of the doors, but he knew that had to be his imagination. After about fifteen minutes, the flame flickered then gave out. The four men examined the slowly fading glow on the door. One man leaned back and gave it a hard kick. They looked like they were talking it over, then turned and came back to the wall. One-by-one, they climbed over, and two of them went to report in to another group of men waiting outside the wall under a huge tree.

"Rodriguez, tell Gunny that they've given up. Looks like good old American workmanship has prevailed. American workers one, Indian workers, zero." He hung up the phone and looked back into the crowd, which had grown smaller in the night. Smaller in number, maybe, but the atmosphere of those remaining seemed a little more intense, a little more focused.

Chapter 35

Wednesday Night, US Embassy, New Delhi

"Sgt Nii says they've given up." PFC Rodriguez announced to the Marines surrounding the door. Gunny stood where he was crouching alongside Post 1 and slung his weapon. The rest of the Marines, except for PFC Van Slyke who was left with the president, and LCpl Saad who was left in the Cultural Affairs office, stood up along with MAJ Defilice from their hasty positions and moved toward the door.

LCpl Kramer reached out to the point where they had heard a dull thud a few moments before. "Hey, it is a little warm. I can feel it!" Sgt Chen and PFC Ramon moved up to feel the spot too, nodding in agreement.

"Why did they try to come through the doors? Those are about the strongest things there. Why not through the embassy walls themselves?" LCpl Steptoe wondered aloud.

Gunny felt a sense of foreboding at that thought, but it was coupled with a sense of determination. "Well, I guess they are playing their hand. And that is that." He considered for the umpteenth time bringing everyone back to the admin office to concentrate his resources, but Post 1 was too valuable a piece of real estate to give up. Even if the security cameras did not work any more, the post glass was bullet proof, and while there were no firing ports, the slots for accepting ID cards and papers could be used for outgoing fire and gave pretty good coverage down both passageways and the hatch to the stairwell.

"Sgt Chen, you and Fallgatter stay here at Post 1. The rest, we're going to back to the admin office. We need to make sure our shit is together on this."

Chapter 36

Wednesday Morning, The White house, Washington, DC

"Madame Vice-President, Director Lin is here." The vice-president looked up from the television where she was watching Dani Craig, the press secretary, at the press conference. That woman was good, she thought. She was conveying confidence while saying absolutely nothing. That was one woman who needed to stay on in her administration.

She had handled the Pitt situation well. When denied landing rights, Secretary Pitt had had his pilot declare an airborne emergency, so he had been allowed to land. He had not been allowed to debark his plane, though, and was still sitting on the tarmac. Craig had made it sound, without actually lying, that Pitt was in India working to diffuse the situation and bring the president home.

She leaned toward the intercom. "Send her in please." David looked at her, raising one eyebrow in a question. She motioned him to keep in his seat.

She would keep Craig, to be sure, but the Director of the CIA was another story. Quite frankly, she didn't trust her. The woman had the ear of the president, and she was unnaturally smart, but her almost stilted way of speech and her obvious affection for the president did not bode well for a future working relationship. And while she may understand the technological aspects of gathering intelligence, she did not have experience in the human side of intelligence gathering. Yes, Dr. Lin would be one of the first to go.

Kai-yen Lin walked into the office and stood in front of the vice-president's desk. "Please sit, Dr. Lin," she indicated a seat in front of the desk. She started to get up to join her, but at the last second decided to stay where she was.

Dr. Lin sat on the outer edge of her seat, back straight, a typed report in her lap, hands folded on the report. She waited.

Vice-President Wright inwardly sighed. "Dr. Lin, I asked you to see me to give me your input on this. Not what you gave at the meeting, but your take. The president just asked me to ask you."

"Yes, Madam Vice-President." There was a pause.

"Well then, can you give it to me? I am due to talk with him again in fifteen minutes."

Dr. Lin cleared her throat. "There has been a significant degree of increased activity in all electronic spectrums. This is to be expected, but there has been an interesting pattern of electronic activities in the wavelengths commonly associated with communications between this building," she paused to pass the vice-president a satellite photo of a large, non-descript building, "and to the area surrounding the embassy."

"And what is this building?"

"That is the Council of Ethnic Preservation. It is a pseudo-governmental organization with strong ties with the ruling party and the labor unions. Its funding comes from official government grants and private donations. We do have some ground assets outside the building now, and there has been increased traffic of persons whom we believe to be associated with both security and military agencies., albeit no one at an executive level." She handed over some more photos of various men in civilian clothing entering the building.

The vice-president smiled. It was the same everywhere. Military men in civilian clothes always looked out of place. Even with different styles in clothing in different countries, they stood out like sore thumbs.

"It is our assessment that the Indian government is at least giving tacit support to the takeover. It certainly has not marshaled troops into any place where they could take action. In fact, two Indian army divisions, the 32nd Armor and the 5th Infantry, have been moved out over the last week for supposed previously scheduled maneuvers, and most of the aircraft at Hindon Air Force Base near New Delhi have been flown elsewhere. I have a list here of the types of aircraft that have left and what is remaining." She looked up expectantly at the vice-president who waved her off.

"The tone of the news media has been muted. There have been some outspoken critics within the parliament, such as Virag Dasmunsi, who have been publically advocating for a full response by the police, but the primary response seems to be silence. I must point out that Dasmunsi's vocal posturing may be merely a platform for the Indian Nationalist Party to damage the ruling party."

"Do you think Mr. Dasmunsi has any real power in this? Can he affect anything?"

"The Indian National Party has risen in the polls since the last election, and if there was an election held today, it is possible that Mr. Dasmunsi could become the new Prime Minister. That is purely conjecture, of course. Polling data in India is notoriously unreliable."

"So for the $64,000 question, why would the current government be giving any support for this? Why risk serious repercussions within the diplomatic community?" She folded her hands into a teepee and placed the tip of the teepee up against her mouth, tilting her head down slightly to look at the director.

Kai-yen Lin looked more uncomfortable, if that was possible. "We do not have any ground assets at a level high enough to be in on discussions within the Party's inner circle. However, due to the current unrest, and coupled with rising anti-American sentiment within central and northern India, most of our analysts agree that this move might be intended to raise nationalistic sentiments and shift public unhappiness from the Party to the US."

"And how far will the Indian government go with this?"

"There are patterns within communications transmissions that might be indicative that the situation has gone on further that it was intended. And our ground assets at the site outside the embassy are reporting that there seems to be some degree of disagreement among the aggressors there. There as been hesitation and, until recently, no firm move forward into the embassy grounds, although there seems to be preparation for such a move. This would also support the concept that the Party does not know itself how this situation should be resolved."

The vice-president took that last bit of information in with some interest, although she hoped she hid that. Was it possible that the prime minster would loose his dogs and let them attack?

Wanting to change tack, she leaned forward. "What do you think of Dr. Ryan's assessment of the efforts of other nations' efforts?"

"The Arab League offers the most reasonable chance for a peaceful resolution. They have had considerable success in Africa, as you know, and in the last incident in Kashmir. It is our assessment that the League is truly trying to bring this situation to a conclusion. The Vatican is a non-player in our assessment. Of the others, perhaps Thailand might have some pull with their effort, but not much."

Thailand? I hadn't heard about that. When and what was that?"

"The Royal Thai ambassador to India, Dr. Amarin Suphantarida, was able to get an appointment with the Minister yesterday at 16:30 local. Thailand, as you know, is heavily dependent upon Indian investment and as a customer, so there is a reasonable connection. But we don't see too much happening here."

David discreetly coughed. "Madam Vice-President, we have your call to the president in five minutes. I suggest that we go into the conference room?"

"Very well." She stood up. Came around the desk, and offered her hand to Dr. Lin who awkwardly shook it. "Thank you Dr. Lin. Please keep me posted. You can reach David here at any time."

Hand still in the grasp of the vice-president, Dr. Lin faltered. "Well Madam Vice-President, as I said, there had been no firm move into the embassy until recently. I want to report to you that about twenty minutes ago, there was some degree of activity at the embassy. At least four men with what appeared to be a propane torch approached the embassy front doors. We could not see what was being done there due to the overhang, but the light reflections we could see were consistent with an attempt to cut open the doors. That effort evidently failed as could be expected, but this signifies a significant rising of the intensity of the situation."

The vice-president kept her face neutral as her heart gave a flutter. Was the end game approaching? She dropped the director's hand. "Well, as you say, they weren't successful. Keep me posted on anything further." She turned and walked down the hallway, flanked by her secret service agents.

Chapter 37

"You all know none of this is going to happen. Contingency 'A' possibly, just being a platform to whisk the president away. But all this planning for a forced entry? Never going to happen." CDR Steve Kinney looked at the rest of the planning group.

LtCol Saunders rubbed his eyes and looked at the overhead before looking back at the glaring commander. "You're right, it probably won't come to anything. But it sure doesn't hurt to plan it now, does it? My commandant, your admiral, the wing commander, and the ship's CO are discussing that possibility right now, but they have given us our marching orders, so I suggest we get to it. Mr. Evans, you were saying?"

Clyde Evans was the State Department rep aboard the *Reagan*. An ES1, he technically outranked everyone in the compartment, but to LtCol Saunders, he seemed to let the military-types run the tempo and direction of the meeting. At 32 years old, he was reportedly an up-and-comer, but the other officers had told Tye that Clyde didn't care for the military and hoped this stepping stone would quickly pass and he could get back to the "real" world of State.

"Well, as I said, embassies are usually considered to be the sovereign territory of that nation. There may not be an actual basis for this is most cases, but this concept has been generally honored throughout modern history."

"So you are saying that if we bomb or land troops at our embassy, then the Indians can't say anything?" CDR Shelly la Porte, the squadron OPS O asked.

Evans grimaced awhile bobbing his head side to side. "Well, sort of. But to get there, you have to cross Indian airspace, and if you drop bombs on the embassy, what if a bomb falls outside on the street and kills someone? That could be considered an act of war."

"And that, my friends, is why we can't just go in and carpet bomb all around the place, then send in these Marines to pick up the esteemed passenger." CAPT Ted Ngata, the Battle Group G3 remarked. "OK, let's look at what we have." He held out one hand and pointed to the forefinger with his other.

"Asset Number 1: The *Honolulu* steamed ahead while we were puttering along with our 'bad' shaft and is in position about 10 miles offshore on corridor 'Santa Fe.' She is there to provide support, but she can also be used to rescue downed aircraft or even to affect an air-to-sea transfer of the president. I don't think we have ever done that between an Osprey and a sub, but it certainly should be possible."

He put out another finger. "Asset Number 2: Our Big Eye. I have no idea how the Old Man got her, but she is sitting in a secure hanger at Farkhor and can be on station when our own birds arrive."

The third finger came out. "Asset Number 3: we have almost 100 Marines and four Ospreys. Certainly we can do something with them."

The fourth finger made its appearance. "Asset Number 4: we have a damn carrier here with a full compliment of aircraft, ordnance, and men and women. This is what the *Reagan* was built for. I suggest you put your heads together and come up with a viable plan to give to the old man. Even if we never use it, we need that plan. That is why they call it a 'contingency plan.' Got it?"

There was a chorus of "aye-ayes" as pubs were re-opened discussion re-joined. After hours of work, there were still many more ahead. It was going to be a long night. LtCol Tye Saunders hoped that there was plenty of good Navy coffee in the pot.

Chapter 38

Early Thursday Morning, US Embassy, New Delhi

Thirst was overwhelming, and Sgt Niimoto did not know how much longer he could last. He had drunk his urine twice during the night, but still, he could think of nothing else but getting something to drink. He tried to sleep, but the fitful catnaps he grabbed hardly qualified as that. At one point, he stared over the walls at the men gathered around, and he could see bottles of beer being passed. Once again, he contemplated just walking over and asking for something to drink. If they took him, they took him. At least his thirst would be over, one way or another.

But he wasn't seriously tempted. Instead he snuck back down the ladder to try and scrounge up something, anything to drink. He found nothing. He brought up the medical kit where he had found the cough syrup and went through that. Nothing to drink. He tried taking some cotton pads and rubbing them on the surface of the bell, hoping to mop up and nighttime condensation. While the cotton seemed damp, he could not squeeze anything out. He found an oxygen cylinder in the kit and took it out of its case, hoping some dew might form on its metal surface.

As the sun's rose-colored fingers began to reach across the dawn sky, he realized that he had maybe one more day left. After that, he was either going to try and make the embassy or just lie down and fade away. He was going to tell Gunny this morning he was going for it after dusk.

There were far fewer people over the wall as there had been before, but they seemed more determined, more focused. A few buses had come by and carted people off, from the looks of it to the new stadium down Sadar Patel Marg, but that was too far away to be sure of that.

A group of men approached the ladder on the Indian side of the wall and started over, carrying a bundle. Sgt Niimoto could not quite make out what the bundle was. They made it over the wall and began to scurry across the courtyard. Sgt Niimoto reached for the phone.

PFC Rodriguez responded, but Sgt Niimoto could not croak anything out. He tried to lick his lips, but to no avail. Finally he was able to force out his message. "Rodriguez, there are bunch of men at the doors. I think they are going to try something. Let Gunny know."

"Sure Sergeant." He could hear Rodriguez relay the message and Sgt McAllister's acknowledgement, then he heard fading footsteps as the PFC ran down the passage.

Sgt McAllister came on the line. "How you hanging, Korea Joe?" concern in her voice.

"I'm OK. Could use a little drink of something though."

"I hear you, buddy. Oh, here's Gunny." She handed the phone off.

"What do you got this time, Tony?"

"Well, there are three guys at the door. I can't see what they are doing." The light was getting brighter, but it was still hard to make out. "They've got a bundle that they are putting down at the base of the door, right in the middle. Now they are… shit they're running! Get back Gunny, I think they're trying to blow it!"

He could hear the Gunny react, yelling at everyone to get back. The seconds seemed to drag on. Sgt Niimoto crouched with just the top of his head over the edge of the cupola wall. What if he was wrong about that? He felt dizzy and lightheaded and wondered if he was thinking straight. A huge blast, felt more than seen, exploded against the embassy doors. Sgt Niimoto was flung down, a huge hand pushing on his chest. He sat stunned for a moment, then scrambled up, rifle ready to take out anyone trying to enter the embassy.

As he peered through the settling dust, he could see the door standing as normal, nothing out of place. He let out a dry chuckle. He guessed that was why they called them blast doors. He crawled to other side of the tower and looked down on the angrily gesturing men who perched on the wall and seemed more than a little peeved that their entrance had not been blown.

"Better luck next time, Mowgli," he muttered with a smile on his face.

Chapter 39

Thursday Morning, US Embassy, New Delhi

The blast was a muffled thud that barely shook the security door. A little dust fell from the overhead, but that was about it. Heads began to appear from where the mad scramble to get out of the way had taken everyone. Gunny, Kramer, and Steptoe had ducked in back of Post 1, and now they stood up, along with Sgt McAllister and Rodriguez who were inside the post. LCpl Saad and Sgt Chen had made it further away and were now getting to their feet a good fifteen meters past Post 1 down the north corridor.

Gunny turned around to see PFC Ramon standing in the stairwell, putting down her hand to MAJ Defilice, who smiled and took it, standing up. Drayton was in there as well, a look of unadulterated excitement on his face. He looked like he was at some sort of amusement park.

Down the south corridor, toward the ambassador's office, PFC Fallgatter still lay prone, his arms over his head. "Hey dipwad, you want to join us?" Kramer shouted at him as everyone gathered in front of the door.

They could hear PFC Van Slyke yell a slurred "Everything all right?" from the Admin office where he had been left with the president and Loralee. Gunny stepped back to look down the passage where he could see four anxious faces peering back at him.

"Steptoe, go down and let them know everything is fine, and ask the president to get back in the office. We don't need him to start wandering around."

As LCpl Steptoe ran down the passage, they all stared at the door. "Man, that is some damn good door," Sgt Chen exclaimed. He stepped up and gave it an experimental shake.

Gunny slung his weapon and put his hands on his hips. "Well, I guess their intent is pretty clear. I think it is time we moved the president. Major, if you wouldn't mind, would you please get him and Loralee and escort them to the vault?"

"Sure thing, Gunny." He slung his weapon as well and started down the passage.

"And let's get SSgt Child down in the vault, too, while we have chance. Kramer and Chen, can you get him there? Wait a minute, though, before you go. LCpl Steptoe, you take Fallgatter and go into the Cultural Affairs office. I know that is a change, but it is closer to the stairwell than the ambassador's office, and you might need to beat a hasty retreat. Keep your eyes peeled and let us know what is going on. Everyone else, into the stairwell. We've got McAllister, Rodriguez, and Kramer as the fireteam at the top of the well, then Chen and Saad at the bottom with Steptoe and Fallgatter when they get there. The rest of us will be in vault. OK? Just like we planned. Right?" He looked at Little Mac, still inside Post 1. "Give Korea Joe a call and let him know what we're doing."

"Uh, Gunny? Rodriguez and me, well, we've been thinking. Post 1 has the best fields of fire. We sort of think we need to stay in here."

"Pat, we went over this. If anyone stays inside Post 1, well, they won't be able to retrograde to join us. They'll be cut off."

"Fifth General Order, Gunny."

Gunny let out an exasperated sigh. "I am properly relieving you."

"How about if me and Rodriguez just wait here a little longer? I mean, look. It is what, ten, twelve meters to the stairwell. If we have to get there, it'll take us a second or two, especially if the rest of the team covers us. Besides, the door is holding, so there is no rush now."

Gunny hesitated. He had made his plan, and he really wanted it to unfold as he envisioned it. But he also did not want to have any dissension now. So he decided he could adjust a little here. "OK, stay here for now. But when you get the command, fall back to the stairwell immediately. You got that?"

"Sure Gunny. Do you think we want to get our asses shot off? Kramer, just don't you go and plunk us when we come to join your own sorry ass."

"I would never do that to a Sergeant of Marines! Now a PFC, however..."

The group broke out in laughter.

"OK, our fun meter is obviously pegged. Let's get going. We know what we have to do, and if anyone really insists on inviting themselves in for tea, well, we are just going to have to dissuade them." Gunny turned and started up the passage where the president, Loralee, and Mr. Dravid were being escorted down the passage.

"Gunny, the president needs to report this escalation. Where is Steptoe?" MAJ Defilice asked.

"LCpl Steptoe, get out here!" Gunny shouted, his words echoing down the passage. After a moment, LCpl Steptoe stuck his head out the Cultural Affairs office. "Front and center, Steptoe."

"The president needs to use the com again. How's it looking?"

LCpl Steptoe grimaced. "We are almost out of juice. The battery may have recharged itself a little after we last powered down, but there isn't much left."

"There is no getting around that now, soldier. I want to get back to DC now." The president came up to stand beside him.

"Marine, sir, Marine," muttered Gunny. The president heard but chose to ignore the comment as LCpl Steptoe powered up.

"I am going to give it right to you, sir. No use me wasting any juice on this." He watched the small screen for a moment and handed it to the president, who put the earbud in his ear. The rest crowded around to listen.

There was a short wait. Then his eyes lit up and he started, "This is President Eduardo. Give me the vice-president." There was a very short pause, and then evidently the vice-president answered. She must have been right there. "OK, OK, wait there. I don't really care now who gave whom the OK to negotiate with anyone. None of the negotiations have worked. We've got people trying to blow up the doors here to the embassy, so I think they have made their intentions clear. Has there been any movement on the Indian government's part?" The president paused, nodding as he listened.

"Then what about the military option? What is going on with that?" He paused again.

Suddenly he shouted into the PDA, "I don't give a good goddamn about that. This is already an act of war, or hadn't you noticed? We have got a number of people here who have to be evacuated now! I am making an executive order here, Vice-President Wright. Let me be clear. All US military forces are to take whatever action they can to rescue us immediately. Am I clear?" The president's face was getting red as he shouted, and specks of spit flew out of his mouth. He listened for a few seconds.

"No excuses, just do it. I know the *Reagan*... the *Reagan*... hello? Hello?" He looked at the PDA which had suddenly gone dark. "Shit!"

LCpl Steptoe grabbed it and looked at it, hitting a few buttons. "That's it sir. It's dead."

The circle of people crowded in a little closer, staring at the PDA. Their last window to the US had just been cut off.

Chapter 40

Vice-President Wright was beside herself. Just who did this arrogant piss-ant ambassador think he was talking to? She looked around the table where no one seemed to want to catch her eye.

When she had heard that the ambassador from Thailand had initiated negotiations with the Indians, she has demanded to know who had authorized that. No one seemed to have an answer for that, so she had Dr. Ryan contact the US ambassador to Thailand who told her that he had actually spoken to the Thai ambassador to India. Dr. Ryan reported that back to the vice-president who demanded that the ambassador be put on the phone. She ran that into the speakers. Now, the ambassador, Case, his name was, was calmly acting like nothing was wrong.

His voice came over the speakers. "As I told you, Madam Vice-President, this was an act of a sovereign nation which was further acting on a request from the rest of ASEAN. We had nothing to do with that."

"And once again, ambassador," she made the word "ambassador" sound like a pejorative. Do you think the Thai government should be representing us, representing us without us even knowing he is doing so?"

"Technically, he is not representing us at all. He is representing ASEAN and the Royal Thai government."

"But you spoke to him, didn't you, before he got in to see the Minister."

"Yes, Madam Vice-President, I did."

"And if this is solely an ASEAN matter, why would you speak to him first?" She looked around the table in triumph.

"Madam Vice-President, according to the US-Thai Cooperation Treaty, I am bound to inform the Thai government of the presence of any operational forces in Thai territory. I merely informed Ambassador Suphantarida before he met with the Minister so he would not be taken by surprise should that fact already be known." No one could see the ambassador, but the exasperation was beginning to show in his voice.

"The Reagan Carrier Group had been cleared a month ago to pull liberty in Thailand, so I don't know why you would have to call to inform him about that." She genuinely looked puzzled.

"I am not talking about the *Reagan*. I am talking about the Marines who transshipped through here."

"What do you mean, the Marines?" She looked over at General Litz who looked up with a confused expression on his face.

"The 100 or so Marines who flew in to U-Tapao and then flew off for destinations unknown, Madam Vice-President."

She reached over and hit the speaker mute. "General Litz, what is this about?" She thought about it and realized that there hadn't been a Marine guard outside the conference room as normal. A Secret Service agent was now taking those duties.

General Litz looked over to the three other four-stars in the room, none who seemed to have anything to say. "I am sorry Madam Vice-President. I don't know anything about this. But I will find out." He motioned to one of his aides.

"COL Shriver, call down to Col Lineau at Quantico and find out if any of his Marines flew into Thailand."

The vice-president turned off the mute. "Ambassador, I'll be getting back to you. Remain accessible to this phone." She hung up before there was a reply.

"I want to know what's going on. With the president out of the picture, I am in charge. Is that clear?" There were nods around the conference table. "And in order to be in charge, I have to know what is going on. No half-baked cowboys doing things their way." She glared, taking everyone in.

The person manning the com link to the President suddenly stood up. "Yes sir, Mr. President," and flipped the switch which brought the president to the speaker. "Madam Vice-President...?" he looked over to her.

She quickly moved closer to the intercom on the table in front of her. "Mr. President, this is the vice-president. How are you, sir? And let me assure you that things are progressing, but we are trying to figure out who authorized the Thai government to negotiate for your release and return..."

"OK, OK, wait there. I don't really care now who gave whom the OK to negotiate with anyone. None of the negotiations have worked. We've got people trying to blow up the doors here to the embassy, so I think they have made their intentions clear. Has there been any movement on the Indian government's part?" The president's voice sounded strained.

"We have not been able to get a meeting with anyone other than their ambassador, and he doesn't seem to be in the loop. The Arab League has been able to see the key players, but nothing concrete is getting done."

"Then what about the military option? What is going on with that?"

She looked around the room again before answering. "We have the Reagan Carrier Group close to India now. And we have our forces on alert in Korea. But we don't want to provoke anything with a rash act."

The president's voice screamed over the speaker, "I don't give a good goddamn about that. This is already an act of war, or hadn't you noticed? We have got a number of people here who have to be evacuated now! I am making an executive order here, Vice-President Wright. Let me be clear. All US military forces are to take whatever action they can to rescue us immediately. Am I clear?"

Everyone stared at the speaker as if the president was going to climb right out of it. "Mr. President, perhaps you should rethink that. Do we want a shooting war with India now?"

"No excuses, just do it. I know the *Reag....*" The speaker went silent.

The com tech jumped up. "We've lost the signal, the one from New Delhi to Katmandu!"

There was stunned silence in the conference room.

General Kantres broke the silence. "Well, we heard the man. Can we move the Quick Reaction Force now? We have them standing by, and they can be in the air in thirty minutes."

The vice-president looked over at David. They had discussed this possible situation. "General Kantres, we appreciate your Ranger's readiness. But we need to make sure the president is in the legal position to make valid orders, given his situation. I have asked the attorney general to look into this." She looked up at the man, who seemed uncomfortable with the question. Good, if he was uncomfortable, then maybe David's assessment was correct after all.

There was a general uproar as everyone started to talk at once. The Army colonel who had left came back in and whispered to General Litz. He nodded and looked up.

"Madam Vice-President. It seems that the Marines have left. Quantico is empty."

A sense of foreboding came over her, and she wasn't quite sure why. Just what the hell was going on with the Marines?

Chapter 41

Wednesday Morning, The USS Reagan, The Indian Ocean

Rear Admiral Conners looked up at CAPT Ngata at the podium. "Thanks Ted. I think we can all see that this is a good start, a basic NEO, but we also know it needs lots of refining. So let's take this bad boy back and iron out the wrinkles we've brought up." He looked around the space. "Any saved rounds?"

Col Lineau cleared his throat. "As you know, the Marines have been out of the ordnance loop for awhile, and I know I should have kept up with innovations on my own, but can someone please go over this Mk402 again? I am still not quite sure how this is supposed to work."

CAPT Ngata pointed toward the back of the space. "Commander Scali, would you like to take this?"

Lieutenant Commander Frank Scali, a 35-year mustang and the ship's ordnance officer, stepped up to the podium. "Well sir, the Mk 402 is a weapon designed to incapacitate troops in the open with little damage to structures. Upon detonation, it attenuates in applied directions and consumes available oxygen in the fireball while creating an overpressure." He paused to look at the colonel.

"Uh, can you repeat that so a dumb grunt can understand?"

"Yes sir." He paused to think. "OK, the Mk 402 is a warhead on an iron bomb. When it detonates, the blast can be sort of aimed to push out in most directions. When it explodes, it burns up all the oxygen in the area and creates a shock wave that can rupture eardrums or even lungs, depending on how close someone is to the point of detonation."

Colonel Lineau had a visceral image form in his mind of bodies on the ground, their lungs ruptured, a bloody froth coming out their mouths. It did not sound like a good way to go

"As our SJA briefed, if we can limit the effect on target to only those people and structures that are in the embassy grounds, well, that is an attack on US soil, not Indian. So we think the Mk 402 is the best bet. Because of the embassy building itself, the consulate, and the embassy walls, if we can get a vertical strike in the courtyard, we can 'aim,' so-to-speak, the blast back upward, and the embassy structures should work to limit effects beyond the embassy grounds. Anyone in the courtyard or outside the buildings facing the point of impact, well, their lungs are going to burst. Some people in the building itself may lose consciousness due to oxygen deprivation, but the embassy building is pretty strong, so there should be no major damage. If the president is in the center of the building, as we have been briefed, well, the inrushing oxygen should replace the burned oxygen before any permanent damage has been done."

"And when we land 60 seconds after impact, we won't be affected?"

You shouldn't, sir. You should be fine."

" 'Shouldn't.' I like that, especially when it is our asses on the line." There was a general chuckle around the space at that. "And what about the hostile-types who aren't in the grounds when your bomb goes off?"

"Well, sir, the attenuation won't be perfect. Anyone near the walls might become casualties. Even if they are not, they certainly won't be combat-effective for at a little while, at least. They should be rather dazed."

"OK, I am going to take your word on it. I do have another saved round, though." He looked up at the admiral, who nodded.

"I understand the need for us to limit bystander casualties. But I'm pretty nervous on shutting off the Big Eye for two minutes, ten minutes before we hit the LZ. Isn't that going to make us pretty vulnerable?"

The Air Force liaison, Maj Godwin, jumped up. "I'll take that one, sir." He moved to the podium. "I am not an expert on all the black box toys, but you understand how the Big Eye is going to work, right?"

Col Lineau gave a half-hearted shrug.

"Well sir, the Big Eye is going to basically block all electromagnetic emissions along a set path. This one will be about 100 miles wide by 200 miles long and will follow you along your route as well as cover the CAP. While you're in this path, nothing can see you except eyeballs on the ground. And if eyeballs see you, what can they do about it? They can't call anyone. But the Big Bird can somewhat regulate the type of electronics it will jam. So, we are going to keep all military detection equipment jammed hard, but we'll open up the telephone frequencies. That will allow us to get a warning out for people to clear the area as well as warn the president and your Marines to get as deep in the embassy as possible."

"And you think the Indians will have stopped jamming the embassy themselves?"

"There is a good chance they will. We don't believe they know about Big Eye's capability, and they shouldn't know anything is being employed. If they lose their own signals, we think they'll assume that it is their own jamming equipment, and they are going to turn it off. They need to communicate too. "

"OK. Thanks. Give me a rifle and a target. All this other stuff is magic, as far as I am concerned." Another laugh swept the space.

"OK people, let's get this thing refined. CAPT Ngata, how about…" the admiral looked at his watch, "another brief at 1100?"

"No problem sir." He gathered his papers, motioned to his combined planning staff, and left the space. The two friends sat there for a moment.

"What do you think, Jeff?"

"Well, it isn't too refined, but a gorilla with a club is not too refined, either, and I wouldn't want to face one of them."

"Yea," he chuckled. "I guess you're right. You've got your Marines bedded down?"

"My commanders are getting briefed now, but yea, the troops are trying to grab some z's. Hey, that Big Eye is something, isn't it?"

"You bet. Have you even seen it? It is not very big, about the size of a Viking. But it can paralyze a small country, and it can stay on station forever."

"How did you get it anyhow? That's a strategic asset. You don't have them in a carrier battle group."

"Ah, it's all who you know. You remember that Air Force firstie, the wrestler, the one who caught me in the third period after I was leading him and pinned my ass? Back when we were second classmen?"

"You mean the guy who knocked you out of Nationals?"

"Yes, that asshole. Well, we've kept in touch, and he is STRATCOM now."

"One year ahead of us and he is a four-star? Fucking Air Force pukes!" he said without real conviction.

"Yea, well he's actually OK, all things considered. I called him up and told him he owed me for that match. Well, actually I just told him we needed it and not to ask questions. And he came through. Not bad for a bus driver who needs an entire airfield to land an itty-bitty plane."

There was a knock on the hatch, and before the admiral could respond, the Com O and SJA came rushing in. "Sir, we've got another message from the president. The Indians tried to blow the embassy doors, but you have to read this." He handed the admiral a slip of paper.

Rear Admiral Conners read the paper, then passed it to Colonel Lineau. He looked back up to the SJA. "So, the President of the United States has given an executive order to the military to use all available means to affect a rescue. Am I reading this right?"

A broad smile crossed the SJA's face. "Yes admiral, you are. And that just might be your out."

"Do you think that might hold up?"

"It might sir, it just might."

The admiral turned and said with faux formality," Well, Colonel of Marines, it seems like the situation has escalated. Do you think we should obey this executive order?"

"Damn right I do!"

"My feelings exactly." He turned to the SJA. "Please inform Captain Ngata that no further refinement is necessary. We are going with what we have." His tone took a serious bent. "I want the first launch of the Ospreys and Col Lineau's Marines in 30 minutes. Make it happen." He looked at Col Lineau. "It's showtime!"

Chapter 42

Thursday Morning, US Embassy, New Delhi

Since the blast, Sgt Niimoto almost forgot his thirst. He scanned the crowd below. Groups of men had come over the wall and up to the embassy building and back, some glassing the embassy through the gate or from makeshift stands that allowed them to look over the wall. Men had gone into the consulate as well.

Outside the walls, a crowd had begun to gather but were standing around watching while men in civilian clothes seemed to be organizing. Although their clothes may have been civilian, their no-nonsense air was that of military or police.

A sudden increase in shouting below the tower caught his attention. He sidled over to the courtyard side and peaked over. His heart dropped. About fifteen men were manhandling the Marines' 106 out of the auxiliary armory.

While the Marines were re-arming after the embassy takeovers, some Army supply officer found the old mothballed M40A2 106mm recoilless rifles. These were ancient pieces, first introduced during the Vietnam War era. The rifle fired a 106 mm shell, either HEAT, high explosive plastic-tracer (HEP-T), or antipersonnel-tracer (AP-T) flechette rounds. The rifle had an effective range of about 2500 meters, but a good gunner could hit targets far beyond that.

The weapon was brought on target by a ballistically-matched

parallel-mounted M-8C .50 cal. spotting rifle. The trigger was a round knob. Pulling on the knob fired the .50 cal, and when the spotter round hit the desired target, the knob was pushed to fire the 106 mm round. Theoretically, the 106mm round would impact where the .50 cal round had impacted.

The rifle was recoilless because the recoil was not stopped by the breach. Rather, the gases formed by firing the round were ejected out vents in back of the weapon. During weapons training, the instructors had put a wooden ammo case behind the rifle before firing. The backblast smashed the case into splinters.

The weapon was sort of a dinosaur, but one of the powers that be decided that an impressive piece of what looked to be artillery might someday intimidate a violent crowd. No Marines had had to use one yet, but they stayed in the inventories of some 24 embassies.

The weapons were old, but the rounds had been re-packed into plastic casings. Only the flechette rounds were deemed necessary, and each embassy was given 10 rounds.

The rifles themselves were too large to be stored inside most embassy vaults, so a secondary armory was constructed at most embassies near the entrances, and the weapon and rounds were stored there. The spotting rifles and sights were stored along with the other weapons in the main armories.

And now, right below him, the men were manhandling the beast into the courtyard. They got the rifle up on the tripod and pointed it at the door. Sgt Niimoto slowly brought his rifle up and sighted on one of the men. But then he thought that if the satchel charge hadn't damaged the doors, then a flechette round certainly would not. He lowered his weapon and waited.

There was obviously some discussion going on. The Indians probably hadn't seen a recoilless rifle, and they were trying to figure it out. Loading the beast was fairly intuitive, and without too much trouble, a round was loaded and the breach locked into place. One man seemed pretty adamant that he had found the trigger, and he squatted beside it. Without sight, though, aiming the weapon was problematic.

With a growing sense of disbelief, Sgt Niimoto watched as one man squatted in back of the rifle, using his eyes to take general aim on the door. He motioned right and left, up and down, as the rifle was aimed.

Still squatting, he gave a thumb's up to the gunner who reached out and pressed the trigger. There was a huge explosion and dustcloud, and just like the wooden box back at Quantitco, the man in back of the rifle was blown to bits. A mangled torso blew up against the embassy ground's wall. Some men who had been watching over the wall ducked back at the blast. Now they had looked back over and were pointing at the body below them. Others in the gun team walked over to look at the man.

Sgt Niimoto stifled a chuckle. *"Dumbshits,"* he thought. He looked over to the embassy doors, and sure enough, they seemed fine. There might have been a scuff mark high and to the right, but it was not too noticeable. At least the Indians didn't seem to notice it.

He really wished he could understand Hindi. The discussion was getting heated below him. The group of men came back to the rifle, and to Sgt Niimoto's profound amazement, they turned the rifle around so the breach faced the embassy and the muzzle pointed at the wall. They loaded one more round, and a new man stepped up to sight down the barrel and bring the breach in line with the embassy doors. Once everything was aligned, he gave the signal, and the gunner once again pushed the trigger. The blast was just as deafening, but this time the man aiming the weapon took 106 mm of flechette round right below the chin. There was a huge crash as the round continued its course unabated and smashed into the embassy ground's wall. Chips of plaster and brick flew everywhere, some flying up in the air before falling and pattering around Sgt Niimoto like small pieces of hail.

A sound almost like a donkey braying briefly echoed around the courtyard for a moment. Some men looked up trying to see the source, but in the confusion of the moment, they quickly lost interest.

Chapter 43

Thursday Morning, US Embassy, New Delhi

With a sudden click, the lights flickered on. Air began to move as the air conditioner started up. Loralee Howard groaned with pleasure. Gunny felt a moment of elation as well, but the he realized that this was probably not a good sign. Unless it signaled the end of the siege, the power was on because the Indians needed it for something. And after hearing from Sgt Niimoto about the 106 incident (which brought peals of laughter from the Marines and Major Defilice), it didn't look like the siege was over.

He rushed up the ladder and went to Post 1. The screens were flickering to life, the security cameras coming online. Both Little Mac and Rodriguez were watching them as if they could will them to stabilize quicker.

At the edge of the front entrance camera's view could be seen some feet milling about. "Sgt McAllister, get me Niimoto." She pressed the code and handed the phone through the window slot.

"Tony, we've got power now. What's happening out there?"

"Gunny, they've brought in some heavy duty stuff there. It looks like a huge cutting torch."

On the monitor, a group of men pushed the huge cylinder forward. One man put on a welder's helmet and lit a torch. A jet of fire appeared on the screen, a jet of pure white. He raised it up. And as he moved it towards the door, he went out of camera view.

"Maybe it will be an ineffective as the last attempt." Gunny Mac turned around to see the president looking out the ladderwell.

"Sir, I really need to ask you to get back down below. Let's see what this situation will bring."

All eyes turned toward the door. The tensions seemed to ease somewhat until a small puff of smoke appeared inside the entrance.

"Shit," someone said. Gunny wasn't sure who it was.

Gunny picked up the phone again. "Tony, what can you see?"

"I can't really see what the cutter is doing, but I can see people clapping each other in the back. It doesn't look good. Do you want me to take them out?"

"Not yet. I need you up there. And that cutter might give out. If they make an entry, we're going to engage. So wait until we tell you or you hear our shots, then engage them. Try and hit the tank and see if you can get it to blow or something."

"Aye-aye, Gunny. Can do."

Gunny Mac turned around to look at his Marines. "OK, it looks like they might have figured a way in. Sgt Chen, get Steptoe and Kramer. Major Defilice, can I ask you to go down to the vault and stay with the president? Van Slyke, you and Ramon go with him."

The major shrugged and went down the ladder with Van Slyke following. PFc Ramon looked daggers at the Gunny before following

What the fuck's with her? he wondered. Oh well, he had other things to worry about.

"Pat, you and Jesus, there, watch that monitor. We need to know how many are out there and where." As Chen returned with the other two, he turned to them.

"Sgt Chen, take your team and get a good angle. If they open up a hole, fire through it, take them out."

A grin spread over Chen's face. "Gotcha, Gunny." He began to place Steptoe and Kramer, trying to figure out the best positioning.

"Fallgatter and LCpl Saad, join me here in the ladderwell. We are the covering fire."

Everyone moved in position and slowly fell silent. The waiting began. Despite the air conditioning coming back on, sweat began to trickle down Gunny Mac's back. Another puff of smoke appeared. Then a dull orange glow began to diffuse around that spot.

Suddenly, a spark shot through the door and bounced around the deck before fading. PFC Fallgatter let out a yelp, drawing glares from the rest. He looked sheepishly down.

More sparks started shooting in, a steady stream of them. Sgt Chen looked back. "Gunny!" he shout-whispered, "I can almost see outside. I am going to engage!"

"That's your call." Gunny tightened his grip on his weapon.

Sgt Chen crept forward. He looked at the monitor through the Post 1 window, noting the position of the men outside the door. He made a mental adjustment and moved to the left, angling his M18 toward the left. He pushed it forward and blindly fired a three-round burst through the sparks. The sparks suddenly ceased.

There was a whoop from inside Post 1. "You got one of them Chen!" shouted Little Mac. And the rest are clearing out. There were a few shouts from within the embassy, and LCpl Kramer slapped Sgt Chen on the shoulders.

"Quiet everyone. They'll be back, so let's not get too carried away with ourselves. Nice shot, though." Gunny wiped the sweat from his brow. He knew they would return.

Chapter 44

The vice-president rubbed her gritty eyes. She felt disgusting and could really use a shower. She looked around the conference room. Empty coffee cups littered the place, and a steward was bringing in yet another tray of sandwiches. Small groups formed, broke, and formed again, like shoaling fish, discussing, yelling even, pointing at computers or printed reports. For the moment, she was a spot of calm amid the chaos.

She caught the eye of Arnold Hatch, the president's chief of staff, and nodded slightly. He was the only other person seemingly alone at the moment. David had been slowly pushing him aside as events progressed, and no one seemed to notice. No one except for Arnold and the vice-president, that is. Arnold just stared at her for a moment, then looked away.

General Litz, General Kantres, Admiral Keogh, the Navy CNO, and General Johnson, the Air Force Chief of Staff were the center of a group of mostly uniforms in the midst of an animated discussion. General Litz forcefully pointed at the CNO who shook his head, pointing at a printout. The chairman kept glancing up at her, then back at the people surrounding him. He called out to Paul Lefever, who came to join them, and handed him the printout. The secretary started to read the printout when a look of shock came over his face.

"*Well, this can't be good*," she thought. With a little hesitation, the secretary made his way to her followed by the flags. He handed the printout back to General Litz, offering him the floor.

"Madam Vice-President, we just got an op order forwarded to us from PACCOM. It seems that the Regan Battle Group has launched a NEO to rescue the president." He stopped, waiting for her reaction.

She was stunned. "You are telling me what?"

"Ma'am, at 0730 Z, the *Reagan* launched four Ospreys with a contingent of Marines and fighter escort to conduct a NEO."

"Marines? They don't do operations anymore. What are you ...," she trailed off. Of course, now she knew to where all the Marines had disappeared. She looked back up. "And just who authorized this NEO?" Her eyes burned into General Litz.

"Well, according to this op order, it seems that the president did." He handed the vice-president the first page of the printout. "See here? In the Mission Statement? It says '...in compliance with the direct orders of President Michael Eduardo, Commander in Chief....'" He looked at her for a reaction.

"And just when did the president give the Battle Group such an order?" Her tone was demanding.

The general swallowed. "Well, he did, sort of. During our last communications with him."

"That was not a legal order. We have determined that while the president is under duress such as he is now, under isolation as he is now, it's just as if he is under surgery or otherwise temporarily incapacitated, and his orders carry no legal weight. He doesn't know the big picture and cannot make a reasonable decision." She seemed to be reciting this more to convince herself than the others. "Besides, just how did the *Reagan* know about this?'

There were some downcast eyes. "Well Madam Vice-President, we don't know at this time. But we are looking into it."

"Do that. But first, we are not going to war over this. Get a hold of the *Reagan* and pull the plug on this thing." There was some shuffling of feet, and the vice-president felt a pang of apprehension.

"Madam Vice-President, we regret to inform you that we have been out of touch with the commander up until now..." Admiral Keogh held up a satphone. "... we were already going to do that, but the NEO task force, well it is completely out of communications. They've got a Big Eye," he looked furtively around the room, "and it has put a dead zone around them. The Big Eye can cut off all…"

"Yes, I know all about the Big Eye, General. I helped fund the prototypes. I know what it can do. General Johnson, the Big Eye is one of yours. Contact the crew and shut this off."

"There seems to be a temporary communications problem with the Big Eye." She looked embarrassed. "We haven't been able to raise it."

"Temporary problem?" So that was how this was going to be played. The vice-president began to feel control slipping away.

"According to the op order, there will be a window, at 0947 Z, that is a little over an hour from now, where the Big Eye will shut down the telecommunications jamming. They want to try and contact the president and also give out a warning to bystanders to get away because they are going to drop a Mk402. They want to minimize casualties. We can use that window to shut this off." General Litz looked hopeful.

"And where is this task force now?" she asked dryly.

"General Litz looked back to one of his strap-hangers who whispered in his ear. The general turned back to her. "According to our calculations, it should be over Indian air space now. We are trying to get a visual with our satellites now."

"Who is the commander of the Battle Group?"

Admiral Keogh stepped up, satphone in hand. "Rear Admiral Joshua Conners. Do you want to talk to him? I've got him standing by." He held out the phone helpfully.

The vice-president sat in thought for a moment. The dice had been thrown. If she picked them up from the table now, history would look on her as a weak. If the NEO could somehow work, she would be the strong vice-president who took forceful action. And if the NEO failed, well, she would be hanging her hat at 1600 Pennsylvania, and she could worry about weathering the storm from the pacifist crowd later. It was time for damage control.

"I don't know about any of you, but I am sick-and-tired about all this BS stonewalling we are getting from the Indians. It is time to put an end to this. If the *Reagan* and some Marines have found an opportunity to get this down, then we sure the hell are going to back them up."

The faces around her were stunned, to say the least. She looked at Dr. Ryan, who had pushed her way into the group once it was obvious something big was up. "Get word to the bystanders around the embassy somehow, that they need to get out of the area. But don't do it too early. Just give them enough time to move back. A Mk 402 does not have that big of an effective casualty radius. Then prepare statements to give the Indian government through our friends stressing that this is not an act of war, but merely a NEO on what is officially our sovereign soil. Oh, and get Secretary Pitt off the ground now. I don't want him still sitting at the airport when this all goes down."

She paused for a moment. "General Kantres, maybe it's time to move the Quick Reaction Force. The barn door may already be open, but you never know.

"Come on people. Let's get going on this. What else do we need to do to ensure a successful operation? Let's go!"

There was an explosion of noise as people rushed to phones and computers.

Chapter 45

Thursday Morning, US Embassy, New Delhi

More and more men were coming into the courtyard with a sense of purpose. Sgt Niimoto watched them flank the door and take positions behind the columns. There were probably fifty or so men crowded down there. One man had picked up the torch again, lit it off, and was trying to sidle up to the small cut and enlarge it while staying out of the line of fire.

"Aye-aye, Gunny. I'll wait. I'll try for the cylinder first, and it that doesn't work, I am going to start taking them out." He placed the phone down and raised his weapon. The last exchange had happened too fast for him to get off a shot, and he was not going to be left holding the bag this time.

The metalworker did not have a good angle for a nice clean cut, but the opening was nevertheless getting longer. Everyone was focused on the cut. A burst of muffled gunfire rang out, almost too muffled for his to hear up in the tower, but the sudden hail of return fire left little doubt as to what had happened. Sgt Niimoto focused on the cylinder and slowly squeezed off a shot. Nothing happened. He could see rounds chips of plaster and stone fly as rounds from inside the embassy and rounds from outside which impacted the doors ricocheted around. He sighted again and squeezed off another shot. Again, nothing. It looked as if his rounds didn't have enough penetrating power to do anything to the heavy cylinder. OK, he would shift to more lively targets.

As he acquired a target, a man with a black t-shirt crouching behind a column, the volume of fire slowed, then stopped. Men peered around at the door, and the metal worker picked himself up from where he had hit the deck, picked up the torch, and tentatively with encouragement from the others, started his cut again. He worked a small circle, and with a big shower of sparks, that circle fell into the embassy, leaving a rough 12-inch hole in the door. Someone gave a shout, and the Indians started firing into the hole. One man, tall and rangy, approached from the side with what looked to be a grenade. Sgt Niimoto shifted his aim, and as the man reached out to throw the grenade in, he took the shot.

The round, traveling at over 1200 feet per second, impacted the man's right shoulder and entered his chest cavity. He staggered, dropping the grenade. A few men must have thought he had thrown it into the hole as they started firing again, but the shot man understood. Sgt Niimoto could clearly see the look of resignation on his face as he fell to a sitting position, staring at the grenade. There was an explosion, and Sgt Niimoto instinctively flinched. When he looked back through the scope, he could see the battered body of the man up against the embassy wall, blood welling beneath him. Another gunman, one of the ones in back of a column, was writhing in pain, clutching his leg. Sgt Niimoto could hear the man's shouts from up in the tower. There was an increase fusillade of fire as two men ran up and grabbed the wounded man by the shoulders, dragging him out of the line-of-fire from inside the embassy.

Something small and round came out the hole. One of the Marines had thrown his own grenade. With a shout, the gunmen threw themselves flat. Trying to compose himself, Sgt Niimoto took aim at a gunman, and when the grenade went off off, he pulled off a shot. He quickly re-acquired the target only to see nothing. The man was unharmed. He has missed. Pulling off a shot accurately was much harder than squeezing off a shot. He gave a grunt and slapped himself alongside his head. He had to do better.

He looked down at his remaining rounds: eight more in the clip and ten more arrayed in front of him. He had to make these count.

As the metalworker edged his way forward again, Sgt Niimoto put the scope's crosshairs on the man's shoulder blade. Reconsidering, he moved the aiming point to the man's spine. At this flat angle, he didn't want the round skipping along the man's shoulder blades. The man nervously crept forward, then reached out again and started cutting. Another man crept up along the opposite side of the cut and reached his weapon around, firing into the hole without exposing his body. Sgt Niimoto let out half a breath and squeezed this time. The rifle chuffed and kicked against his shoulder. He quickly shifted aim and squeezed again, aiming center mass at the gunman firing right into the embassy.

The first round impacted the metalworker directly on his spine, on the C7 vertebrae. The 178 grain round shattered the bone, sending shards throughout the unfortunate man's lungs and heart. He was dead before he knew he had been hit. The second round also entered its target's back, but lower and to the left. The gunman dropped, then tried to crawl out of the way. Another man rushed over to help him.

Two men crept up the grab the feet of the metalworker and drag him alongside the edge of the embassy building. A large, heavyset man met them and turned the prone body over. He seemed to notice something, then quickly tore off the dead man's shirt. Sgt Niimoto has a sinking feeling as the man checked the body for an entrance wound on the chest. He flipped the body back over, pulled the bloody shirt back, and touched the wound there. Sgt Niimoto could clearly see the confused expression on the man as he checked the dead man's chest, then the understanding dawn on is face as he looked at the dead man's back. Hand still on the wound, he suddenly looked back over the courtyard and up. With one of the odd chances in combat, he happened to look directly at the tower and caught sight of Sgt Niimoto aiming down at him.

He brought his rifle to bear, not wanting to fire like this, to expose himself. He never really thought to drop back down out-of-sight as that would only prolong things. And he really did not want to hide anymore. He wanted to face his enemies. Through the scope, Sgt Niimoto could see the man's eyes widen, a shout beginning to form as he started to swing his own weapon around. Tony Niimoto smoothly pulled back on the trigger sending the boattail round down from the tower, across the courtyard, and into the man's throat. The man fell as if pole axed, and Sgt Niimoto swung his weapon to take aim on one of the two men who had dragged the metalworker. To his surprise, he jumped back and started pointing back at the embassy door. Somehow, they thought the round which had taken out the man had come from inside the embassy. Sgt Niimoto sighed with relief.

Over the next 15 minutes or so, Sgt Niimoto became a machine. Pick a target, wait for fire, then squeeze off a round. He took out a replacement metalworker with a headshot, but most were other gunmen. Fifteen shots, fifteen hits. Twelve obvious kills. He had contemplated keeping the last round for himself, like they do in the movies, but he realized that that would help nobody in the embassy, so he used it to take out an automatic rifleman who was pouring fire into the hole.

He had called into the embassy to let them know he was out of ammo and to ask what he should do. They were understandably a little busy, but through PFC Rodriguez, Gunny told him to hold fast and wait. So he was waiting now. Yet another metalworker was cutting away at the door now, making progress. He had at least three quarters of a large square cut out, an opening which would be large enough to let at least two men enter abreast. And Sgt Niimoto didn't have way to stop him.

He looked back on the other side of the wall. There were a dozen or more men up on the makeshift stands, watching the progress of the men at the door. As he watched, one of the men seemed to be having problems with his phone. He kept looking at it. Then trying to call someone. He tapped a man next to him and said something. The man handed him his phone, but that one didn't seem to be much better. Bad com will kill you, he thought, as he moved back to watch the bad news. Now that his killing mode had passed, he was thirsty again. But somehow, that didn't seem so important anymore.

Chapter 46

Thursday Morning, US Embassy, New Delhi

When the first piece of the door fell in, a small circle of about 12 inches in diameter, incoming fire had intensified, and a round skipped off the deck to hit Sgt Chen in the calf. He seemed more angry than hurt, and he returned fire, cursing up a storm. But Gunny could tell that the shock was now setting in. Chen was quieter, somewhat distant. But he refused to go below.

The first grenade to come flying in somehow took them by surprise, despite the fact that they expected it. But when it happened, it still came as a surprise at the moment. Somehow, no one was hit. The second grenade had dinged LCpl Steptoe, though. Nothing serious, but sobering none-the-less.

And now Sgt Niimoto was out of the picture. He had probably single-handedly kept the gunmen out of the embassy for the last twenty or thirty minutes, but there was nothing he could do now. And the Marines watched almost mesmerized as the new cut line slowly grew along the door. LCpl Kramer had tried to get enough of an angle to take out the man on the torch, but the hole was too small, and the volume of incoming drove him back. It was only matter of time now before the opening was cut.

No one had thought to disable the security cameras, so they could

189

see on the monitors the gunmen massing to storm the embassy. A mass of fire suddenly came in the opening.

"Mother fucker! Again!" Sgt Chen grasped his calf, right where he had been hit before. Another round had hit him, almost in the same place. Kramer rushed over to where Chen lay in back of Post 1.

"Chen, you OK?" asked Gunny Mac.

"Oh sure, Gunny, if you count those cocksuckers shooting me in the goddamn leg again as being OK." He muffled some curses and Kramer bound the leg again, wrapping the bandage right over the existing one.

More rounds came to ricochet around the entrance. This position was becoming untenable. He heard a shout from below him. "What's happening up there?" It was the president, followed by a sheepish-looking Army major.

He shouted down, "Mr. President, can you please go back to the vault? We can't do our job here if we have to worry about you. Major Defilice, can you please escort him back?" They looked up at him, then moved back out of sight. Probably not back to the vault, he thought, but it was better than nothing.

He moved back to where he could see out the ladderwell hatch. The opening was getting close to being cut through. Well, he had to make some changes.

"OK, everybody listen up. We'll pull back to the ladderwell and try to secure the hatch here. When they get in, they'll probably take time to search the ground floor, and that'll give us time. We're going down to the bottom deck where we can mass our fire. You know, like the Spartans when they fought the Persians. Let them come at us in small numbers. Sgt Chen, we need to carry you. I don't want your blood to leave a trail to the ladderwell. OK? Let's move it."

"Uh Gunny?" It was Sgt McAlister, speaking through the voice grill of the post. He turned around with a questioning look.

She looked at PFC Rodriguez who gave a slight nod. "Well, like we told you before, me and Jesus here, well, we kind of figure we should stay here."

"No, I want you to fall back. We can't stay here."

"General Order Number 5, Gunny."

"I told you before, I am relieving you."

"Well, we don't see it that way." She paused, taking a deep breath. "Look Gunny, we can cover that opening there, when they get it. We can fire right under the document slot and cover the whole thing. This glass here is bulletproof, so what can they do to us? You need the time, and we can give it to you. "She paused again. "You know we are right."

Gunny's mind raced. He wanted to pull them back, to keep them safer. His thoughts flashed for a brief second to Colonel Parks, trying to teach his very green driver so long ago what it meant to be a leader. Now he knew what the colonel meant.

The cut line on the door was getting close to being completed. The rest of the Marines were waiting on his decision.

"Besides, Gunny. We're all probably going to catch it today, and we'd rather go out on Post than hiding in some dark vault, probably getting shot in the ass by Fallgatter or Ramon." She laughed.

He made his decision. "Roger that, Sergeant. Man your post." He raised up his arm in a salute. Both Little Mac and Rodriquez came to quasi-attention and returned the salute.

"You've got balls, Pat. You too Jesus." He turned to the others. "All right, let's move it."

LCpl Kramer and PFC Fallgatter picked up Sgt Chen and carried him to the ladderwell and down below. LCpl Steptoe wiped up a few drops of blood dripped from Chen to the deck. Gunny Mac turned to look one more time at Post 1 before closing the hatch, but both Sgt MacAllister and PFC Rodriguez were attentively watching the embassy door. The hatch swung shut, cutting off his view of them.

He hurried down the ladder, a two flight set of stairs with a landing between. When at the bottom, he could see the first floor hatch by looking up the middle between the sets of steps. Gathered at the bottom was the rest of the party, everyone except for the two in Post 1. They all looked to him.

"Well, they're almost in. I don't know how long we can keep them out, but we are sure going to try. Sgt McAllister and PFC Rodriguez have volunteered to stay at Post 1." He could see Loralee quickly lower her head in prayer. "Frankly, I don't know how long they can hold out, but it's a good position."

"Well, we can keep them under observation, at least. So we know." Major Defilice looked at the Gunny.

"What do you mean, sir? How can we do that?" Then it dawned on him "Yes! The auxiliary security closet." He rushed down the passage almost to the vault and opened a small room full of monitors. This was a redundant monitoring station that monitored inside various embassy spaces. It was not under Marine control, so it had slipped his mind. Others following him tried to crowd inside, but the space was too small.

"Sgt Chen, take Kramer and Fallgatter and take a position at the bottom of the ladder. We need to hit them if they get that far."

Everyone else crowded the best they could to get a view of the second monitor, the one which showed inside Post 1. Both Marines were alert and ready. Sgt McAllister had her hand on Rodriguez's shoulder. Inside the space it was silent, the only sound the breathing in and out of nine sets of lungs.

Suddenly, Rodriguez pointed. The monitor had no sound, but his shout was evident. Both Marines put the muzzles of their weapons out the document slots and pulled the triggers. The reports could be heard in the distance, coming past the closed hatches, then down the ladder well and passage. They could hear the answering fire as well.

The glass of the post seemed to shudder as Rodriguez ducked, then he straightened up and reloaded before firing again. A sound of an explosion reached the watching group. A grenade must have been employed, but the Post was pretty strong.

"How long can they last?" It was the president, concern evident in his voice. To Gunny, it seemed like the concern was actually for the two Marines, not for his own personal safety.

"I don't know, sir. It depends on what weapons they have."

"Shouldn't we go do something?" It was Ramon, who sat clutching her M18, looking oversized in her grip.

"No Ramon, we shouldn't. If we open the hatch, they'll know where we are, and that's that. Those two Marines have pretty good protection now. And they knew what they were doing. We won't John Wayne it and let their decision go to waste."

Talking ceased again as they watched the screen. Coolly, Sgt

McAllister and PFC Rodriguez took turns firing out the port. It looked like they were on the range without a care in the world.

Gunny's pocket started to vibrate, an awareness that crept up on him, so intent he was on the monitor. Puzzled, he reached into his pocket and pulled out his phone. It was ringing as if nothing was wrong. The incongruity struck him. He flipped it open. "Hello?"

The woman's voice on the other end seemed frantic. "Gunny McCardle, is that you?"

"Yes it is. Who is this?"

"Hey, I've got somebody," he could hear her shout to someone else before she came back to him. "Gunny, this is Major Rogers. Is the president with you? Is he OK?"

"Yes ma'am, he is. As far as OK, well, we're under attack right now, and frankly, I don' know how long we can hold out." He knew the major, of course. It was a small Corps. And the voice did sound like hers.

"Gunny, we don't have much time. I'm surprised we got a hold of you as it is. You've got to hold out longer. "In…" There was a pause. "In twenty-two minutes, the Navy is going to drop a big-ass bomb on the embassy, danger close. This is a Mk402, and it won't destroy the embassy but it will mess up anyone outside and suck up a lot of the oxygen. Get everyone as close to the center of the building as possible. We'll be there right after that, so get ready."

He was a little confused. "You're coming?"

"I'm out to sea, but the Colonel has every swinging dick he could find and they're coming in to get you. Look, we'll be cut off any sec. Where do you have the president?"

"On the lower level, in the vault."

"OK, I'll tell them, if I can raise them. Get in that vault and hunker down." The line was cut.

"Who was that? I thought the phones didn't work," LCpl Steptoe asked curiously.

Gunny stared at the phone for a second. He couldn't believe it. Rescue?

"Everybody, listen up. The 'Dant is coming to get us. I don't know how. But that was Major Rogers on the phone. So all we have to do is hold on a little longer, and we're home free. "

There was a sudden explosion of sound as everyone tried to talk at once. "Quiet everyone!" he shouted. "We need to move back to the vault. They've got some sort of bomb they are going to use to prep the place."

He thought of the two Marines in Post 1. He hoped the Post would protect them from the bomb. They just had to hold out a little longer. If they could, then this was going to work. He looked back up the monitor. McAllister and Rodriguez were still calmly alternating their shots, one covering the other while that Marine reloaded.

His hopeful optimism fell as on the screen, they could see Sgt McAllister fall back, hand to her throat, then fall out of camera range to the deck. There was a collective shout in the closet. A seeing eye round must have found its way through the slot and into the post. They could see PFc Rodriguez turn around and look down at her, then they could see him shout and move to the slot and empty his clip. As he fumbled with this clip to reload, he looked up and out the post glass, yelling. Several barrels poked into view, through the document ports, and muzzle flashes filled the screen. They could faintly hear the gunfire above them as they saw PFC Rodriguez fall back.

There was muffled shouting in the deck above them, celebratory shouting.

The president seemed shocked. "They're gone! Just like that!"

Gunny tried to think. He needed time, and he had to act now. He grabbed LCpl Steptoe and Saad and rushed back down the passage to the ladderwell. He looked at the three Marines there. "Look, Post 1 just fell. But the 'Dant is coming with the rest of the Marines to get us out of here. We need time, though. In about twenty minutes, there's gonna be one mother of a bomb landing on us, but it isn't going to bring the place down. So we need a diversion." He looked at Chen. No, Chen couldn't run. "Kramer, Steptoe, Saad, I want you to quietly go up the ladder. Go to the second deck. If and when these yahoos open the hatch, light them up, then run like hell. Keep them chasing you. We've got three more decks up there, make them chase you. But in seventeen minutes, get into a closet or head in the middle of the building and hunker down. Keep them away from the president. You got it?"

All three nodded. "Then go. Quietly now. Remember, they're

right outside that hatch there." The three Marines started carefully up the ladder.

"Sgt Chen, you take Fallgatter here and cover the bottom of the ladder. And keep quiet!"

"I think I'll join them here. It sounds like fun." It was Drayton. He was smiling, but his hands were trembling and his face pale.

Gunny clapped him on the shoulder. "Roger that."

He ran back down the passageway. "Mr. President, I have to insist on you getting into the vault now. You too, Loralee."

"Where did those three soldiers… sorry, Marines go?"

"Sir, we need more time, so they'll draw anyone to the upper decks and away from you."

"So they are sacrificing themselves, too?" He seemed distraught.

"I hope not, Mr. President. I hope they buy us all enough time to get out of here."

"Gunnery Sergeant!" It was Mr. Dravid. Gunny Mac kept forgetting that he was around. "You need these attacking men to go upstairs?" Without waiting for an answer, he ran down the passage.

Gunny instinctively brought up his weapon, but realizing that fire would draw attention to them, he held off. He tried to signal Sgt Chen, but by that time, Mr. Dravid was already climbing up the ladder. Gunny rushed to look up, but Mr. Dravid passed the first deck hatch and kept on up. Gunny hoped that was a good sign.

He looked at his watch. They had fifteen minutes until the prep fire. He wheeled back and ran as quietly as he could back to the vault. Major Defilice and PFC Ramon were at the hatch. Inside, Loralee had taken an M18 off a table where the extra weapons had been put and was loading it. She looked up and caught the Gunny's eye. "You think I'm just going to sit here?"

The president looked at her. "I think I'll take one, too."

Gunny looked to Van Slyke. "Prep the president on that. Make sure he knows how to use it." He looked around. "We need to be ready to pull this hatch shut. I'll get Sgt Chen to lock it."

The vault had a unique safety feature, one which made little sense to the gunny. While it had a safety release inside the vault, it could not be locked from inside. It had to be locked from the outside. So if worst came to worst, and they needed to seal the hatch of the vault, to lock it, then someone had to be outside of the vault to do that. It had to be done from the outside.

A flurry of motion caught Gunny's eye. It was Sgt Chen, motioning up the ladderwell. There was a burst of fire from above, and then Mr. Dravid's voice could be heard shouting something. Hindi-sounding voices responded, then there was the sound of rushing footsteps going up the stairs.

Gunny crept forward. No one seemed to be coming down. He hoped the ploy would work, and he hoped his Marines would survive their efforts. Sporadic gunfire echoed from above. At least they hadn't been caught yet. He looked at his watch. Eight minutes.

He moved back to the security closet and looked in, but not much could be seen on any of the screens. A few passing bodies, a few shadows.

He barely heard a plunk, plunk, plunk as something came down the ladder, bouncing on step after step. He looked up just as a quiet "shit" echoed down the passage. The explosion was deafening in the confined spaces. Shrapnel whined as it flew down the passage towards them. The blast stunned him for a second, then he gathered his wits and looked down towards the ladder.

Sergeant Greg Chen, Private First Class Michael Fallgatter, and Drayton Bajinski lay shredded at the end of the passageway. PFC Fallgatter gave a moan and moved his arm when a burst of fire ripped into him.

Gunny whipped around and dived toward the vault. With Major Defilice, he pulled the hatch partway shut. As a shape came into view to inspect the bodies, both men opened fire, and the body fell. Gunny looked at his watch. Six minutes.

A rifle came around the corner and sprayed down the passage, hitting nothing before being pulled back. Gunny fired on the rifle, but missed. He knew what had to be done.

He looked around the vault, at each face there. He finally settled on Van Slyke, his face still bandaged. He was a good man. "PFC Van Slyke. You and me. We're going to go out there and secure the hatch." There was an explosion as another grenade was rolled down the ladder. "Major, if I can ask you to keep the president safe here. Hopefully relief will get here soon." He got up as Van Slyke came forward.

"No!" It was PFC Ramon. She took a deep breath. "You've ignored me since I've got here, you have ignored me for the last two days since this stuff started. I'm a Marine, dammit, and not a 'Princess.' Peter can barely see out of his eye, and Gunny, you're as bad a shot as I am. But you need to be in charge here. It's the mission that is important here. Greg and I are going." She indicated Major Defilice, who stood there with a wry look on his face.

"No Ivy, I want you to stay here. Van Slyke and I will go."

"Dammit Gunny, didn't you hear me? For once, you'll let me be a Marine!" She glared at him.

"Gunny, I don't think I'd stand in her way." It was the major. And I think we need to go pretty quick." He whipped off another shot down the passage.

She stared at him for another moment, then swept her arm, clearing off files from a heavy table. "Greg, help me with this." They started pushing it toward the door.

"Wait a minute." The major walked up to her and stood her up. He bent down and picked her up, her feet dangling a good eighteen inches off the ground. He looked at her for a moment, then kissed her solidly on the lips. Her arms curled in back of his neck. They stopped, and stared in each other's eyes for a moment before he put her down. Without comment, they pushed the table out the door.

Loralee's eyes glistened, and she quickly wiped them. "Well," was all she could say.

As the door started to close, Gunny hit the side of his head with his hand. *How could he have forgotten Tony?*

"Wait!" He grabbed the landline and dialed up Sgt Niimoto. "Come on, answer, answer!"

MAJ Defilice fired down the passage again. "Uh Gunny, a little urgency?"

"Yea?" Niimoto here."

"Tony, no time. In three minutes, the embassy is going to get hit with a Mk402. You've got to take any cover you can. Any!" The line went dead as the door of the vault was shoved shut, cutting the wire.

Chapter 47

The vault door closed with a sense of certainty. Major Defilice put his shoulder to it and hit the keypad to lock it. Somehow, though, PFC Ramon did not feel alone. She looked up at the major and smiled. Well, it was time to get going. She turned around and started pushing the heavy metal table.

"Ivy, let me push, you cover me." She was still hyped for standing up to Gunny, and she bristled for a second before relenting. He was right. He could push this easily alone. He bent down, and he pushed the table along edgewise, so the top of it preceded them like a bulldozer blade. It was a heavy metal table, and should stop quite a bit of anything thrown at them.

Ivy followed, weapon at the ready, pointing over the table. Twice, she fired as they made their way down the passage. Almost there, a grenade bounced down the steps. "Down!" she shouted. The impact was loud and the shock wave actually moved the table a few inches. They both instinctively stuck their heads over the edge to check it, but nothing penetrated the heavy tabletop. They smiled at each other with relief and started moving again.

As they approached the opening, they both sidled to the front wall. An arm came around the corner with a rifle, and Ivy snapped off a burst, surprisingly hitting the arm. With a shout, the arm was yanked back while the rifle it had been holding fell to the ground, bouncing until it came to a stop on top of Drayton. Ivy felt a little gorge rise in her throat as she looked at the four men lying there, the three Americans and one Indian gunman.

Greg looked at her, grabbed her hand and gave it a squeeze. Despite the intense circumstances, she felt a wave of affection roll over her.

He positioned the table and gave her the signal to cover him. She stood up and fired up the ladder while he pushed the table out to block the bottom. Sgt Chen's body served to help anchor it in place. It may not have been much of an obstacle, but maybe it would stop the grenades from being rolled down on top on them.

There was a shout from above and a thud of descending feet. Greg stood, cool as a cucumber and fired. Ivy ducked under his arm and fired her own burst. Two bodies fell to the landing, just a couple feet away from them. They both ducked back as return fire peppered the ladderwell. The burst stopped and was followed by a small cascade of spent brass, which bounced down the stairs.

There were some voices from above, then the plunk, plunk, plunking of a falling grenade. They both leaned back as the grenade lodged against the table and detonated. Except for her ringing ears, Ivy was untouched.

She could feel Greg's big body lean against her, hard and powerful. This was a man. She looked at him and knew then that this was the man for her, the one who could meet her expectations. She wanted to spend the rest of her life with him.

There was another mad rush down the stairs. Again, they both popped out, one low and the other high. Again, they forced the retreat. The major looked down at the private first class and smiled. "Some fun, huh?"

They could hear discussion in Hindi going on above them. As it stopped, several grenades came bounding down the stairs, exploding against the table. As soon as they detonated, a bum's rush of steps came down. They both struggled back up to engage, firing up the ladder. Without a sound, Maj Defilice fell back, rifle falling from his hands. Ivy stopped and looked. A round had hit him high on the forehead. His eyes were open, but looking at nothing. Just like that, he was gone.

More men rushed down the steps firing into the major's prone and unmoving body. A sense of rage engulfed her. Even here, even now, she was being ignored. She turned and fired into the mass of men, dropping two of them.

"I am a Marine! Remember that! Private First Class Ivy Huertas Ramon, USMC!" One man stumbled and fell down the steps to come up against the table. Ivy leaned over and crushed his nose with a vicious swing of her rifle butt. She felt a sharp pain high in her chest and looked down in amazement at the small flower of red blossoming up over her left breast. It hurt, but not as much as she might have imagined it would, and otherwise, she felt fine. Somehow, the round had not hit anything vital, but the bright red blood welling on her white t-shirt made for a vivid image.

The man who shot her looked at her in amazement as well. Ivy swung up her weapon and put two rounds in his chest.

The next round took her low and in the stomach. She felt the mulekick and sat down, in back of the table, confused. Her breathing became difficult, and she glanced down to see a growing red stain along her belly. She looked over at Greg and leaned over, head on his chest. She slowly reached over and touched his face, feeling the stubble, taking in the strong jaw, strong now even in death.

"Oh Daddy," she thought, " you'd have liked him so."

She slowly faded away. She never felt the shock of the huge explosion that rocked the embassy.

Chapter 48

Thursday Morning, US Embassy, New Delhi

Tony Niimoto watched the battle unfolding beneath him. The cut which finally made an opening in the door had come accompanied by a cheer from the men outside the embassy. Now men were leaning in, firing, and falling back. Others reached around to throw grenades, which echoed oddly across the courtyard.

He felt elation as some of the men fell. A few were pulled back alongside the edge of the wall, but three lay on the ground, across the threshold of the door, quite obviously dead. Someone in there was kicking some ass, and for every gunman hit, Sgt Niimoto felt a lift.

Those small lifts could not overcome the feeling of helplessness and despair overtaking him, though. Being able to see and hear a battle, one in which his fellow Marines were engaged, and not being able to do anything, well, that was its own kind of hell.

He had contemplated trying to sneak down to the 106, still in the courtyard below him, thinking somehow to turn it on the men assaulting the doorway. But the number of men in the courtyard and on the embassy walls covering those inside made him realize that any move there would be useless.

Three gunmen seemed to gather themselves. They shouted at each other, and in a concerted rush, ran into the opening. All three fell before even getting into the embassy. One stumbled on one of the bodies already lying there and was hit. The other two managed to get to the threshold before falling. The bodies were piling up.

A voice from on top of the wall shouted across the courtyard. One of the men cupped his ear, and the voice repeated itself. There was an acknowledgment. Then several men got prone and crept up along the edge of the wall. They reached out and began to pull the bodies back. A burst of fire challenged them, and one man was hit in the arm, but the bodies were cleared and dragged out of the way.

A group of a dozen or so men climbed over the wall and sidled forward, out of the line of fire. They joined the other gunmen and conversed for a few moments. All of them moved forward into position just to the left of the opening. Several grenades were thrown in, and upon their detonation, the men made a mad rush into the embassy. Several fell, but at least fifteen made it in. There was a furious exchange of fire for about 30 seconds, then the fire ceased. A moment later, a gunman came to the door and out onto the steps, signaling the men on the wall. There was a cheer from the men there, and another couple dozen hurried over the wall, across the courtyard, and into the embassy. Several of the men pushed in the cutting equipment that had made the breach in the door. Sgt Niimoto's heart fell.

Sick, he sat back down, back against the cupola wall. There didn't seem to be much hope. He began to wonder what he should do. He really hadn't thought he would be in this position. Surely someone would have noticed him by now. Heck, when he laughed out loud over the 106 firing, he thought he'd blown it. But he was still sitting in the tower, unnoticed and ignored.

He could hear a few bursts of gunfire from deep inside the embassy, but he didn't bother to look. He couldn't bear it. He wondered at his chances if he simply walked out and tried to act like a bystander. It was probably his best chance. He moved over and looked at the crowd outside the embassy grounds.

Well, it looked as if whatever problem there had been with the telephones was over. People were now talking on them. There were about a hundred of the military-looking men there, many peering over the edge of the wall or through the gate now that fire from inside the embassy had ceased. There were also a couple hundred people just watching from outside the walls, unable to actually see inside the embassy compound. Some were taking photos or videos, some were just chatting. One man was wheeling a cart with some sort of fried snack, not getting far as people kept stopping him to buy. Well, he was just going to have to try and mingle and slowly move through the crowd and to one of the other embassies.

An official-looking car came rushing up from the distance, tires squealing. Two men jumped out and began to yell at the crowd. One of the military-looking types came over to challenge the men, but one of them grabbed his arm and began gesturing with huge expansive weeps of his arms. Bystanders began to gather around. Sgt Niimoto wondered what the heck that was about when he saw his phone flashing with a call. He picked up the receiver listlessly.

"Yea?" Niimoto here."

It was the gunny, his voice elevated with stress. "Tony, no time. In three minutes, the embassy is going to get hit with a Mk402. You've got to take any cover you can. Any!" The line cut off.

Sgt Niimoto started at the receiver. He really had no idea what a Mk402 was, but it couldn't be good. And only three minutes? There was no way he could get down the stairs, confront the men on the wall, and somehow get out of there. And with the access to the consulate sealed, he could not even make it there.

"Shit, shit, shit, shit, shit!" What was he going to do? He looked about the cupola wildly. He wondered if the walls of the campamile would protect him. They were pretty strong. He crept over and crouched down against the wall. He felt awfully vulnerable.

Crouching there, his eyes caught the bell. That was a pretty strong piece of gear there. He scuttled over to the bell and crawled underneath it. There was a gap of about 18 inches between the bottom of the bell and the deck, but at least he'd be protected from overhead fire, he thought. But that gap seemed pretty big now. Awfully big. But how could he lower the bell?

He could hit the red lever on the wall, of course, but then he'd be outside. How could he do it from the inside? He climbed partway out from under the huge bell, then grabbed the first aid box, expecting the incoming bomb at any second. He quickly pulled it in and opened it. Bandages, splints, the oxygen bottle, ointments. He grabbed a roll of bandages. Would that work?

Feverishly, he unrolled the bandage. It certainly looked long enough, but did he have enough time? How long did Gunny say? He took a deep breath and made his decision.

Scooting under the edge of the bell, he ran over to the control lever, standing upright despite being in view of those below. He tried to tie the bandage on the lever and gave it a short tug. The bandage came undone.

"Shit!" He told himself to calm down, then he tied a more substantial knot. That should hold. Carefully, he unraveled the bandage as he made his way back to the bell and crawled back under. He carefully and slowly pulled the bandage. The lever moved, then held up. Taking a deep breath, Sgt Niimoto put more pressure on the bandage. He could see it start to untie, but the lever suddenly slipped into position, and the bell began to drop. Sgt Niimoto slid back to the middle of the bell as it slowly came down. Eighteen inches, twelve inches, eight inches, six inches. There was a huge pressure wave which slammed the belfry, and an outrushing of air. Sgt Niimoto felt the explosion more than heard it, then he felt nothing more.

Chapter 49

Thursday Morning, Sadar Patel Marg, New Delhi

D r. Amarin Suphantarida felt frustrated, useless and tired. He had
been in to see the Minister twice, but beyond some platitudes,
nothing was really said. He had an interesting meeting the evening
before, though. Along with Mohammed Kalhil of the Arab League,
he had been asked to meet with representatives of the Indian National
Party. There, they had been told that the continuing situation was an
anathema to international relations, and that they were appalled that
there had yet to be a peaceful resolution. The undercurrent Pui felt
was that they wanted the two of them to let the Americans know that
this situation could be laid at the feet of the current administration, and
should their party somehow slide into power, they would be stalwart
allies of the US.

But from the current government, there was really no concrete
action. So the siege at the US Embassy was still underway, and the US
president may or may not even be alive. No one knew for sure what was
the situation at the embassy. Both CNN and BBC, which had been
broadcasting live satellite views of the embassy grounds, had been cut off
in India a few hours before, and now with the phones out, he couldn't
get updates from back in Thailand.

He had taken his driver to try and get closer to the embassy to see
if he could get a better feel of things, but he had been stopped and told

to wait by the stadium where an Indian spokesperson would supposedly brief the foreign press.

He sat sweltering in the car as the temperature slowly climbed. Even for a Thai, New Delhi sure could get hot. Much to his surprise, his phone suddenly rang. He grabbed it, almost tearing his pocket in his hurry to get it. "Hello?"

"Pui, this is Rick. Don't ask questions, but where are you? Are you at the site?"

Surprised, he answered "At National Stadium. Why? What…?"

"Look. In about nine minutes, the US military will drop a Mk402 bomb on the embassy grounds. Most of the blast should remain within the embassy grounds. Don't ask me how. But there's concern that people close to the grounds may be within the casualty radius. The bomb sucks up the oxygen, and there can be internal damage to people too close. We need someone to get over there and get as many people away from the embassy as possible. Can you do it?"

The Thai ambassador looked at his phone. If there was some sort of big bomb coming, well, quite frankly, he wanted to get as far away as possible. He was at least a thousand meters from it now, but more sounded better. Instead, he calmly responded.

"Of course, Rick. I am on it right now." He hung up and told his driver to rush to the embassy.

His driver protested that they could not get there, so Pui took the extra fifteen seconds to explain the situation. To his credit, the Indian driver took off, and when an armed policeman tried to stop them at a roadblock, he blew right past him.

The embassy could barely be seen down the tree-lined boulevard, but people in front of it certainly were evident. He was mentally counting down the seconds as they rushed up.

A couple of hundred meters from the embassy, the driver pulled the car into a sliding stop. They both jumped out, and the driver started yelling in Hindi. For a moment, no one seemed to pay attention to him. The slowly, people began to gather. An officious-looking man, in black paramilitary-type clothes and carrying a rifle, came up and began to shout. His driver shouted back, nonplussed. The ambassador looked at his watch.

"Look. I am the Royal Thai Ambassador to India. In less than a minute, there is going to be a huge explosion at the embassy, and anyone too close is in danger. You've got to get your men back as well as all these people."

When he mentioned an explosion, at least one of the bystanders understood English, because he shouted out to the crowd in Hindi. There was a gasp, then people started to push back. They moved slowly for a few seconds, then some people began to run. People who weren't even there looked up to see the people running, so they jumped up from what they were doing and began to run as well.

His driver continued to extort people, and it became a mass exodus. People were screaming and shouting. Some of the men dressed in black paramilitary gear also began to run, some of them jumping off the embassy walls to do so. He looked at his watch one more time and shouted to his driver that they needed to get out of there, too. Both of them turned to run.

He kept glancing at his watch as they ran, being elbowed by other panicking people. A young woman fell in front of him to be kicked by several people. His driver stooped to help her up, and the ambassador took her other arm as they managed to half-drag her along. As nothing was forthcoming, he wondered what would happen if he was being played, if he was starting a panic for no reason.

He needn't have worried. A huge explosion erupted behind him, pushing him to the ground where he landed on the woman he was helping. There was an odd sensation in his chest as if he couldn't breathe for a second, but then an inrush of air seemed to fill his lungs. He gasped and looked at the young woman who was sobbing, arms covering her head. He helped her up to sitting position. A food cart lay on its side a few feet away, hot oil spilling onto the road. He looked back.

Near the embassy walls, he could see some people prone. But further out, closer to him, people were struggling to their feet.

He could hear something coming, a whup-whup. He turned around again to see a huge helicopter, no, one of those hybrid plane-helicopters the Indonesians used for pirate interdiction, but with "U.S.MARINES" emblazoned on the sides come directly over head and move off to the embassy. He could see the huge rotors tilting as the machine slowed down and began a descent into the embassy grounds itself. Three more of the planes flew over to circle the embassy. There was a burst of fire from one of them into the grounds.

Ambassador Suphantarida had done what he could. Now he decided to sit down, right there in the street, and just watch the show.

Chapter 50

Thursday Morning, 25,000 Feet Above New Delhi

L T David Littlehawk was in his element, flying his Lighting II. The warrior blood of generations flowed through his veins. The air this high seemed unnaturally bright and clear. Down below him, over the vast metropolis, a ground haze almost obscured the details of buildings, roads, parks, and all the things which make a city a city. He didn't need sight for this mission, though. He simply watched his HMDS to know that he was on target.

A military history buff, he smiled at the thought of being on an actual weapons run. He felt a kinship with the brave Dauntless pilots at Midway, diving down on the Japanese carriers. Of course, he wasn't going to be diving his big F-35C. Nowadays, with smart ammo and guided munitions, when in the attack mode, all the plane had to do was to get in the cone and the munitions would do the rest. Further, unlike the Dauntless pilots, he didn't have Zeros ready to jump his tail or a barrage of anti-aircraft trying to bring him down.

The Mk402 he carried needed to have a near vertical drop for the blast to have the desired vertical attenuation, so there had to be as little lateral drift as possible. And while air friction would essentially eliminate most of the drift if the release point was high enough, the intent here was to get that drift to zero. But with smart ordnance, the bomb itself would take care of that. All LT Littlehawk had to do was to pickle the bomb at the right time. So, it wasn't exactly like flying a Dauntless, basically using the plane to aim the bomb. His HDMS would tell him where to fly and when to release. He didn't want to admit it, but it was almost like being on autopilot. He could have been on a training run back at China Lake.

With the more experienced pilots needed to fly CAP, it was left to one of the junior pilots to take the run, and the skipper thought it ironic that having almost missed the mission, he should be the one to take it in.

His HDMS flashed, and he adjusted the heading of the big bird to match the optimum flight path as computed by his navigation system. "Cougar, this is Chickenhawk. Commencing run now."

"Roger Chickenhawk. God's speed." His CO's voice came over the com.

He kept his Lightning II on the steady heading. His track monitor kept him honest as he approached the target. The screen on his PCD, set to maximum magnification, could pick up the target through the ground haze now, the middle of the embassy courtyard, right on one of the abandoned vehicles there. Of course he couldn't pick up the laser painting on the vehicle now, courtesy of his wingman, some thousands of feet below him and off to the side, but he knew it was there.

The numbers in his HDMS kept getting smaller, getting to the point of release. His thumb hovered over the pickle. Now! He pushed the pickle and the Mk402 detached and began its solo descent.

He immediately pulled up and started to climb. He was in no danger from his own ordnance. But now that he had released it, he wanted to get back up and do what a fighter pilot did, shoot down planes. Let anyone try something, and this warrior would knock them out of the sky.

Chapter 51

Thursday Morning, US Embassy, New Delhi

The door shut with a sense of finality, cutting the communications line. Gunny stared at the phone receiver for a moment, hoping Sgt Niimoto understood his hurried warning. He slowly placed the receiver back in its cradle and looked around the vault.

The president and Loralee Howard were looking up at him. Loralee had her M18 and seemed confident. The president looked a little lost. He could see SSgt Child's feet on the deck behind the last set of shelves where they had laid him down. Child was still unconscious but still alive, his strong body unwilling to release its hold on life. LCpl Van Slyke moved toward the closed door and took up a position facing it. Outside, they could hear a muffled burst of fire. They all looked at each other, wondering, hoping.

More shots rang out, then an explosion. Gunny put his hand on the door as if that could help him see how Ramon and the major were. Part of him wanted to rush out and join them, but it was too late for that. He could not leave even if he wanted to without jeopardizing those left inside the vault.

The president and Loralee came up to join them at the door. They stared uselessly at it. They could not see anything, they could not do anything, yet the four of them stood there.

Another set of explosions could be heard, fuzzy and muffled as if they were far, far away, then some shots. And incredibly, seemingly a voice yelling out. They could not quite make out what was said, but it sounded like Ramon. A few more gunfire reports, then nothing. The vault became silent, only their steady breathing sounds making their presence known.

Was it over? They looked each other in the eyes, that thought weighing heavily on each of their minds. Suddenly, a low rumble filled the air and the vault shook, items falling off the racks. Loralee fell to one knee, and Van Slyke quickly reached down to help her back up. Gunny took an involuntary breath, afraid there would be no oxygen, but the seals on the vault were good.

"That's them! We just need to hold out a little longer." There was a palpable sense of relief among themselves.

"Van Slyke, come here. Let's clear this other table here and use it as a barricade in front of the door." Both of them started shoving electronics and manuals and extra weapons off the table onto the floor where it joined the items already shoved there by Major Defilice and those which had been knocked down by the explosion. They started shoving the table into place when a set of hands joined them to help. The gunny looked up into the president's eyes.

Between the three of them, they managed to jam the table around a rack and into place on one edge in front of the door. "OK, let's see what we can pile up in front of this." He started rummaging through the electronics, books, and other odds and ends.

As gunny lifted two heavy pieces of some sort of testing equipment over the edge of the table, the president asked "Why not put those on this side of the table? That makes more sense to me."

"Well sir, if we do that, and if a round penetrates through the table, then all of this can become shrapnel. All this glass and metal and plastic, well it can just fly around. On the other side of the table, most of that should be stopped."

Loralee nervously chuckled. "He's got you there!"

The president almost seemed to begin to glare at that, but he suddenly relaxed and laughed. "I guess you're right. And maybe he should be making the decisions here, not this dumb California boy."

It really wasn't that funny, but all four of them broke out in laughter. In the stress of the situation, the knowledge that they may be the only ones left alive, and now the hope to a possible rescue, well there was sense of hysteria to the laughter.

"Peter, cover the left side of the door there." PFC Van Slyke merely nodded, his swollen face too mangled by now to say much. "Loralee, if I can ask you to sit here in back of this table and cover the middle, and I'll take the right."

Still chuckling, Loralee got between the two Marines.

"What about me?" Gunny felt a tap on his shoulder.

"Sir, maybe you should just move to the back of the vault over there and get down. We'll cover you the best we can."

"Do you really think that will make any difference if they get in before our people do?" Gunny had to agree and shook his head. "Then I'm going to join you here. I've got this rifle here, and Peter has shown me how to fire it."

"Roger that, sir. I guess you're right, and the more firepower we have here the better." He moved over a space to let the president move in between him and Loralee.

"Thank you, Gunnery Sergeant."

Gunny placed his weapon butt on the deck and took the president's M18. He hit the magazine release and caught the falling magazine, checked it, and slid it back into the weapon. He pulled back the charging handle and released it before handing the weapon back. He took another full magazine out of is pocket and handed it to the president as well.

"It is on safe now, sir," he said, pointing. "Push it up, and you are hot. Pull the trigger when you have a target. You are good to go."

The president nodded and slipped between Loralee and the gunny. They stared at the door, listening for any sound. "Why did they do that?"

The other three looked at the President. "Why who, sir?"

The major, Major Defilice, and that woman Marine, Ramon. I don't understand why they did that." He looked confused.

Loralee elbowed Gunny McCardle, raising her eyebrows. She was a civilian, but she understood. Perhaps it was because of her brother, or perhaps it was just her makeup.

Gunny looked over at the president. "Mr. President, I really don't know if there are words to explain that. It's almost something you have to feel, and in order to feel it, you have to experience the same training, the same camaraderie, the same feeling of family we have. You would do anything to protect your kids, wouldn't you?"

"Yes, but that's different. They're my flesh and blood. Any animal will protect its offspring. That is nature. But those two and the soldie… Marines who went upstairs, and the two in the guard booth, they aren't family. They aren't flesh and blood. But none of them hesitated. And that little Ramon, she is just like some of the high school girls I remember. You were going, and she backed you down. She went. And the major went with her."

"Yes, they went. But you're wrong sir. We are flesh and blood. Maybe not by genetics, but we are family. Our bonds are greater than mere genes. And Major Defilice? OK, he isn't a Marine, but we'd be damn glad to have him as one. He understands what it's all about."

Some voices came through from the passage. Did they sound Hindi? They seemed right outside the door. Everyone froze, then relaxed somewhat as the voices seemed to fade away.

The president picked it back up. "But they must have known they were going to die, right?"

"I imagine so, Mr. President. But they both, well, all of them, Major Defilice, PFC Ramon, Sgt McAlister, PFC Rodriguez, Sgt Chen, Drayton Bajinski, and probably the three who went above decks as well, they knew they probably would not be making it. To be honest, I don't know if we are going to make it. But Marines do their duty, no matter what. "

Loralee added, "My brother Ian, the one I told you about, the Marine who lost his legs in Afghanistan? You now, all he tried to do was to go back. He kept appealing his decision, trying to show that he was every bit as able as any other Marine despite his two prosthetics. He had a 70% pension, tax free, and VA benefits, but could he stop and move on? No, he had to get back with his unit before their next deployment. It was his biggest regret that he didn't make it."

There was a small thud against the door. Then some voices. The four froze, not moving a muscle. A soft glow appeared on the door, then a puff of smoke followed by a stream of sparks. An acrid cloud of smoke came into the vault and eddied around the ceiling.

"Get down!" Gunny ordered needlessly. All four crouched behind the table, protected from the steady stream of sparks shooting into the vault. There were four simultaneous clicks as four safeties were clicked to "fire." Sweaty hands nervously gripped the weapons.

While the vault door was pretty heavy alloy, it was not made of the same material as the embassy security doors. The torch being used made pretty good progress. They watched the cut line get longer and longer around the lock as whoever was doing the cutting tried to isolate it. When the lock was completely cut, it still did not budge, so after a moment, the cut line started to descend between the door and the vault wall itself. As the lines of the cut met, the locking mechanism fell away, leaving a small gap in the door. PFC Van Slyke started to raise his weapon but Gunny pulled it down and motioned for all four to get down. As they crouched behind the table, they could hear Hindi voices at the small opening as if someone were looking in.

The torch started up again, and a cut was being made at the very top of the door, cutting through the heavy steel bar there. After a moment, the bar was cut, and the torch shifted to the locking bar on the floor.

There was a shout of triumph, then gloved hands came in to grip the door at the new opening. Gunny motioned to the other three, and they came up, weapons aimed. As the door was pushed open a crack, Gunny opened fire, followed by the other three a split second later.

At least one set of hands was hit as the other two sets jerked back. There was some furious shouting down the passage and footsteps running from further down toward the other offices. They could hear an excited exchange right outside the door. A hand appeared around the edge of the partially opened door and threw in a round object.

"Down!" shouted Gunny as the four crouched behind the table. A horrible four or five seconds followed, which stretched for an eternity. There was a deafening blast as the grenade detonated. Gunny and Van Slyke immediately sat up, weapons over the edge of the table. Three men tried to rush in, but their concerted burst dropped all three in their tracks.

Gunny looked down at the men, one in plain view, the other two partially obscured by the door. He has just killed a man, maybe more. He was glad the man in front of him was face down. He didn't want to see him, to get any feelings for him. The two other bodies jerked as they were dragged out of sight, but one in front of him stayed, a testament of some sort.

"Good shot, you two. Thanks." Loralee coldly looked down on the gunman.

The voices outside stopped. Gunny knew they were regrouping, ready to try and end it all right there in the bottom deck of the embassy.

"Do you despise me?"

Gunny looked to his left in surprise at the president. The president had his weapon pointing up, and there was an almost sorrowful look on his face. "Sir?" he paused for a few seconds, not expecting such a question at a time like this and not quite knowing how to respond. "With all due respect, I am kinda focusing on the next few minutes. I don't think this is a good time for a retrospective."

"No, I really want to know. I need to know. You've been telling me for the last two days about the Marine Corps, how important it is to you, to them," he waved his arm as if to encompass the entire embassy. "Now all of them are dead. And I'm not stupid. We can't hold out here much longer. And we can't hope for rescue. So now, I want the truth. I was the one who took away your Marine Corps. Me. Michael Antonio David Eduadro. So I am asking you, do you despise me?"

Both PFC Van Slyke and Loralee sucked in their breath. Gunny turned to look back at the small opening in the door. He thought for a second or two. "No sir, surprisingly I don't. Oh, I was pissed when you wouldn't let us fly the Corps colors for your honor guard two days ago. That was plain disrespect. But about our Corps, I guess you did what you thought was right at the time, and you can't fault a man for following his conscience. Not that it makes much difference now."

There was some gathering noise from out in the passage. All four turned to the opening and raised their weapons.

"Thank you, Gunny. And for the record, I think now I may have been wrong. I can see that sometimes, government is not all about dollars and cents. It is about heart and soul. And I know this may mean nothing, but if by some chance we get out of this, I'm going to bring back the Corps. I swear it."

"Mr. President, I appreciate that. But I'm afraid you just might not get that chance. Here they come!"

Loralee Howard, diplomat's wife and sister to a Marine, Private First Class Peter Van Slyke and Gunnery Sergeant Jacob McCardle, United States Marine Corps, and Michael Eduardo, President of the United States of America, lifted their weapons and faced their incoming fate.

Chapter 52

Thursday Morning, 1000 Meters From the US Embassy, New Delhi

Sitting in the jump seat, Col Jeff Lineau could see the first Osprey flare out and land in the embassy courtyard some 1000 meters ahead. There had been some discussion about FAST-roping, but he had decided that letting the embassy walls protect the debarking Marines was more important. Well, Marines and Navy. There had been some last minute additions to the mission. A SEAL team was included in the first bird. They were going to take position in the bell tower as a sniper team and cover the operation from there while Captain Kreig's 3d Team secured the courtyard.

There were some other additions as well. Each bird had a corpsmen from the *Reagan* to supplement Doc Hollister, and both the Colonel's bird and Capt Mahmoud's had a flight surgeon as well. There were two Indian-American sailors with them who could speak Hindi and Urdu. Each bird had a Navy "co-pilot," pilots who had at least flown rotary wing planes before, and each door gunner was a Navy gunner's mate, freeing up four Marines to join the others entering the embassy. There were also two deck controllers or "yellow shirts." The Ospreys didn't have enough seats for all the pax, so some had sat on the deck between the sling seats for the entire trip. Hopefully, more people would have to sit that way on the way back.

Peering through the Osprey's windshield, he could see the tell-tale flashes of the door gunner engaging something, then the big bird almost disappeared behind the distant wall. He started a mental count. Five seconds, ten seconds, fifteen seconds. He wished his com worked, but the area was back under blackout. Suddenly, the first bird rose fully back into sight and pulled away, just as the second bird, with LtCol Ricapito's team aboard, flared in from the other side of the embassy for a landing on the roof of the embassy.

As they flew closer, he glanced down through the windows beside the co-pilot's feet. There were quite a few people down there on the street, many of them pointing up at them. For the hundredth time, he hoped that none of the people besieging the embassy had anti-aircraft weapons. At this height and speed, his bird, in particular, due to its approach lane, was pretty vulnerable.

As they came up to the embassy, the second bird pulled up and out. In the light's angle, he could clearly see the newly painted "United States Marines" and US flag, which had been hastily applied to cover the Indonesian markings. His own Osprey rushed in, ramp already down.

Col Lineau quickly unbuckled and followed the rest of the Marines out, his headquarters on the heels of Major Roberto's team. As soon as his foot hit the courtyard deck, the Osprey jumped into the air to go and take its place in the orbiting station above the embassy.

The embassy grounds looked surprisingly in good condition. The various plants and trees had obviously suffered a big force, and the embassy itself looked a little scorched and had some broken windows above the first deck, but frankly, he had expected worse. There were, however, quite a few bodies, perhaps thirty or more, lying motionless around the courtyard. As he ran up to the embassy's front door, he passed several bodies that had blood froth coming out their mouths. Not a pretty way to go, he thought.

He looked up into the bell tower to see the SEALS getting in position. Capt Kreig already had most of his Marines up on the wall, weapons pointing out, but no one was firing.

The fourth and final Osprey took off after debarking Capt Mahmoud and 1stLt Hoins. Capt Mahmoud quickly moved his Marines out to the consulate building to keep anyone there from coming over to the embassy itself. Hoins quickly took her team up to join the colonel at the steps to the embassy.

There was a flurry of shots from inside the embassy. He rushed up to the front door itself when LCpl Neller, 1st Team's runner came running from inside.

"Sir! We've run into some bad guys in there when we tried to clear the first deck. Major Roberto thinks we can take them, but that's gonna keep us from checking below for a few minutes. He wants to know if Colonel Ricapito can get there."

The plan had been for the Major Roberto to sweep in the embassy from the front, then rush down the main passage to check the two offices where the president was last known to have been. He was then to send a team down to the lower deck to check out the vault where there was also a possibility they had holed up. He wished he had been able to get confirmation on where they were from Major Rogers. He wasn't all that confident that the major would have even been able to reach them during the break in the jamming, though.

LtCol Ricapito's team was to land on the roof and blow an opening there, then make its way down, clearing the building and then covering the retrograde from that vantage point.

There was a rattle of fire and a few rounds pinged around them. Col Lineau swore and spun around to see most of Mahomoud's Marines and some of Kreig's firing en masse into a broken window on the consulate building.

Just then, there was a blast from somewhere above him on the embassy roof. He looked up to see a Marine leaning over the edge, waving small green flag. Colonel Ricapito was in, but how fast could he adjust? He needed to get the word, then move down five decks.

He looked to Capt Mahmuoud, but he and his Marines were engaged with somebody, and with the people he saw outside the embassy grounds, he wanted Kreig's presence on the walls keeping them back.

"Neller, tell Major Roberto that he has to get into those offices now. Whatever it takes. If they're clear, he needs to check all the others. We'll take below decks. McNair, get over there and tell Captain Mahmoud to give me ten Marines. Have them meet us below on the bottom deck."

As PFC McNair took off across the courtyard, the colonel turned to the lieutenant. "It's us Stacy. Let's get your team down the ladder in there and do a search. They could be anywhere, but the vault is our best chance."

She turned to her small team and gave a quick command, then led them into the embassy. They all knew where the ladder going down below was, but knowing on paper and in real life can sometimes be a little different. As they rushed in, they veered to the left somewhat before spotting the ladder and rushing to it, a few rounds pinging around them from the gun battle going on down the long passageway there.

Colonel Lineau was right on their heels. As he rushed in, the Sergeant Major caught his eye, sitting on the deck, back up against the bulkhead, holding his left forearm while one of the *Reagan*'s corpsmen worked on the biceps. He had chosen come in with Major Roberto's team and had evidently taken a hit. His anger was a palpable force, and as he rushed by, Col Lineau knew the Sergeant Major would not let something like that keep him back.

He rushed past the shattered Post 1, not taking the time to look in, and dashed into the ladderwell just as some rounds came bursting up. He ran through the opening, dragging LCpl Luc with him and to the steps leading up and out of the line of fire. One of the lieutenant's Marines was just standing there, rounds pinging around. He grabbed her by the body armor and swung her out of the way as well.

Leaning over the rail, he looked down to see the lieutenant, the master guns, and two Marines standing almost elbow to elbow on the landing below, exchanging gunfire with a handful of men standing at the bottom of the ladder. Almost in slow motion, he could see the master guns stagger, then one of the other Marines as well. But with their body armor stopping the rounds, neither went down, and the gunmen at the bottom of the fell one by one until none were firing back.

Colonel Lineau vaulted down the steps with the other two in tow. He had to leap over another Marine, Cpl Smith, who had taken a hit to the leg before he could join the other four rushing to the bottom. There were several dead gunmen there and a table blocking the way, which had to be straddled. On the other side, there were several dead Marines: Sgt Chen, PFC Ramon, and that was probably PFC Fallgatter. There was a rather large military-looking man (secret service?) and another civilian there. There was barely enough time to let all of that register. They rounded the corner and saw three gunmen, rifles in hand, at the far side of an ajar door to what had to be the vault. His heart sunk. Were they too late? His gut told him that the president and any others were in there, and from the gunmen's attitude, it did not look good.

As they came into sight, one gunman saw them and tried to scramble into the vault to get out of the line of fire, but as one, the now seven Marines opened up, and the three men had no chance. They were cut down where they stood.

Ten Marines from Capt Mahmoud's team came stumbling down the ladderwell behind them. With a tremendous sense of loss, Col Lineau moved forward with the others to look into the vault, knowing what they would see.

Chapter 53

Thursday Morning, US Embassy, New Delhi

Two rifles appeared around the edge of the door, firing wildly in. The rounds ricocheted around the vault, but no one was hit. All four of them fired on the rifles, but seemingly none of them were hit either. This happened twice more before one of the rifles dropped on the floor. Gunny didn't know which one of them had hit it.

Some fingers came around the edge of the door and started pulling it open wider, but this time, a round hit the target, sending a piece of the finger flying off to land on the deck, clearly in view of those inside. They could hear shouts of pain.

The inside of the vault was becoming full of smoke, and the bitter acrid smell was getting overwhelming. Loralee's M18 started to waver, and she finally slid down to take a knee. She looked up apologetically and coughed.

There was in increase of fire, and PFC Van Slyke grunted, slapping the back of his butt. But he kept upright, returning the fire. His magazine emptied, and with a calm collectiveness, he slipped in another mag. It was hard to see, but it looked like several people rushed past the door to the other side. His ears were ringing so much that he didn't trust Van Slyke to respond to words, so Gunny pushed Van Slyke over to the left a bit to give him a better angle to fire at anyone coming from that direction.

There was another increase in the volume of fire, and the three of them shot wildly out through the door. He didn't think he was hitting anything, but he couldn't stop. He was at his end game. Smoke obscured his vision. As he changed his magazine at the same time as the president, PFC Van Slyke held up his hand. The firing had stopped for a moment. OK, they needed to use their ammo smarter. They slowly aimed out the door, waiting for a real target.

PFC Van Slyke shifted his point of aim further to the right and fired off a double tap burst.

"Shit!" a voice rang out in English.

It was immediately followed by a different voice "US Marines, US Marines! If you are American, we are here to rescue you. Identify yourselves!"

Gunny couldn't believe he heard right. His ears were ringing, but the words were unmistakable, and the accent sounded right. In fact, it sounded like Master Guns Chung!

"This is Gunnery Sergeant McCardle. We are holding our fire." He put out a hand to push down the muzzle of the president's weapon.

A head peaked in. It was the master guns. "Is the president here with…." He saw the president standing there, unshaven, dirty t-shirt, and holding an M18. Nonplussed, he said, "Mr. President, can you come with us please? We have a flight ready to take you out of here."

Marines came in and helped the four of them out. Colonel Lineau was there himself, and he caught the Gunny's arm. "Anyone else in there?"

"Just SSgt Child, sir, in back of the rack there, on the deck. He's hurt pretty bad and isn't conscious. I think that's all." A tremendous wave of despair and fatigue washed over him. His det, his Marines. Only Van Slyke and he made it. And Child, if you could count that as "making it." How could he explain his failure to keep his Marines alive?

His mind was a blur as they were hustled down the passageway to the ladderwell. Marines were already picking up the bodies. One Marine he didn't recognize picked up PFC Ramon, her limp arms swaying lifelessly as the Marine moved. Tears came to his eyes.

"Them too," he told them, pointing out Drayton and the major. SSgt Pierce, from the KL det, simply nodded.

In a daze, he made it up the ladder, assisted by someone who didn't register with him. They got up to the entrance, and he could see the damage inside Post 1. Two other Marines were at the glass, looking inside with somber expressions. Marines were moving about with a sense of purpose. Major Roberto came out of the passageway leading toward the ambassador's office.

Gunny Phelps from Quantico was there, and he gave Gunny McCardle a thumbs up. He saw the president then, and rushed out shouting to someone. They half-dragged the president to the opening in the door, finally getting him to release his M18.

Gunny Phelps came back and spoke to Major Roberto. "It's clear sir. I think we need to go now."

"Roger that, Gunny. Get that bird down."

Gunny Phelps turned to what looked like a sailor in a yellow jacket, like they had on carriers. "Petty Officer Martin, bring her in." He looked out the opening at someone else. "You two, cover him!"

Gunny Mac leaned against the bulkhead. His mind was floundering, like it was stuffed with cotton. He sat there alone despite being surrounded by Marines. He could hear a loud noise growing from outside. A Marine poked his head through the opening.

"It's landing now!"

A half-a-dozen Marines surrounded the president and moved him outside. Not knowing what else to do, Gunny Mac followed, but stopped as he got through the opening. A huge Osprey was landing, "US MARINES" emblazoned on its fuselage. Gunny Mac hadn't seen one of them for years. The Marines ran the president down to the bird and up the ramp. Others pretty much carried Loralee to the bird. She raised an arm and waved to him as she was carried up the ramp. Other Marines poured in. The sailor in the yellow jacket waved two ping-pong paddle-like signals, and the Osprey fairly jumped into the air. Another Osprey started to come in for a landing.

Colonel Lineau stood next to him, watching the president leave. Gunny turned to him. "Colonel, we've got three Marines in the reefer in the ambassador's pantry. We've got three Marines somewhere above deck. And we've got Sgt Niimoto up in that bell tower. All of them come with us. We are not leaving anyone behind."

Without pause, Colonel Lineau called up LCpl Luc and another

Marine. "McNair, go tell those SEALS to bring Sgt Niimoto's body with them. Luc, tell Colonel Ricapito to bring the Marines in the reefer and whoever is above decks. He may have already found their bodies, but they come with us."

A second Osprey landed in the courtyard. Colonel Lineau looked at him. "You two get on that one. I want you out of here."

"Begging the colonel's pardon, but no sir, I need to stay until all my det has been loaded on board. I need to know that they're going back to the US for their families."

The CO put his hand on his shoulder and nodded. He gestured to PFC Van Slyke, who was being attended to by a corpsman. The two made the walk together, the corpsman still working on him as they moved, and boarded. An orderly line of Marines formed up and quickly got onboard. The yellow jacketed sailor waved his magic wands and the Osprey took off, a small windstorm buffeting those left.

Half of the remaining Marines left their positions on the wall to begin to form again. LCpl Luc came running up to the CO. "Sir, Colonel Ricapito has the three Marines from the reefer and will have them on the roof in three mikes. They've found the other three Marines, too. They are ready to take off as soon as your bird leaves."

"Thanks, LCpl Luc. You get ready, you and McNair. Stick on my ass. I don't need you two wandering off."

A third Osprey landed in the courtyard, and Gunny could see another coming in to apparently land on the roof of the embassy.

PFC McNair came running up. "The SEALS, they are coming down now, but they said there are no Marine bodies up there."

Gunny looked up in confusion, then a little anger. "Bullshit! I spoke to him just a little while ago, right before this place got hit. He is up there!" Or could the blast have knocked him out of the tower? Or even burned his body up? He looked at the bodies lying about the courtyard. None seemed too terribly damaged from outward appearances, so no, his body had to be still around somewhere.

Master Guns Chung walked out and called to the CO. "Colonel, we've got to go. There is some movement over the wall, maybe a force coming here."

"We're not going without Tony!" Gunny shouted, running into the courtyard, around the Osprey and through Marines starting to board.

LCpl Luc ran after him. They ran into the broken hatch to the bell tower and almost collided with a group of four SEALS coming down.

"You, come with me!" His tone brooked no argument.

The six of them crashed up the steps and finally through the broken hatch into the cupola. Gunny looked about in desperation.

"Uh, just what are we supposed to be doing here?" It was the SEAL lieutenant, looking perplexed.

"We've got a Marine here, and we're taking him back." He looked around, then over to the edge where he could see out over the embassy wall. He couldn't see a body on the ground there.

"We told the other Marine, there is no one here. No body, nothing."

He rushed over to the other side. He could see nothing on the ground there, either. He could see an Osprey on top of the embassy, Marines boarding. He could see the Osprey below him in the courtyard, almost everyone evidently onboard, the colonel standing there looking up at him, gesturing.

"Sorry, but we're leaving." The SEALS started to move out.

Gunny looked back into the cupola. Despair struck out at him, almost a physical blow. Then he noticed something was out of place. He couldn't figure it out for a moment, but then it struck him. The bell. It was flush on the deck. He wondered how that happened. Did the blast do that? He moved up to it. A small tangle of rolled cotton was coming out from under the bell, ragged and torn.

"Get back here! Now!" He started to push at the bell, to tip it over, but it was too heavy. LCpl Luc started to help.

The four SEALS exchanged glances, then rushed over. The six of them moved to one side, then tried to push up. The bell tipped, then fell back down with a thud.

"OK," one of the SEALS shouted, "on my command, heave, then you Marine," he pointed to LCpl Luc, "stick your radio under the edge. Then we can grab it. OK, HEAVE!"

The bell tilted up six inches, and LCpl Luc was able to jam his useless radio under the edge. The six men lowered it onto the radio, shifted their grips, then grasped under the edge of the bell. With one concerted heave, the bell came up and over to crash on its side up against the cupola wall.

Lying on the deck where the bell once covered, Sergeant Anthony Niimoto looked up in a daze, a small medical canister on his chest slowly feeding oxygen around his face with a soft hiss, a medical kit open beside him.

"Hey Gunny," he croaked out, "do you have anything to drink?"

Chapter 54

Saturday Morning, The Whitehouse, Washington, DC

The President of the United States of America sat in the chair in front of his desk in the oval office and looked at the three others there. This was the first time he had a chance to meet with them, his trusted advisors.

Well, the old Chinese curse of living in interesting times was surely upon him. The last three days had been a hectic whirlwind of activity, and only today were things sinking in. Sitting in the oval office right now, in some ways, it seemed like the last week had never happened, it had been a dream. But President Eduardo was a changed man, and that brought reality into focus.

After his hurried evacuation from the embassy, the flight back to the *Reagan* was almost anti-climatic. He found out later that the plan had been to lower him from the Osprey to a waiting sub, but the complete lack of Indian response had prompted them to return to the *Reagan* directly, and, in retrospect, much to his relief. He hadn't envisioned dangling from the bird to get on a sub. Instead, the Osprey had made a graceful landing on the *Reagan*, and he had walked off to the cheers of hundreds of sailors on the flight deck. The unreality of it was such that he actually stopped and shook hands with as many sailors as possible, as if he was back on the campaign trail.

He was taken up to the flag officer's stateroom where he called his wife, her tearful cries of relief almost overwhelming him. He made some other official calls while wolfing down a pastrami sandwich handed to him, then got a quick shower, shave, and change of clothes (he never did find out whose clothes those were) before being whisked away back down to the flight deck where a waiting C2 was there to fly him to Diego Garcia.

On the way down, he saw Gunny Mac in mess decks and went up to him. Gunny stood up to face him. The president simply put his arms around the gunny in a bearlike hug, then stepped back. No words were exchanged. None needed to be.

He took the flight to Diego Garcia, surrounded by an escort of Navy fighters, where he met up with Secretary Pitt. Pitt's plane was re-designated Air Force 1, and together, they made the long flight back to the US. It wasn't a relaxing flight, of course. There was numerous phone calls to the US and with various heads of state, there were several briefings on what had and was still happening, a brief stopover in Hawaii for refueling, and only a few hours of sleep.

The landing at Andrews was almost festive, with music and huge numbers of officials and press. He felt like a returning hero, but in his heart, he felt that this "hero" was an imposter. He really hadn't done anything heroic. Others had done that.

A quick stop at the White House for a carefully choreographed press conference and medical check-up, then it was off to Camp David with his family for the night and next morning. As he looked around Camp David, it seemed odd not to have Marines there. Secret service agents had taken over each of the Marine details.

That afternoon, it was back to the White House for meetings and more meetings, with the vice-president and Cabinet, with the Senate and House leaders, with his staff. Then he insisted on calling the families of all those killed in the takeover and rescue. That was pretty rough, but he knew he wanted, no he had to do it. Finally, he was able to get upstairs and to sleep.

Now, after his morning briefings, he had the Director of the CIA, his National Security Advisor, and his chief of staff sitting around him. He pondered what Bo Waters had just said. "So that is the way it needs to be?"

He looked over to Arnie, who nodded. He put his hands in back of his head, elbows out. He swung around al bit so he could look out the window. A Marine was there, standing at parade rest, back toward him. The president didn't know his name, but he must have just made it back from India himself. A sense of security tinged with affection washed over him. He smiled, then turned back.

"We don't hold the Indian government responsible? At all?"

"Not quite, sir. We have gotten assurances that they will pay for all the damage to the embassy as well as make payments to the victims' families. But we cannot make the takeover out to be an overt act by the Indian government. That would be tantamount to war."

"But it was an act of war. An attack on US soil."

The National Security Advisor agreed. "Yes, it was, sir, but with the snap elections called for, well, this particular government looks like it is going to be out on its ass."

"And that looks like a pretty sure thing?" He looked over at Kai-yen.

"From our projections, I would have to assume it will be a significant win for the Indian National Party. Popular backlash against the Prime Minister and the ruling part is growing, and that was most likely the tipping point for his dissolving Parliament and calling for new elections. He probably thinks this is his best chance at retaining power, i.e., before full disclosure of his party's support of the takeover."

Despite the seriousness of the conversation, the president had to smile. Kaiyen was an old, old friend, but she was perhaps the only person he knew who would actually use the phrase "i.e." in a conversation. He was actually surprised she didn't use the full Latin "id est."

"I have also spoken with Viraq Dasmunsi personally. He assures us that India is and will remain a close ally, and he hinted he is willing to re-open past negotiations, such as opening up their financial markets, under his new administration. He made what I understood to be an appeal to help keep this situation as what has been described in the Indian press."

"So, we act like this was a mere group of terrorists, which acted due to Indian armed forces being elsewhere on previously scheduled exercises. This 'terrorist' group saw an opportunity and grabbed it, and the Indian government was slow to respond due a fear of loss of escalation and loss of life? And that they invited us to conduct the actual evacuation due to it being US soil?"

"Pretty much so, yes sir." Arnie sat back, watching him.

"And that will fly?"

"Well, the government did send in the police as soon as the Marines started landing. They arrested over a hundred people. But no, this won't fly with most of the world's leaders. On the other hand, it really only has to fly within India and within the general American populace. The rest of the world will just accept what we agree to say." He paused. "And that's the value of modern diplomacy. People act as if outright lies are the truth without batting an eye."

"Oh, I know we have to do this. But it really sticks in my craw. If you were there, if you had seen those young men and women die, well… well, that's over and done with. Arnie, I want Secretary Pitt briefed on this, and I want him to take point. I want him in bed with soon-to-be Prime Minister Dasmunsi. Let's make this fade away as soon as it possibly can. Pitt is a good guy, by the way. I want him brought in closer to the circle in the future."

"OK, I've got another meeting in a few, right Arnie? So quickly, about those other things. The awards? Do we have Congressional sponsors yet?"

"Yes sir, "Arnie nodded. "Congressman Birch requested to sponsor all of them."

"Good. I want this done quickly, not going through a couple years of DoD approval. But push DoD them on those other awards, too. I want these people to feel our deep appreciation. My appreciation."

"And the Marines?" He looked a little apprehensive.

Arnie laughed at this one. "Mr. President, I have made a few calls. This one is going to sail through without a problem. The Marine Corps is pretty popular right now, and there were already a lot of people, people in Congress and out in the constituency, who rather thought the Marines should never have been down-sized. Even if you hadn't promised what you did, I think someone on the Hill would have hitched their wagon to this train."

The President looked a little relieved. Hopefully, this was a promise he could keep.

"You being a bona fide hero too isn't hurting matters. We don't have too many presidents personally fighting terrorists, you know," Arnie said, motioning over to where the M18 the president had used in India was already framed and hung on the wall.

The president felt guilty about that, posing, in his opinion, as a hero. But he also understood political capital when he saw it, and he did feel a certain pride in having stood up and traded rounds with an enemy.

"And I still want your input on the bloodletting. Lefever is gone." The president raised a hand to cut off his chief of staff's protest. "Oh, I'll wait a little bit, but that asshole is out of here within two months. I am willing to take your advice on Wright. She can stay out her term. But I want your input on who may have been acting out of their conscience and who was acting for political gain. And then, what you think we should do about it."

The president stood up. "Thanks for your support. You have served your nation, but I personally appreciate your loyalty." He shook each hand in turn.

As he they left, he walked back to his desk. The Marine was outside, still at parade rest, his dress blues tight against his broad back. The President of the United States smiled.

Chapter 55

Two Months Later, HQMC, Quanitco

Brigadier General Jeff Lineau sat in his office, listening to the hubbub going on outside the hatch. He realized the office had gone silent.

"Excuse me? I didn't catch that."

LtCol (Col Select) Tye Saunders looked back at his notebook, then back up. "I just told you we are authorized to approach all former Marines now serving in the other branches about returning to us. We really are going to need a senior cadre to help guide this expansion, and the Chiefs of Personnel of the other branches have pledged their support."

General Lineau smiled. "I guess it helps getting that support when the Commander in Chief himself asks for it." There was a general chorus of laughter.

Tye added, "I spoke with Major General Lawrence this morning. He has decided to give up his second star to return to the Marines as our new FSSG CG. He told me one star with the Marines was much better than any number of Army stars."

There was a chorus of "Ooh-rahs" at that quote.

" That's really good news. I knew General Lawrence, back in the day when he was still a Marine. He is a great logistician, and it will be nice to have him back and out of his Army greens. He is going to help a lot in getting us back on our feet. I am glad he saw fit to give up his Army career and that second star." General Lineau felt a big sense of relief at the news.

The Sergeant Major, arm still in a sling, spoke up. "On a related note, we are starting to interview retired Marines about coming in for temporary orders. This afternoon, I've got an interview with that Staff Sergeant, the one who lost his legs in Afghanistan, the brother of Loralee Howard. If he is fit to sit in back of a desk, I'll send him into see the XO for final approval. But, as you say, if the request comes from the Commander in Chief, I guess we're going to find that this Marine still can serve." Another round of laughs went around the office.

"Speaking of Ms. Howard, I haven't heard back about her move. We had Marines helping her?"

Major Mahmoud spoke up. "Yes sir. The entire S-1 and S-4 sections showed up Saturday and packed her up. Her belongings should probably be half-way back to her hometown now. She said she was going to visit a sister, then head on back. She just didn't want to stay in DC anymore."

"OK, let's keep track of her. I especially want her to be here for the Birthday Ball. You know, I talked with her on the *Reagan* and then again while flying back to CONUS. That is one amazing lady."

Cpl Tyson knocked and stuck his head in the hatch. "Sir, Admiral Conners is here to see you."

"Send him in!" He looked at the others. "Ladies and gentlemen, can you give me a few moments?"

The others got up and started to leave when Joshua Conners walked in, looking out of place and a little lost in civilian clothes. Tye Saunders reached out to offer his hand. "Good to see you Admiral Conners."

Conners took the offered hand. "That is just Mr. Conners now, I'm afraid."

"Begging the admiral's pardon, but no it isn't. You are Rear Admiral Joshua Conners, Friend to the Corps. You will always be an admiral to us. And we'll never forget what you did for us." The others nodded in agreement.

It couldn't be true, but it seemed like a small tear formed in the admiral's eyes, a tiny bit of moisture. "I'll take the 'Friend to the Corps' title with pride." They looked into each other's eyes before the XO turned away and followed the others out of the office.

The tall man in civilian clothes hesitated a moment, then turned to his old classmate, hand out. "That star looks good there!"

Well, it's only temporary. It hasn't been officially confirmed yet, and they could still come to their senses any minute now and kick my ass all the way back to North Dakota. But the President says wear it, so I wear it."

"So what happened to 52-and-a-wake-up?"

"Bastards won't let me retire now. Something about needing me to build up the Corps again."

"Well, that's good for you. I can't see you sitting on your ranch pushing cows around. Julie would be bossing you around unmercifully."

"You've got that right!" They both laughed and sat down. The silence carried on a little bit too long for comfort.

"Josh, you know how much that sucks. I can't believe they did that."

"Oh, we both knew our careers were over after this. We both went in with open minds. You came out a hero, and I'm not being funny here. You really were. And I am happy you escaped the headman's axe. But we both knew what was going to happen, and OK, it happened. I still would not change a thing."

"But we saved the president. If we hadn't acted, he'd be dead by now, and we might be at war. You were the one who did that. You made it possible."

"But I broke the cardinal rule in the Navy. I acted without telling my chain of command. They don't trust me. Audrey Race at PACCOM chewed my ass, and the CNO? You don't want to know what went on in his office. Oh I know," he said forestalling Jeff's protest, "I am getting the Distinguished Service Medal for the action, but the CNO left no room for interpretation. I was told to retire. So I did."

"And I told you, let me talk to the president. I think I can get his ear for this."

"And I appreciate that. You can't understand how much. But no. I am done. I'm going home."

The silence stretched out again.

"But now you've got your star." He brightened. "A real Commandant. So they are bringing back a whole division?"

"Yep, and the FSSG. No air wing, though, for now at least. We are in negotiations with the National Guard now to take back Camp Lejeune."

"Hey, that is great."

"We're getting back the Marine Barracks in DC from the Park Service, and General Litz says he wants me there. But I want to be in LeJeune. I can't command from DC!"

"Heavy is the crown. Well, you'll have to be a politician now, and get somebody else to do command. Just think if it, though, you should get another star. Both of us making two stars. I never would have believed it."

"Three," he responded quietly.

"Three? Three what?"

"Three stars. I have to wait until the division is stood up, but I'm going to get three stars." He looked apprehensive.

Josh Conners threw back his head and laughed, standing up and rushing over to give him a bear hug and pound his back. "You bastard! Three stars! Who did you blow for that?"

The Commandant of the Marine Corps gasped for breath. "I never said they knew what they were doing! Hell, all I care is that the Marines are back. Even if we owe it to a Navy puke like you, the Marines are back!"

Chapter 56

Three Months After the Embassy Takeover,
Wisconsin Avenue, Washington, DC

First Sergeant Jacob McCardle drove the staff car up Wisconsin Avenue, past the trendy restaurants and bars. As the light turned red, he slowed the Ford down. through the side window, he saw a good lunch crowd eating at the sidewalk tables at the Mumbai Café. Two young women were sitting in the sun, laughing, drinking what looked to be mango lassis. He wondered if they would like Thumbs Up colas. Probably not. No one except him did. The light turned green, and he continued north.

The ceremony had been well organized and was touching, he had to admit. The Rose Garden looked peaceful and serene. The white chairs for the attendees had been placed with care. Four placards on silver frames had stood to the left of the podium with photos and bios of the four honorees.

First Sergeant McCardle got there early, then stood in the back as the dignitaries and guests filed in and took their seats. He saw Loralee Howard, so he sat down beside her, disregarding the name tag on the seat assigning it to someone else. She reached out and squeezed his arm. Finally, all were in place, and the doors to the oval office opened. The President, General Lineau, the Speaker of the House, and the immediate family members came out and made their way to the garden.

The First Sergeant hadn't seen the family members since the funerals, but their images were imbedded in this mind. Some of the immediate grief present at the funerals might be missing now, but a sense of solemnity, sadness, and yes, pride now was evident.

The cameras rolled as people took their seats and the president went to the podium to speak. And it was a good speech. Hearfelt, earnest, and respectful. Good politicians could do that, but the First Sergeant thought that this was not an act, that it really was from his heart.

Then it was time for the awards. The President called each family in turn up by the order in which they fell and presented the wreathed star with the sky blue ribbon. Sergeant Tracy Ann McAllister. Private First Class Jesus Emilio Rodriguez. Major Stanley Paul Defilice. Private First Class Haydee Huertas Ramon. All presented with the Medal of Honor.

Each family solemnly accepted their loved one's award with both sadness and pride. Little Mac's father, a sun-weathered cowboy, thanked the president and stoically accepted his hug. PFC Rodriguez's grandmother, the person who had raised the young man since he was a toddler when his mother was sent to prison, openly cried. Major Defilice's young son stepped up, clearly not understanding the importance of the ceremony, his small, innocent face looking back at his mother, the major's ex-wife, to see what he was supposed to do. And Pedro Ramon, Princess' father, took the award in his hands, looking at it for a long moment before crossing himself and looking heavenwards, quietly mouthing his pride to her, his only daughter.

Normally, a Medal of Honor took a year or two to get approved, but by having a Congressional sponsor recommend these in a special session of Congress, these four were shoved through the system in record time. Not that anyone in DoD was complaining.

The evening before, First Sergeant McCardle had gone up to Arlington to see the graves of PFC Ramon and Major Defilice. They had been buried side-by-side there, and the grass already covered any sign of the digging of the graves. But the small images of the medals were already on the tombstones. Someone had already had them emplaced. The First Sergeant had just stood there for half an hour, lost in his thoughts before leaving and going back to the hotel reserved for the ceremony guests.

He continued his drive north. He thought about all that had happened since that fateful day. The sense of despair at losing his Marines, the sense of joy when he saw LCpl Steptoe and LCpl Saad on the *Reagan*. Yes, those two had made it. LCpl Kramer hadn't. He had been shot while trying to free Mr. Dravid, who had been leading the gunmen on a wild goose chase, and when they figured that out, they held him down to execute him. LCpl Kramer wasn't going to allow that, and he rushed from a closet to save him. Eight-to-one odds might work in Hollywood, but they don't usually work in real life, and Hank Kramer was cut down, soon to be followed by Mr. Dravid. But Steptoe and Saad were able to draw the men up one more flight of stairs before the bomb hit, and both had been knocked unconscious. LCpl Steptoe had recovered enough to catch the attention of LtCol Ricapito's Marines as they came pouring in through the hole in the roof. LCpl Saad had taken some fairly serious cuts from flying glass, but he was quickly attended to and brought back to the *Reagan* without problem.

Getting back to the US was a blur to him. Then there were the debriefs, the funerals, the press interviews. He had taken a week's leave, but he felt lost back home, so he had come back to Quantico three days early. His promotion to First Sergeant was a surprise. No more "Gunny Mac." "First Sergeant Mac" did not have the same ring to it. Everyone called him "First Sergeant McCardle."

There had been another smaller ceremony at the Pentagon that morning before the Medal of Honor ceremony. The new Chairman of the Joint Chiefs, General Kantres, and the Commandant had presented the awards to the rest of the det.

Navy Crosses went to Tony Niimoto and Hank Kramer. Hank's father accepted the award for him. 2ndLt Tony Niimoto looked good in his new bars. He was reporting to OCS at Ft Benning in two weeks. Soon, the Marines would have their own OCS back, but for now, it was still the Army school for new lieuies.

Corporals Steptoe and Saad were both presented the silver star, posthumously. Both had very large extended families at the ceremony. Sergeant Chen and Private First Class Fallgatter were also presented the Silver Star. It hurt the First Sergeant to see that no one was there to accept the medal for Chen. His mother had been contacted, but she refused to come, saying she had better things to do. Loralee Howard, who had become somewhat of a den mother to the Marines, took the award instead. Her brother, SSgt Cannon, looked a little old for a staff sergeant, but he stood proudly beside her in his uniform. You could not even tell that he had prosthetics under his trouser legs.

LCpl Wynn, SSgt Child, Cpl Crocker, and Cpl Ashely were awarded the bronze star. There had actually been some tension about that at the Department of the Navy. Some people felt that while Their loss of life and injuries were deplorable, except for Wynn, they hadn't actually done anything to earn a medal. But this had taken on a political life of its own, and the medals were awarded.

Midshipman Fourth Class Peter Van Slyke also was awarded a bonze star. His face was still pretty disfigured, and he had already had two surgeries, but he had been appointed a midshipman at the Naval Academy. It was a presidential appointment of course. It looked like the line of Van Slyke officers in the Marines was going to continue unabated.

And First Sergeant McCardle? He was awarded the Silver Star. He looked down at it, hanging off his dress blues blouse. He couldn't decide if he felt guilty or proud for having it. He had been offered a field commission as well, but after thinking long and hard about it, he turned it down. He was enlisted and he was proud of that. That was what he knew how to do.

And he was going back to India. A First Sergeant normally did not lead a detachment, but the embassy was being repaired and would open again in two months, and he requested to go there and bring the det back. Cpl Steptoe also asked to return, and the rest of the det would come from various other posts.

He pulled in the large circular drive at Bethesda Naval hospital and off to the right where he found some official vehicle parking. Getting out of the car, he made his way to the front and walked in.

"May I help you?" The older man at the information desk asked before he took in the First Sergeant's face. He had been on the news enough lately, and with his dress blues and silver star hanging there, he was immediately recognized. "Oh, First Sergeant McCardle. Welcome to Bethesda Naval Hospital. Can I help you?"

"No, thanks. I know where I'm going." He had come to visit Van Slyke and Saad while they were there, but he hadn't been to where he was now going. But he knew the way. He went down the main passageway, then to the elevators in the far back, on the right. He took one up to the third floor and walked down to the ward on the end. The nurse at the desk looked up to help, but he waved her away.

He slowly walked to the third room on the left, 3002C. He knew the number already. He stared at the number for a minute before he steeled himself and walked in.

Staff Sergeant Joseph Child lay on the bed, a respirator in his mouth. The formerly huge, impressive figure seemed shrunken and withered. A purple heart was still in the box at the small table beside the bed, and on the bed, between his feet, was the bronze star. His father must have left it. His father lived in Bethesda now, taking care of his son. He had accepted the bronze start that morning without a word, but he had not gone to the Medal of Honor ceremony.

The Physical Evaluation Board and just made a determination that SSgt Child was no longer fit for duty in the Marines. He was given a 100% disability and a retirement date of the first of next month. He would be moved to the VA Hospital in Detroit where he would live out however long he had left in a room there.

First Sergeant McCardle stood there, watching the slow rise and fall of SSgt Child's chest, listening to the wheeze of the respirator. This was the man of whom he had been, quite frankly, in awe. A better Marine than him. He wondered for the thousandth time that if their roles were reversed, would Child have brought back more of the det home?

He walked to the side of the bed and reached out, taking Child's hand in his. It was limp and cool, so unlike the man who had moved it, who had controlled that hand before. This was why the First Sergeant hadn't been able to come up to this room before. He couldn't accept what this man had become. But now he had to face it, to say goodbye. SSgt Child was a hero, a real Marine. One of a long line of heroes. But now he had passed the torch. And Ramon, Rodriguez, and McAlister had taken him up on it. Niimoto and Kramer. Van Slyke, Saad, and Steptoe. They would take that challenge into the future, bringing that tradition of honor and courage with them to a new generation of Marines.

And yes, he admitted, so might he. That was his mission now. To prepare for the future of the Corps.

He took an envelope out from inside his blouse and opened it, taking out a photo. It was a photo of the detachment in front the Marine House, taken a week before the presidential visit. He had downloaded it on his phone, and when he got back to the US, he had printed it out. Before, the eyes of the Marines who had died seemed to look at him accusingly. But now, as he looked at it, it looked more like they were looking at him in support. They were family, after all.

He placed the photo neatly on Staff Sergeant Child's chest. Taking a step back , he came to attention and saluted. Holding the salute for a few moments, he brought it down sharply.

"Good bye, Joe," he whispered.

He did an about face and marched out of the room and into his future.